THE FALLEN

THE FALLEN

A Novel

Mark Terry

IPSWICH, MASSACHUSETTS

ISBN: 978-1-933515-75-5

Published in the United States of America by Oceanview Publishing,
Ipswich, Massachusetts
www.oceanviewpub.com

10 9 8 7 6 5 4 3 2 1

PRINTED IN THE UNITED STATES OF AMERICA

For Ian and Sean

"We all shine on like the moon and the stars and the sun."

—John Lennon, "Instant Karma"

PART I
SECOND COMING

CHAPTER 1

Lieutenant Charlie Walker tracked the van rolling down the road toward Checkpoint Delta through his M24 sniper rifle's scope. He had the crosshairs centered on the driver's head, finger caressing the trigger. *Pow!* he thought. *Pow. Pow.* Calm. Like target shooting. Not real flesh and blood. Not a person. Not a human being. Just a target. He rehearsed the kill in his mind. Two shots through the driver's head. Shift so he could watch the passenger jump out. *Pow.* Pick him off. Anybody in the rear? Shift to the right, catch them as they scrambled out of the back.

Wearing a ghillie suit, a Nomex flight suit camouflaged with leaves and brush, he hid on a hillside overlooking Cheyenne Hills, a sprawling five-star resort outside Colorado Springs at the foot of the Rocky Mountains. A member of the Colorado National Guard's 19th Special Forces Group, Charlie was invisible among the shrubs and underbrush that covered the slopes.

Darkness covered the hillside, the sun still blocked by the surrounding mountains. The thin Colorado air was cold for mid-June. At sunrise the temperature would jump dramatically. It would be damn near impossible to lay out in a ghillie suit in scorching eighty-degree sun. He wasn't looking forward to it. It would be a long, hot day. Already he was coated with a slick of sweat. His stomach grumbled. He had a peanut butter energy bar in his pocket and a canteen of lukewarm water. But he knew a cold six-pack of Coors was waiting for him when he was done.

He also had to pee. When this van passed through, he would crawl over to a stand of aspen and relieve himself. He had considered the aspens for his sniper nest, but it had a partially obstructed view of Checkpoint Delta. In the hot daytime sun, he might consider it, at least part of the time. The open sunlight would be brutal.

Charlie peered through AN-PVS 7B night vision goggles, everything glowing green. He slowly swiveled his rifle, tracking the vehicle, a red panel van. The National Guard manned checkpoints at strategic sites along all entrances to Cheyenne Hills in preparation for the G8 Summit. The summit officially began at ten a.m. with the arrival of twenty heads of state and their entourages. Checkpoint Delta was just west of Cheyenne Hills West, one of the fancy castle-like resort buildings on the west side of Double Mirror Lake.

The red panel van slowed to a stop by the checkpoint. Charlie focused the crosshairs of his rifle sights on the driver's-side door and waited. How many times tonight? Twenty? Thirty? A hundred? Over and over during the night he repeated the routine and nothing exciting happened. He didn't think it would. This G8 thing was a big, big deal. The Secret Service ultimately ran security, overseeing Brigadier General Frank Cole's command of the National Guard troops. From what Charlie could see, Cheyenne Hills was zipped up tighter than a plastic baggie.

Charlie had only two minutes to live.

CHAPTER 2

Sergeant Sandy Kosell stepped around the barrier at Checkpoint Delta, holding up her hand to the approaching red panel van. A white sign on the door advertised Rowan & Ogilvie Spirits & Fine Wines. Traffic through the night had been sporadic, as expected.

Although they all knew the importance of security for this event, a part of her — the less professional part — thought this was boring. What terrorist would be crazy enough to try to attack an event like this? F14 fighter jets enforced a no-fly zone with a seventy-mile radius around Cheyenne Hills. Nothing larger than a blue jay was entering this airspace except for commercial flights into Colorado Springs Airport, and that was going to be shut down when the dignitaries flew in and out. Every road into the resort had multiple National Guard checkpoints.

Cheyenne Hills itself was crawling with Secret Service agents and Bureau of Diplomatic Security agents from the State Department. Her team even met a couple of Israeli guys, Mossad or something, and some spooky Russian agents with flat eyes and serious bad attitudes. There were leaders from twenty countries coming to this thing, and each one had a slew of their own security people.

She didn't think anything was going to happen here.

The van slowed. Kosell saw at least two men inside. She kept her M4 carbine ready as she cautiously approached the driver's side. Three of her fellow soldiers covered her back. Sandy had the laptop out, ready to double-check the van's security pass.

The doors opened and a man stepped out on the far side of the truck. She got the driver, the talkative one. Lanky, broad-shouldered, in black slacks and a lightweight windbreaker, his eyes snapped with energy and charm. A straw cowboy hat tilted at a cocky angle on his head. He seemed vaguely familiar to her, but she didn't know why. He was good looking in a bad-boy sort of way that she found appealing.

He grinned at her. "Hey, good morning." A touch of Texas laced his voice. "Are we in the right place? This Cheyenne Hills?" He laughed. "Like I don't know from all the other checkpoints. You're not gonna frisk me, are ya darlin'?"

Kosell relaxed. Just a good ol' boy who was a little stuck on himself. She smiled back, willing to play the game. "Only if you want me to, sir."

The Texan said, "Well, now, there are worse ways to spend the evenin' than bein' patted down by a pretty gal such as yourself."

Sandy felt herself relax even more. But something from her briefing popped into her head. *Look at their hands.* This guy's hands were tucked into the pockets of his windbreaker. And it was also a little unusual for people to actually get out of their vehicle. She straightened up, back to business.

"Sir, please —"

Both hands popped from his pockets. With a nonchalant toss he threw one object at her, the other over her head. The man on the passenger side of the van also flung something. She raised her weapon. The man spun so his back was to her. A massive flash of light, like being at the center of the sun, exploded around her with a sizzling pop. An acrid odor bit at her nostrils.

Disoriented, Kosell stumbled. Blind, but unhurt. *"What — ?"*

Then she thought — flash grenade!

The last thing she felt was a silenced bullet exploding into her skull.

CHAPTER 3

Lieutenant Charlie Walker watched the red panel van slow to a stop. The National Guardsman — a woman — walked forward, hand up. Even from a distance, he liked how she looked — oval face, blonde hair tucked under her helmet. Her three backup spread out a little bit so they could cover the vehicle. Doors opened on each side of the van and two men climbed out.

The guy on the driver's side looked casual, nonthreatening. Charlie kept the sights of his scope on the driver, just below the brim of his cowboy hat. *Pow*, he thought. Charlie moved his crosshairs directly onto the cowboy's chest and said, *"pow"* in a soft whisper.

The cowboy pulled his hands from his pockets. He tossed something directly at the woman, and threw something else behind her. On the other side of the van the other figure also tossed something. The rear doors of the van popped open and two, no, three figures —

A surge of adrenaline burned through Charlie's veins. Something was —

The world exploded in an electro-chemical flash. It was a silent flash from Charlie's distance, but that didn't matter. The night vision goggles he wore utilized infrared, heat, and light magnification. He was watching through the LM setting, the apparatus magnifying light intensity by hundreds of times. The flash of light turned his world into a green-white explosion that seared his eyes before the circuit breaker cut in and compensated.

In the brief explosion of distraction and blindness, the man in a matching ghillie suit, who had been silently stalking him for the better part of the last hour, leapt up and fired a silenced bullet into the back of Charlie's head.

The man rushed over and studied Charlie for a moment before he reached down and removed Charlie's radio set and whisper microphone. He focused his own goggles down toward Checkpoint Delta.

When the flash grenades exploded, the four National Guardsmen were momentarily blinded for about thirty seconds. An eternity as far as trained assassins were concerned. The two men outside the van and the four who leapt from the now-open doors raised their silenced assault rifles and ruthlessly gunned down the soldiers in an eerily soundless display of violence.

It took far less than thirty seconds.

Four of the assassins moved in an unhesitating, rehearsed manner, dumping the bodies of the guardsmen into their Humvee, which was pulled off to the side of the road. The four assassins wore identical camo and took up the post alongside the barricade, almost as if nothing had happened.

The leader of the assassins — the cowboy — said into his throat mic, "Check in by the numbers."

Up in the hills surrounding the resort, additional members of the group called in, confirming that they had taken out their snipers as well. "One here. *Cobra*."

"Two here. *Chacal*."

"Three here. *Vibora*."

The assassin who had so deftly taken out Lieutenant Charlie Walker said, "Four here. *Lobo*."

Through his goggles, Number 4, *Lobo*, saw the cowboy — The Fallen Angel — nod in satisfaction and climb back into the panel van. A moment later he heard The Fallen Angel say, "First perimeter. On schedule."

Number 4, *Lobo*, began a slow crawl to a different location in his ghillie suit. He wanted to move a good distance away from the dead National Guard sniper. Nobody would see the body, the way it was camouflaged, but in the rising heat of the day it was going to stink and attract flies and maybe even vultures.

He considered a stand of aspen. Yes, that would work. A nice shady area.

CHAPTER 4

The cowboy they called The Fallen Angel drove the van for Rowan &
Ogilvie Spirits & Fine Wines along Pikesview Road and turned into the
entrance to the Cheyenne Hills Resort. It was a sprawling, five-thousand
acre complex surrounding a small lake split by a bridge. The main
complex, The Cheyenne, was a meandering stucco castle, ten stories tall
at its main tower. The leaders of the G8 — or G20, as the summit had become — would be living in The Cheyenne for the duration of the summit,
scattered among its many wings and floors.

The Fallen Angel, who had been born Richard Coffee, grinned at
that. They wouldn't be living long.

He didn't head over toward The Cheyenne, however. Instead he cut
left and drove past the tennis complex toward Cheyenne Hall, the International Center, and Colorado Springs Hall. It was a three-building complex where the actual meetings of the G8 Summit would be held.

There was another roadblock. This one was manned by Secret Service. They all wore black camo, their MP5s and Uzis held loosely in their
arms. One of the agents approached with a mirror held on a long handle
so he could check underneath the vehicle for bombs. Another agent
stepped forward with a German shepherd on a leash.

The lead agent, Larry Ferrigno, was a broad-shouldered, muscular
man with a jowly face and blotched skin from too close a shave. Coffee
watched his face, noting the habitual look of suspicion and skepticism.
Remembering his research, Coffee knew he had to be careful with this
one. Ferrigno was a pro, a dedicated patriot. The Fallen Angel had not
found any obvious weaknesses or exploitable quirks in his life; at least
none they could leverage in a relatively short period of time.

Ferrigno said, "Please step out of the vehicle, gentlemen."

The Fallen Angel and his partner, who was designated *El Tiburón*, clambered out. Ferrigno said, "You have your paperwork and identification with you?"

Nodding, The Fallen Angel handed it over to Ferrigno. Ferrigno rolled his shoulders as if to relieve tension as he looked over the credentials. "What's inside the truck?"

"What it says," The Fallen said. "Dom Pérignon, Krug, several cases of wine. They wanted extra, just in case."

Ferrigno nodded. "We were told about the last-minute order." He chewed on his lip, watching his team go over the truck. The agent with the mirror said, "Clear."

Ferrigno nodded. "How's it going, Matt?"

The agent with the German shepherd reappeared a moment later and shrugged. "Seems okay."

Ferrigno appeared relieved. "Okay. You're clear. Go around to the loading dock. The agent there, Vincent Silvedo, will walk you through security."

"Thanks."

The Fallen Angel and *El Tiburón* climbed back into the van and drove toward the loading dock. "It worked," *El Tiburón* said. He was a dark-skinned man, Colombian, with a narrow face, thick mustache, and long-fingered hands as delicate as a girl's.

"Yes." The Fallen smiled. "Of course it did." He took off the cowboy hat, tossed it behind him and ran a thick-knuckled hand through his straw-colored hair. *Of course it did.*

The dogs couldn't sniff through a vacuum. The van was refrigerated. The refrigeration unit contained a compressor. Built into one end of the van was a heavy, steel compartment. In it were guns, C4 plastic explosives, detonators, ammunition, and gas masks. The compressor sucked the air out of the compartment, effectively sealing it.

After loading the gear into the compartment, they had washed down the interior of the van with bleach, then spilled several bottles of wine and champagne on the floor, mopped it out with detergent, rubbed in some oil and grease and mopped that out as well.

But the compartment was only part of their cargo. The champagne bottles themselves were even more important.

CHAPTER 5

The Fallen Angel backed the van into the loading dock area. It was large enough to accommodate two full-sized semis side-by-side, with a loading platform at the back. Unlike many loading docks, it could be shuttered with rolling steel doors. He and *El Tiburón* climbed out and were met by Vincent Silvedo, the Secret Service agent. Silvedo also wore black camo and carried an MP5. The man looked like a walking muscle, his upper body a taut V that stretched his tight black T-shirt and vest.

"Any problems?" he asked, scratching at a bristly five o'clock shadow.

The Fallen Angel shook his head. Silvedo had been an easy recruitment — a combination of flattery and bribery. Hammering in on the man's vanity, his ego — *passed over for two promotions, obviously they don't recognize your abilities, but we will, Vincent, oh yes, with us you'll rise to the top. And we'll make you rich in the process.*

The Fallen Angel reached over to a control panel inside the truck and flipped a switch, cutting the power to the compressor. "We'll just unload things and you can point the way."

Silvedo's teeth flashed. "Excellent." He studied his notepad and scribbled something, then handed the paperwork to The Fallen. "Show this to Agent Bannister inside."

The two men unloaded the truck, moving the bottles of wine and champagne onto dollies. Once everything was properly loaded, Silvedo handed each of them a packet containing the black pants, shoes, white shirt and jacket of the catering staff. Richard Coffee and *El Tiburón* stepped into the van and quickly changed clothing while Silvedo kept watch.

Once dressed, The Fallen Angel knelt by the lockbox, turned a handle, waited a moment as the vacuum released and air hissed in. It opened with a sucking sound. The contents were in three crates labeled Dom Pérignon, but instead contained weapons and explosives. He removed the three crates and hauled them to a waiting dolly. He looked at Silvedo.

"Ready?"

"Absolutely." Silvedo grinned. "This is going to be fun."

The Fallen Angel locked eyes with Silvedo, who instantly calmed down. In a low voice, The Fallen said, "Discipline."

"Yes, sir."

The Fallen nodded. Had Silvedo been too easy? Had he overlooked something when he recruited him as a sleeper years ago? Too late now. But Silvedo wouldn't survive the day. He would make sure of it personally. "Very good," he said. "We'll see you inside."

The Fallen Angel tapped his throat mic. "Second and third perimeters breached. On schedule."

He and *El Tiburón* pushed their lethal cargo into the loading area of the International Center.

CHAPTER 6

Michael Gabriel walked out his apartment door, driving mug of black coffee in his hand, and strode toward his pickup truck. He wore the uniform of the Cheyenne Hills Resort maintenance staff — rubber-soled shoes, khaki pants, and denim shirt. An ID badge hung on a lanyard around his neck and what looked like a normal cell phone hung on his belt, although it was, in fact, an Iridium satellite phone.

He stopped by the truck, a beat-up blue Dodge Ram, marred with rust and Bondo. He stretched his six-foot frame and ran a hand through his thick wiry brown hair. *Just a couple more days. One way or the other.*

He took a sip of his coffee before climbing into his truck, looking toward the mountains. He liked the view: Pikes Peak, the Colorado Rockies. It was beautiful here, but it wasn't home. He wanted to go home. *Just a couple more days.*

"Hey, *amante. Qué pasa?*"

Michael turned with a smile. "*Amante?* What's that mean?"

The speaker was a woman, Maria Sanchez. She worked for the food service at the resort's International Center. Working in the International Center and all over the resort for the last eight months Michael had gotten to know Maria pretty much whether he wanted to or not. Maria Sanchez was in her twenties, with large liquid eyes, black curly hair, and a vivacious smile. She was a flirt and Michael Gabriel knew exactly what *amante* meant in Spanish.

She wore her uniform for the day — a black skirt that stopped an inch or so above her knees, a while blouse, hose, and heels. "You make that uniform look illegal, *querido,*" he said.

Maria laughed, the sound like high-pitched bells tinkling in the thin Colorado air. "All this time you knew!" She threw him a lascivious look followed by a mock pout. "All this time I have been waiting for this tall, dark, and handsome senor to sweep me off my feet."

Michael Gabriel grinned. "Ah, Maria, I've seen you hanging around with your boyfriend, the one with all the muscles. He'd break me into pieces if he caught me smiling at you."

"Oh you!" She linked arms with him. "Aren't you going into work early today?"

He shrugged. "Big day."

"Long day, you mean. All those world leaders pretending to be so proper, to have their moral authority. How many times do you think some prime minister will pinch my *nalga* today, eh?"

"Sell it to the *National Enquirer* for a hundred grand."

"Ah, I wish. Well, I got to go, unless you want to give me a ride?" She flashed him a coquettish look, ever the vamp. Over the last six months he had given her the occasional ride into the resort or back to the apartment. They'd even had a couple of dates. Fun, nothing serious. He wasn't sure Maria was looking for serious, and God knows he kept his emotional distance. If it bothered her, she hid it well.

Only once, eating Mexican food at a place in Colorado Springs called El Azteco, did she seem frustrated with him. "*Ay, Dios mio!* Michael, my tall, dark senor with all the secrets. You never talk about yourself! You are a *bandito* with a dark past, no?"

He had laughed and said, "I am a *bandito* with a dark past, *si*, senorita, and you should be worried about what you don't know about me. I am a bad *muchacho* who would do horrible things to you in the darkness."

She had wriggled in that terribly sexy way of hers and said, "Ooh, senor, what kind of horrible things?"

"Wicked, evil, nasty things, senorita. So you should watch yourself."

They had moved on, and she hadn't again suggested that she wanted to know more about his past than he was willing to give.

"Maria, Maria," he said, arms wide, "I would love to drive you in today, especially with the hassles with parking. My chariot is your chariot. Hop aboard."

With another laugh, Maria ran around the truck and jumped into the passenger seat. Michael Gabriel, whose real name was Derek Stillwater, climbed into the truck, fired up the engine, and headed toward the resort. Despite the beautiful, flirtatious woman in the passenger seat chattering away, he thought, *It's almost over. One way or the other, it's almost over.*

CHAPTER 7

The Fallen and *El Tiburón*, pushing their dollies loaded with champagne, wine, and weapons, moved coolly into the International Center, where they were met by another Secret Service agent who studied their paperwork, double-checked the Secret Service seal on the boxes, and waved them on. Turning a corner, they were met by a member of the catering staff. He was dressed the same way they were, in black slacks, a white shirt and jacket. His dark hair was worn cropped to his skull; a thick black mustache decorated his upper lip. He moved with a bold, athletic, loose-limbed grace, and his manner was nonchalant, almost jolly.

"You made it," he said.

The Fallen nodded and pointed to the dolly containing the boxes filled with weapons. "These are the ones you need to worry about."

"Excellent. Follow me. We'll be setting up in Cheyenne Hall. That's where the initial meet and greet is being held. It's just as we were told."

He took hold of the dolly and walked them around to a freight elevator and punched the button. His name was Alvaro Hernandez, though his current designation within The Fallen Angels was *El Camaleón*.

They loaded the dollies into the freight elevator and rode it to the basement. From the elevator they took a right turn into a tunnel that extended off in both directions. They passed several Secret Service agents. Twice they were stopped, their paperwork reviewed, the Secret Service seals inspected. Silvedo had done his job and there were no problems. Their security credentials and paperwork were completely filled out.

They passed through a pair of steel security doors. The Fallen studied these thoughtfully. As if reading his mind, *El Camaleón* said, "Definitely. I'll take care of it. I haven't seen a flaw yet."

"Good."

Beyond the steel door, the hallway angled upward at a slight grade. Tile walls, acoustical tile ceiling, hard-textured cement, polymer flooring, and harsh fluorescent lighting were the only things to see. The air smelled of industrial cleanser and was thick with humidity. At crossroads a sign indicated an emergency exit to the left. To the right was a hallway leading to the elevators. Straight ahead it said: TECHNICAL WORK AREAS.

They turned right and took the freight elevator to the first floor. *El Camaleón* led the way. They entered a service corridor on one end of the mammoth Cheyenne Hall. Off to the left a hallway led to the kitchen area where the cooks and caterers were preparing for the event. To the right were a series of storage rooms and walk-in freezers. Straight ahead was an undecorated, utilitarian corridor, blank wall on the left, service doors on the right opening into the hall itself.

They pushed their carts forward into Cheyenne Hall. It was a banquet hall filled with round tables covered with crisp white linens. At the front of the room was a raised stage with twenty black leather chairs. A microphone and glass podium jutted above a raised glass TelePrompTer screen. Just below the stage was a compact set of six television cameras that allowed for 360 degree viewing of the summit. An army of similarly dressed catering staff prepared the tables around the perimeter of the room.

El Camaleón pointed to the tables stretched against the walls. "Put the bottles of champagne on those. Stacked appropriately." A faint smile ghosted his dark features. "Make sure you get them on all sides of the room. I'm going to put these boxes in the storage area. Jaime will keep a close eye on them."

He pushed the cart containing the crates filled with weapons and explosives across the room. The Fallen and *El Tiburón* went to work opening their crates and carefully setting the bottles of wine and champagne on the long narrow tables that graced the walls of the room.

The Fallen Angel looked around, feeling the thrill of a plan coming together. He tapped his throat mic. "First perimeter breached. On schedule."

CHAPTER 8

Derek Stillwater eyed the National Guard troops manning the final checkpoint. They seemed professional enough. Four men in camo carrying M4 carbines. They spread out in standard formation, covering the truck. Yet for some reason they seemed different than the guards at the previous two checkpoints. More menacing. Maybe it was just that they were guarding the actual entrance to the resort itself.

Maria said, "I don't like this much. Makes me feel — I don't know, like I'm living in a war zone or something."

Derek didn't say anything, but rolled down his window. As far as he was concerned for the next three days — the duration of the G8 Summit — they *were* living in a war zone. A guardsman walked over. "Only authorized vehicles today, sir." He had dark brown eyes, almost black, and thick eyelashes like a girl. He was a broad, swarthy guy with high cheekbones and a solicitous, but cold, manner.

Derek held out his identification for the resort and handed over Maria's, as well. He also handed over the official paperwork they had been instructed to bring with them. The guardsman took it, studying the identification and the sticker on the truck's windshield.

"You can go."

Derek took the paperwork back, nodded, and drove on. He glanced at the soldiers in the rearview mirror and frowned. Everything seemed okay. Nothing unexpected. But for some reason he had a bad vibe. He couldn't pin it down. *Just paranoia*, he thought. *Pregame nerves*.

Maria, a chatterbox all the way here, was suddenly quiet. She punched the radio back on, a staticky FM station that was playing a hip-hop tune in staccato Spanish. "Shit." She jabbed it off. "I hate this."

"You don't like that song?"

She glared at him. She flapped her hands, encompassing the guards, the resort, the whole world. "No, this! All this!"

"Hey, it's no big deal," he said. "Just some weekend warriors trying to keep the world safe for democracy."

"I didn't like them," she said, voice soft.

It took him a moment to figure who "them" were. "Why?"

She didn't answer right away. They were closing in on the next checkpoint, which was manned by the Secret Service. Finally she said, "I don't know. Something. His accent, maybe."

Derek raised an eyebrow. "Accent? What accent?"

"Something out of the country."

"He looked Hispanic to me. You have more of an accent than he did."

"I have no accent, Michael!"

Derek laughed. "Right. No accent at all, *querido*."

"I don't!"

He laughed more, feeling relieved. "Okay, you don't have an accent. What was this guy's accent? He looked Hispanic to me."

"I don't know. Not Mex. Just — something."

A part of Derek's mind took it seriously. Another part just figured Maria was feeling jittery. Hell, *he* felt jittery.

They pulled up to the Secret Service checkpoint in front of Cheyenne Hall and were asked to step out of the truck. They did, handing over their identification and security paperwork.

The lead Secret Service agent at this checkpoint, Larry Ferrigno, studied Derek's paperwork. "Michael Gabriel," he said, reading from the ID. "What do you do here?"

"Maintenance," Derek said. Ten feet away another agent questioned Maria.

"What part of the complex?"

Derek gestured toward the three-building complex of Cheyenne Hall, the International Center, and Colorado Springs Hall. "Typically here. I mean, I go where I'm needed, but mostly I work here. That's where I'm assigned today."

"Right. I remember seeing your name on the list. Let me double-check." Ferrigno glanced at the screen of a tablet computer and adjusted the cursor. He nodded, tapping a stylus against the drop-down menus, accessing the Secret Service database.

The agent with the dog inspected his truck. Another agent used the mirror to look underneath it for bombs.

"Is there a problem?" Derek wondered how thorough the Service had dug into his background. It was a problem with these National Special Security Events. The Cheyenne Resort had over 1,600 employees. In the case of the G8 Summit, you had to coordinate with about twenty countries' security services and deal with the fact that each country's leader brought along thirty or forty staff members. A background check wasn't going to dredge up every single quirk in each person's history.

Ferrigno shook his head and handed Derek back his credentials. "Nope. Have a good day, sir. Please park in Lot C. You know where that is?"

Derek nodded.

Relieved to have made it through this, he climbed back in the truck, but Maria waved him off. "I'm right here, Mike. I'll just walk in. It's shorter."

"No problem. Have a good one."

"You, too. And thanks for the ride."

She strutted away and Derek noted with amusement that all the Secret Service agents watched her walk away in her short skirt and heels. *Yeah, well, when you've got it, flaunt it*, he thought. Maria was worth watching. He jammed the old truck into gear and headed over to Lot C, which was out of the way and inconvenient to Cheyenne Hall.

He parked in the shade of a huge hackberry tree and took a deep breath before climbing out of the truck. As Michael Gabriel, he was a charming loner, the one few people got to know. His story was that he grew up in Florida, but liked the mountains. He was handy, had a year or so of junior college. He spent the last fifteen or twenty years working maintenance at hotels. He was nobody unusual. Just a guy doing his job.

Derek Stillwater, on the other hand, had a Ph.D., and retired with the rank of colonel from Army Special Forces where he specialized in biological and chemical warfare and counterterrorism. Derek Stillwater was "officially" dead, having died in a domestic terror incident eight months earlier. His job title was "troubleshooter" for the Department of Homeland Security. Whenever there was a potential biological or chemical terrorism event in the U.S., he went along with the FBI to "evaluate, coordinate, and investigate."

He had been undercover for eight months in preparation for a possible attack on the G8 by a terrorist calling himself The Fallen Angel.

Derek knew The Fallen Angel well. They had once been partners. They had once been friends. And he had reason to believe they were going to meet again.

CHAPTER 9

Washington D.C.

President Langston's administrative assistant ushered Secretary James Johnston into the Oval Office. Johnston was no stranger to the Oval Office, and walked briskly over to stand squarely at the feet of the American eagle on the presidential seal. Although he was no longer a general or even in the military, he couldn't quite suppress the urge to stand at attention and salute. He squared his shoulders and waited.

Behind the president were three multipaned windows overlooking the south lawn. This morning a team of maintenance people were mowing and trimming the emerald green grass. "Good morning, Mr. President."

Langston had aged. His sandy brown hair was shot through with gray and his rugged face looked craggy and worn. When he ran for office he had been boyish, vigorous, lean, and handsome. Johnston thought the presidency should come with a warning label: "The Surgeon General warns that the presidency will prematurely age you and has a high risk of early death."

The job always wore on the holders of the office, but the death of most of his cabinet and his wife and children in a terrorist attack added decades to President Langston's appearance. And his mind had changed. He was not the man who had been elected; this new man was angry, distracted, and tired. Wearing a navy blue three-piece suit, President Langston sat behind his desk, peering at paperwork through bifocals. "Hello, Jim. Have a seat. Robert's coming."

"Yes, sir."

President Langston waved him to sit down, ignoring him. Johnston and Langston were not on the best of terms, and never had been. Johnston's political leanings were just a bit too liberal for the conservative administration. But his tenure on the Joint Chiefs, his expertise on terrorism, and the need for the Republican Party to have a military man in the cabinet to make up for Langston's lack of military experience made him a frontrunner for secretary of homeland security.

President Langston finished underlining something in the document he was reading, and set it aside as Secretary Robert Mandalevo was ushered in by the president's chief of staff, Lauren McCullough. President Langston sat back in his chair and gestured for Mandalevo, the director of national intelligence, to take a seat. Mandalevo was a tall, elegant man with a shaved scalp, long, oval face, and grim eyes. Johnston didn't think he had ever seen Mandalevo smile. Mandalevo looked like a scalpel with his lean, straight build and black tailored suit. "Good morning, Mr. President," he said, and settled into a chair next to Johnston. Mandalevo tipped his head. "Good morning, Jim."

Chief of Staff Lauren McCullough swept a blunt hand over her steel gray hair. "Wheels up in one hour, Mr. President."

Langston waved a hand. "I know, I know."

McCullough wore a gray suit and rose blouse and low heeled shoes. Pearl earrings and a matching necklace and a slim Piaget watch were her only jewelry. She was a serious, grouchy autocrat with the personality of a badger and the protective instincts of a momma bear. She knew her business and didn't let anybody forget it.

Johnston made it a point to stay on McCullough's good side though, because she never failed to remember who was loyal and competent, and who wasn't. She never failed to repay political grudges or favors. Her mind was like a political calculator. Johnston liked her. Unlike most Beltway politicians, she would never stab you in the back — she'd look you right in the eyes as she slipped the stiletto between your ribs.

"Yes. Well, gentlemen," she said, "I want your intelligence briefing for summit security. Robert? Why don't you start."

With a nod, Secretary Mandalevo ran through a summary of international intelligence recently gathered surrounding the G8 Summit. He finished with, "There has been some chatter regarding the inclusion of Crown Prince Talal and Minister Shitzak Tichon, but nothing directly threatening."

President Langston scowled. "Damned Palestinians pissed off they weren't invited?"

Always diplomatic, Mandalevo said, "Nobody believes the Palestinian government should be considered one of the economically strongest in the world, Mr. President." It was hard to argue that point, and nobody commented on how deftly Mandalevo sidestepped the actual question.

"So there aren't any major terrorist threats to the summit?" asked McCullough.

Mandalevo frowned. "With an event of this magnitude, there will always be threats. We have no specific threats, however. Security, as you know, is very high for this event."

McCullough glanced at Johnston. "Jim?"

"There are the usual protestors. They're set up in Colorado Springs, and we've got National Guard, Secret Service, and FBI handling things. They're being kept a long way from The Cheyenne. Nobody wants a repeat of Seattle."

"What about that bit of chatter you picked up, when was it, October? About Coffee? There hasn't been any follow-up."

Johnston frowned at the question. "As you know," he said, "we've been keeping an eye on hate groups and militias. The NSA was monitoring phone and e-mail of The Reverend Lt. Colonel Jeremy Sebastian, who ran a group called the Colorado American Rights Delegation. They're a militia, but very militant and they're on our domestic terrorism watch lists. Anyway, NSA picked up part of a phone conservation that we suspect was made to Sebastian by Richard Coffee."

President Langston perked up. "When was this?"

"The call itself was late August, sir."

"What happened? Why wasn't I informed of this?"

Johnston tried to keep his expression neutral. The president had been briefed on this. President Langston was following the hunt for Richard Coffee closely. Was this his way of jamming him into a corner, shifting control to Mandalevo? Christ, he hated the political games in the White House.

"It was a snippet, sir. Part of a telephone conversation. The voice we believe to be Coffee said something like, 'This is your guardian angel. Remember me?' Sebastian said, 'Fallen?' Then starts praising him for almost killing you, sir, but Coffee cuts him off. He says, 'Don't say anything else,' then says 'they're coming back.'"

Langston's dark eyes nearly glittered with anger. "*They* being The Fallen Angels?"

"We believe so, sir. Then Sebastian says, 'Is this about that Cheyenne Hills thing?' and Coffee hangs up."

"So," said McCullough, "you believe —" she paused, thinking for a moment. "How sure are you that the caller was Richard Coffee?"

"The reference to 'Fallen' and 'guardian angels' suggests it strongly. The bureau voice printed it, and compared it to the sole tape we have of Coffee's voice, which, as you know, is very poor quality. They did not give a one hundred percent confirmation."

Secretary Mandalevo interrupted, his voice smooth. "It is, as a matter of fact, well below fifty percent, isn't it, James?"

Johnston slowly nodded. "They estimate it at a twenty-two percent certainty."

Everyone thought about that for a moment. Then President Langston said, "What about this Sebastian? Did you pick him up and question him?"

Johnston hesitated. "Sir, there was a time lag between receiving the recording intercept and analyzing it. The call was made in late August. We didn't receive the report from NSA until early October. As soon as it was analyzed, we sent agents to pick up Sebastian. However, sir, Jeremy Sebastian was murdered two days after the telephone call."

Chief of Staff McCullough was watching the president closely, eyes narrowed, expression troubled. "Sir, we've been through this —"

President Langston leaned forward, elbows on his desk, face flushing with anger. "Why is this the first I've heard of this?"

Johnston glanced at McCullough. She said, "Mr. President, it was in one of your briefings. Everything involving Richard Coffee and The Fallen Angels is automatically put at the top of your security briefing."

"I don't remember this. I damn well would have remembered something this relevant, a real sighting of the bastard who killed my wife and children." President Langston scowled at McCullough, then glared at Johnston.

"Sir," Johnston said, "it didn't go anywhere. All we have is a very vague, unsubstantiated connection between Richard Coffee and Colorado Springs and the G8 Summit. It's nothing more than a rumor. We don't know for a fact that —"

"I understand. But that madman murdered my family! What are you doing about this?"

"Sir, the Secret Service is running security for the summit. They have been fully advised of the possibility that Richard Coffee may try to do something there."

President Langston turned his glare on Robert Mandalevo. "Robert? What do you have on The Fallen Angels?"

Mandalevo tapped his long, thin fingers on the arm of his chair for a moment, gathering his thoughts. "As you know, Mr. President, the members of The Fallen Angels who were arrested have been confined to Guantanamo Bay. They were all recruited from the highest levels of the world's intelligence agencies. They are very professional. And for reasons we don't completely understand, they have proven to be very resistant to our interrogations. None of them have spoken, sir. None."

"What about Coffee? Did you track him?"

"We found evidence, sir," said Mondalevo, "that he slipped across the border into Mexico. In fact, he sent a postcard to Dr. Derek Stillwater from Mexico City. From there, we suspect he continued to move south into Central America. It was rumored that he was in Colombia, but it was never corroborated. That's all we know until that phone intercept."

"Where was the phone call from?" demanded McCullough. Johnston thought the president's erratic behavior was rattling her and she was trying to make up for it by stepping in and taking control of the meeting.

Mandalevo looked over at Johnston, eyebrow raised.

"We don't know," said Johnston.

"What do you —"

"We don't know," he repeated. Those three words he felt were often the three most important in intelligence circles. Most politicians didn't get it; they always felt that an answer was necessary. "It was a cellular call, but the NSA never did track down exactly where it came from."

President Langston stood up. "One question, Jim." His voice held barely contained rage.

Everybody rose to their feet. Secretary Johnston said, "Yes, sir?"

"Do you have assets in place to deal with Coffee, should he make an attempt at the summit?"

"As I said, sir, the Secret Service runs security at National Special Security Events. They have been informed and are doing everything possible."

President Langston banged his fist on his desktop. He growled, "No, Jim. That's not what I asked. Do you have *an asset* in place to deal with Richard Coffee?"

Johnston understood the question. "Yes, sir. I do."

"Very well. Let's move on."

As Johnston and Mandalevo left the Oval Office, Mandalevo said, "What was that about?"

Johnston scowled. He glanced back over his shoulder. In a low voice, he said, "You were there when we briefed him on this. We both remember it. He's getting worse."

"I'm aware of that, but that's not what I'm talking about. *What was that all about?*"

"What was what about?"

Mandalevo stopped and looked at him. "What asset was the president talking about?"

Johnston shook his head. "We have assets in place all over Cheyenne Hills, Robert. It's what the Secret Service does. The service's preparations for the summit are excellent. You've been fully informed of the situation."

"I'm the National Intelligence Director." Mandalevo's eyes narrowed, one of the few signs he gave that he was annoyed or even angry. "I should know what you have up your sleeve. What asset was the president talking about?"

Johnston said, "Robert, you've been fully briefed on security for the summit." He turned and walked away.

You don't need to know, thought Johnston. *The only people who know are me, Derek Stillwater, and President Langston.* Johnston understood something about Richard Coffee that not everybody appreciated, even Robert Mandalevo. If Coffee couldn't seduce people to join him, he would bribe, blackmail, or threaten them. He had fingers into governments and intelligence agencies all over the world. Johnston trusted Mandalevo, but who knew who else might have access to that information? Especially if it was information Coffee really wanted. And one thing Johnston was sure of — Richard Coffee was very interested in knowing if Derek Stillwater was still alive.

CHAPTER 10

Secretary Mandalevo returned to his office in the West Wing and walked past his secretary without a word, slamming his door behind him. He had a window overlooking the south lawn, but otherwise the office was mostly remarkable for how small it was. In the White House, and especially in the West Wing, proximity to the president was the real indicator of status, and he was reasonably close — a short walk down the hall. But windows and size of the office were also indicators of how important you were to the administration, and of your own personal importance to the president, and he knew it.

He stood in his small office and clenched his fists, thinking, stewing. This little skirmish exemplified everything that was wrong with the National Intelligence Directorate — it had been created to increase communication between the different intelligence agencies in the U.S. government after 9/11. Instead, it had inspired everybody to become even more protective of their own turf. He'd hoped that by keeping his office in the West Wing with easy access to the president that it would become symbolic of his importance. That turned out to be wasted effort, and not a day went by that he didn't consider moving over to Liberty Crossing, but thought it would be viewed as an even bigger admission of failure.

Also, every time he considered moving to the national intelligence headquarters, he knew what kind of message that would send to the press — Mandalevo's cutting his losses, throwing up his hands with his frustration with this administration, and hiding out at Liberty Crossing.

Plus, he didn't like the way President Langston was behaving these days. The Fallen Angels were a clear and present danger to the United States, but so was al-Qaeda and a number of rogue countries around the world. You couldn't put all your focus on one enemy or a different enemy would sneak up behind you while you were occupied. He felt his continuing presence in the West Wing and his easy access to the president would only strengthen his point about America's enemies and the need for constant vigilance.

He glanced for a moment at the most important thing in the room —the photograph of his family that rested on a corner of his oversized maple desk. His wife, Laura, who died three years earlier of ovarian cancer. His twin daughters, Megan and Midge, short for Margaret, now grown. Megan lived in Los Angeles, an agent with the Gersch Agency in Beverly Hills. Midge, following her father's footsteps, worked for the State Department in the U.S. embassy in Greece. He was proud of his daughters. He missed them. He missed all three of them.

He turned and stuck his head out the door and said, "Get Bill on the phone," and ducked back inside his office.

A moment later his phone buzzed and Marcia said, "Lieutenant General William Akron for you."

Akron was the deputy director of the National Intelligence Directorate, and worked out of their newly built headquarters at Liberty Crossing in northern Virginia. The former director of the National Security Agency, Akron ran the day-to-day operations of the NID. "Robert, shouldn't you be heading over to Andrews?"

"In a couple minutes. I need you to get some files and e-mail them directly to me on Air Force One ASAP."

"No problem."

"I want everything we know about Richard Coffee and The Fallen Angels. In particular, I want everything we have on an NSA intercept in August between Richard Coffee and the Reverend Lieutenant Colonel Jeremy Sebastian in Colorado."

"Do I need to know what this is about?"

"I don't know. Maybe."

"Okay, Robert. Understood. Anything else?"

Mandalevo thought for a moment. "Get me the file on Derek Stillwater. In fact, here's what I really want to know about Derek Stillwater, Bill. Find out if he's really dead."

"Dead?"

"Check social security, check Homeland Security payroll and benefits records. Anything else that might be relevant. I have a suspicion—"

"Robert? What's going on?"

"Stillwater was always Johnston's go-to guy. Johnston's got somebody undercover at Cheyenne. I wonder if Johnston pulled a switch."

"I wouldn't put it past him. I'll get the information for you. Anything else?"

"No, not for now."

"Yes sir. Have a good trip, sir."

CHAPTER 11

Derek Stillwater pushed his work cart in front of him through the tunnel connecting Cheyenne Hall to Colorado Springs Hall. The three buildings — Cheyenne Hall, the International Center, and the Colorado Springs Hall — were laid out in a rough triangle, making a combined 185,000 square feet of meeting space. Each building was connected by an underground tunnel and the basement areas of each building were a maze of narrow corridors, public meeting rooms, offices, and power plant and technical areas.

His boss, Steven Planchette, had been pleased to see him and promptly sent him over to Colorado Springs Hall to replace burned-out lights in two of the conference rooms, and fix a backed-up toilet in the women's restroom on the main floor. Ah, the glamorous life of the undercover agent, he thought. Yet, in a way, he had enjoyed his eight months here. The jobs were straightforward, short-term, and you could see the results immediately — and generally speaking, nobody tried to kill him in the process.

His work cart was about the size of a garden cart and contained all the tools and parts he might need for these sorts of jobs — screwdrivers, wrenches, hammers, wire cutters, an electric drill, and bits. It was painted a deep maroon. It had his name on the side: Michael Gabriel. The label was twofold: one, so people wouldn't — in theory — presumably poach tools off it, and two, so if he pissed off a guest they'd know who to report. He had added a bumper sticker to personalize it further. It read: WHAT IF THE "HOKEY POKEY" REALLY IS WHAT IT'S ALL ABOUT?

So far he had encountered no guests, but the Secret Service and DSS people were omnipresent. A pair of agents, two men in dark suits, stopped him. One's head was triangular shaped, his chin tapered so he looked like a fox or a ferret. He said, "ID and paperwork," snapping his fingers. Derek shrugged and produced the documentation. The other agent looked bored. Ferret Face looked over the paperwork and gestured for Derek to open the cart. Derek did. The agent poked around and shrugged. "Lot of potential weapons in there."

Derek shrugged back. He pointed to the bulge of the gun under the agent's coat. "Real weapon right there."

"Damn straight," the agent said. "Well, you check out. Move on."

Derek did. He was stopped twice more on his way to his repair jobs. Other agents passed him on without checking his identification. It was unpredictable, which was probably the intention.

Derek moved through the steel doors separating the tunnel from Colorado Springs Hall, took a right, and pushed his cart toward the freight elevator. As he waited for it, a trio of people in dark suits approached. They walked with purpose, deep in conversation. When the elevator door opened, the lead agent, a slim white-blond man in a dark suit, said, "Well, since it's here. Hold up."

Derek obediently pushed the DOOR OPEN button and waited for them to enter. The second agent to enter had a head like a cement block, with gray hair cut short and ears that protruded like handles from the side of his head. His suit was black and had an odd cheap cut that didn't fit him all that well. He scowled at Derek, scanned the cart, then seemed to dismiss him.

The third person was a woman. She had long reddish-brown hair, high cheekbones, green eyes, and an oval face. She squeezed into the elevator. It was tight with the four of them and the cart. Her gaze slid over Derek for a moment before she turned her back to him and stared at the elevator door as they rose to the first floor.

Derek's heart hammered in his chest. He knew the woman. She was with the FSB, the *Federal'naya Sluzhba Bezopasnosti*, or Russian Federal Security Service. Her name was Irina Khournikova. And she knew him, too.

The guy with the head like a cinder block, his voice heavily accented, said, "Everything seems to be running clockwise."

The blond guy seemed puzzled. "Er —"

"Like clockwork," Khournikova said. "Everything seems to be running like clockwork." Her English was nearly perfect with only a slight Russian accent.

"Da. What did I say?"

"Clockwise. In circles," said Khournikova.

The Russian man frowned. "No, no. Like clockwork. Da? Going as planned. On schedule?"

"It's looking good," the blond said cautiously. His hair was so blond it looked almost white, his complexion pale and chalky. Derek wondered if he was an albino.

The elevator doors opened, and the three agents moved away. Khournikova didn't look back at him. Derek pushed the cart out of the elevator and headed in the direction of the women's bathroom. He passed by two more security stations and answered their questions and showed them his paperwork and let them look at his cart. When he finally made it to the women's bathroom, he knocked on the door to make sure no one was inside, then propped it open with a yellow plastic sign indicating the restroom was closed for repairs. He grabbed his toolbox and went to see what the problem was with the toilet.

It looked like somebody had tried to flush a tampon, he thought, and went about unclogging the thing. He heard steps behind him and said, "This restroom's closed temporarily. There's one —"

Irina Khournikova stood just inside the doorway, a gun in both hands, aimed directly at him. Her voice was soft. "Hello, Derek. Been a while."

CHAPTER 12

Derek, on his knees in the toilet stall with a plunger in his hand, glanced over his shoulder and raised his eyebrows. He tried to appear nonchalant. "So you're a bad guy now?"

Irina narrowed her eyes and stepped farther into the restroom. The restroom was slightly larger than a double-wide trailer, broken into two duplicate sections joined by a foyer. It screamed money and elegance, and Derek thought it was rather silly — wine-colored marble, gold-plated fixtures, frosted-glass light sconces. He tried to act casual, but he kept his eyes on the gun.

"So," Irina said, "the U.S. government faked your death — just like they faked Richard Coffee's death. Perhaps your government should stop doing that."

"They probably should. But when it comes to Coffee I'll take any edge I can get." Derek turned and clambered to his feet. "Put the gun away, please."

Irina shook her head. "There was quite a bit of speculation by both our governments as to whether you were actually a part of The Fallen Angels."

Derek took two steps closer to Irina. She backed up, but didn't lower the gun. "Stay where you are," she said.

"You're questioning *my* involvement with Coffee? Don't be an idiot. I have more reason to doubt you than anybody, and you know it. Last time we met you and Coffee disappeared at the same time. That doesn't inspire confidence. Why are you here?"

She jerked the gun at him. "Stop moving in on me."

"Okay." He took a fast shuffling step sideways toward a row of maroon marble-topped sinks, momentarily out of her sight. She spun immediately after him. And froze.

Derek kicked out and swept her legs from under her. She hit the marble floor hard and Derek was immediately on her, one knee pressing down on her wrist, the other on her chest. With her free hand she slammed him in the ribs. With a groan he twisted the gun from her grasp and leapt off her.

She rolled instantly to her feet in a graceful motion, pulling another semiautomatic from inside her jacket.

They stood five feet away in identical crouches, guns aimed at each other.

"I see your knee is better now," Irina said.

"Two surgeries. Now tell me, why are you here?" He shuffled slightly to his right. Irina moved slowly to her right as well.

"I'm part of the security detail. And you?"

"We picked up a shred of chatter that suggested Coffee might be interested in the summit."

Irina blinked. "He's back in the States?"

"We lost track of him in Colombia."

"He went to Colombia from Mexico," Khournikova said. "I lost him in Colombia as well. He disappeared into the jungle. There are a lot of drug dealers there as well as a lot of terrorist training camps. I'm sure Coffee would have found eager converts. There are plenty of unhappy, angry people with guns in Colombia looking for someone like Richard Coffee to come along and show them the light."

Derek cocked his head. "Do you think he's going to show up here?" He moved a little bit to his left this time. The Russian aped his movements.

"I'm intrigued that you think he might." With a shake of her head she put her gun back inside her jacket and raised her hands. "Enough. I don't believe you're — how did you say it — a bad guy. As you know, I have personal business with Coffee. So, tell me."

Derek lowered the gun, hesitated, and handed it back to her. He didn't think she was on Coffee's side, although figuring out exactly whose side she was on could sometimes be a problem. "What's your government's take on The Fallen Angels now?"

"We still want him for crimes committed in Russia, but we've seen no activity since his attacks here in the U.S. As you might say, he's on the back burner."

"And with you?"

"If I see him, I will kill him. I won't talk to him or try to arrest him. I will kill him dead."

Derek frowned. "Coffee was pretty deep into your intelligence agencies. Can you trust the people you have here?"

Her green eyes seemed to glow. "You are asking me *that*? Coffee's collaborators *were* your government. Listen to yourself! One of your own FBI agents tried to murder me at his order. Who of your people should *I* trust, Derek Stillwater?"

He shook his head. "Only one. Me."

She nodded. "And you can trust me — if you're willing."

Derek sighed. "I guess I'll have to, won't I?"

She studied him for a moment. "How do I contact you?"

He tapped the Iridium cell phone on his belt and recited the number. She repeated it, committing it to memory.

"I will be patched into the security network," she said thoughtfully. "Where will you be?"

"I'm not inside with the meetings, but on the immediate advance team. I stay ahead of the main group. The summit begins at Cheyenne Hall. Your president is hosting and will be introduced by his chief of staff. Then President Langston will welcome everybody and set the agenda. There will be additional talks by President Vakhach, EU President Waldenstrom, and Prime Minister Hollenbeck before they break into groups. I will be at the International Center during this time period. You?"

Derek shrugged. "I don't know. It'll depend on where I'm needed. I won't be in the main banquet hall during the activities, but I may be in the basement or the perimeter. If possible, I'll watch on the security cameras in the security center."

She nodded. "Then I can contact you if I need to."

Derek nodded. "And you?"

She recited her number. He quickly memorized it. "All right. But don't tell any of your people who I am."

"I understand. Now you can go back to your toilet." With a bitter, crooked grin, she turned and walked out of the restroom.

CHAPTER 13

Lt. General William Akron, deputy director of the Office of the National Intelligence Directorate, paced around his large office in Liberty Crossing. Because of the sensitive nature of the NID, there were no windows in the offices, but it was a large office. It had also been furnished with some first-class furniture — cherry in his case. The building was nearly brand-new — it still smelled ever so faintly of fresh paint.

Akron was thinking about Mandalevo's request. He had ordered it immediately, but he didn't like it. It smelled of politics. The NID had been specifically created because politics interfered with intelligence; because of all the interdepartmental turf wars between the various intelligence agencies.

Akron thought he was up to date on the Derek Stillwater issue and on the matter of The Fallen Angels and Richard Coffee. But maybe not. The Stillwater issue, he thought, was dead and buried. As he walked past his cluttered desk, he reached out and snagged his coffee cup, taking a sip, thinking not for the first time that he wished his office had windows. Such was the life of an intelligence wonk.

Akron had come up through the army. Served in Desert Storm in '91 and later in Kosovo. Ran military intelligence for a while, then worked at the CIA, and for a while directed the NSA. His career had almost ended during the Clinton administration, the so-called don't-ask-don't-tell period. Akron, who was more-or-less openly gay, had chosen to "not tell" and keep his job, although from time to time the subject came up in terms of national security clearances. He was currently single, and with the demands of his job, pretty much chaste and celibate. He did have a cat named Harley, but aside from Harley, there wasn't a lot in Akron's life except his work.

His secretary buzzed him and let him know the files were here. The chain of custody security issues could be a pain in the ass, so rather than add signatures Akron pushed into his secretary's office and signed off on the thick folder containing confidential files and several computer disks. All were labeled TOP SECRET.

Akron's secretary, an efficient man with a crew cut and wire-rimmed glasses who projected the sense that he would be happier wearing a military uniform, said, "Wheels up in ten minutes. Anything you need the director to know in the next twenty?"

"No." Akron shrugged his broad shoulders, ran a hand through his unruly gray hair and pushed back into his office, shut the door, and opened the first file, the one on Derek Stillwater. It was thick and most of it was made up of conflicting FBI reports and attorney general briefs regarding Stillwater's actions during The Fallen Angels' first terror attack. Akron had been over it before and in his opinion Derek Stillwater had been acting in the only way possible during what turned out to be one of the worst terrorist events in U.S. history. The FBI had gotten their boxers in a bind because they were left looking like idiots.

There was more than an element of a witch hunt on the part of the attorney general, who made no secret that he would prefer that Secretary James Johnston had stepped down for good after the failure of the Department of Homeland Security to predict or prevent the initial attack.

Akron thought the AG had an easy job. Clean up the messes afterward and assign blame.

Scanning the document, something caught his eye. He read it carefully. It was a report concerning Derek Stillwater's death. What had Robert said? *Find out if he's really dead.*

Why would they fake Stillwater's death?

One reason would be politics, wouldn't it? Under investigation by the FBI and the attorney general, the AG hounding after Johnston's job, Stillwater's death would douse the flames of a major political brush fire.

Was Johnston political enough to do that? In Akron's experience, Jim Johnston hated politics and avoided tricky political maneuvering when possible. Akron didn't think much of Johnston's administrative skills, even less of his political skills, but he thought he was possibly a tactical genius. If Johnston ever left Homeland Security, Akron would consider him to run operations at the Office of the National Intelligence director.

Should be easy to prove, though. He picked up the phone and asked his assistant to get him in touch with someone involved in death benefits for the Veterans Administration.

CHAPTER 14

Richard Coffee and *El Tiburón* completed setting out the special wine and champagne bottles around the ballroom. Unnoticed, they slipped into a storeroom and changed out of their catering uniforms and into the uniforms of the Secret Service technicians — dark pants, white shirt, dark tie, and dark windbreakers. They carried credentials supplied by their inside man, Vincent Silvedo. They plugged in the earphones and throat mics for their surveillance kits, which allowed them to stay in touch with their own people, and with a flick of a switch, monitor the Secret Service security network.

The storeroom contained extra chairs and tables and the carts to transport them. It was loaded with boxes and crates containing extra sound equipment, platforms, and backdrops for the stage in the ballroom.

El Tiburón, whose real name was Pablo Juarez, used a pry bar to carefully open the crate containing guns, explosives, and other equipment. Juarez liked guns, but he really liked explosives. C4, Semtex, dynamite, claymores, ammonium nitrate, it didn't matter. He was an expert with them, having been trained by the CIA during the late '80s when he was only a teenager living in Colombia. Trained, rewarded, betrayed, and hunted. He had fallen, and now they would pay for their betrayal.

He moved the explosives into a separate container. Coffee picked up the special device, his pride and joy, and carefully laid it in the center of the crate. *El Tiburón* smiled. He thought Coffee — The Fallen — was a genius. A madman even by his broad standards, but brilliant. *El Tiburón* had learned valuable lessons from The Fallen — have more than one plan; create backups for your backups; make the enemy think one thing while planning something different; think big and think global.

On top of the explosives and other equipment *El Tiburón* placed flashlights, probes, and tools that the service used in preparing a security site. If anybody bothered to check, they would pass inspection, at least for a few moments. If anybody got that close to discovering them, *El Tiburón* and Fallen were prepared to kill without hesitation.

El Tiburón sealed the crate with an official Secret Service seal provided by Silvedo. He looked over at The Fallen, who was studying a floor plan. The Fallen looked different than he had only months before. His hair was blond, his face clean-shaven, eyes covered by tinted wire-rimmed glasses.

"*¿Está listo?*" Are you ready?

The Fallen nodded, folding the floor plan away in his pocket. "*Si. Armenos una trampa para algunos ratones grandes.*" Yes. Let's set a trap for some big mice.

El Tiburón laughed. "*Asi es que es la verdad. Si construye un ratonera major todo el mudno correrá a su puerta.*" So it's true. If you build a better mousetrap, the world will beat a path to your door.

"*Si. Y doblar la rodilla por miedo y respeto.*" Yes. And bow at your feet in fear and respect.

With a mutual laugh, the two men pushed the crate and dolly out of the storeroom and into the hallway.

CHAPTER 15

After finishing with the lights, Derek used his phone to call Steve Planchette, his boss. "I'm over at the International Center. Anything else over here?"

Planchette's voice was as easygoing as usual. The man just never seemed ruffled by anything, even the thought of twenty world leaders and their staffs pissing and moaning about cobwebs or toilets being backed up. "Not over there, but come on back. One of the walk-ins isn't holding its temperature, there're some problems with one of the ranges and there might be a problem with some electrical stuff in the kitchen, too. You mind?"

"No. I'll be right there."

"Thanks, Mike."

Derek clicked off and began the long trod back to the Cheyenne Center through Secret Service checkpoints. He was amused that Steve didn't seem uptight with the kitchen problems. The caterers and kitchen crew must be flipping out.

He'd find out soon enough. As he passed through the tunnel into the Cheyenne Center, he noted two Secret Service agents working in the ceiling area just inside the security doors. There was a dolly loaded with a crate marked SECRET SERVICE. One of the agents stood at the base of a folding ladder. He wore the dark slacks, dark windbreaker, and rubber-soled shoes of the service. His face was angular and bony, complexion swarthy, hair dark. He looked Hispanic, maybe even Native American. His dark eyes locked on Derek.

Derek prepared to be stopped again, but the agent just nodded him past. He glanced up at the other agent, but he stood on the top of the ladder, his upper body hidden within a hatchway to the service areas that ran between the basement ceiling and the first floor subfloor. It was a four-foot-high crawl space of dusty, grimy girders, conduits, valves, wiring, and circuits.

As Derek turned the corner, he glanced back at the two agents. Something inside his head set off a vague alarm, but he wasn't sure what it was. Maybe it was just that he didn't know what they were doing in the crawl space. It had been swept thoroughly in the previous days, and he had even led some of the Secret Service agents around some of the nooks and crannies of the facilities, though it was always hard to tell if they were paying attention. The Secret Service tended to set their own agenda.

Riding up to the main floor, he pondered what it had been about the guy that bothered him, but couldn't put a finger on it. He was used to relying on his gut instincts, but the truth was, he was never meant to work undercover. He had parents and a brother, family. He had a life that he liked, living on a cabin cruiser on Chesapeake Bay, kayaking, working. Undercover, he spent all his time worrying. Paranoia was like a tattoo, once it imprinted on your skin it was almost impossible to erase.

Maria Sanchez walked past the kitchen toward the banquet hall carrying a box of cloth napkins. "Hey, *amante.* Miss me already?"

Derek grinned. "You bet."

"Ah, a tease. What you been doing?"

"Fixing the women's toilet. You?"

"Making the place pretty, of course." Maria made a face. "Of course, William is running around like his hair is on fire. The ice sculpture is melting in the freezer, and a couple of the ranges aren't working. He's *loco grande.*"

"I'm on my way."

"Oh, you poor boy," she said. "Better watch out. William's a screamer."

"I can handle it. See you later."

With a laugh she said, "Promises, promises," and sashayed into the banquet hall.

It wasn't hard to find William O'Grady. All you had to do was follow the snarling voice. O'Grady was as wide as he was tall, about five feet six, in chef's whites. His sweaty, curly hair clung to his round scalp, his complexion as red as a setting sun. Hands on hips, he was screaming at a cook about the way she was cutting carrots for the salads.

"Are you mad? *Julienned! *They have to be *julienned! *That means like matchsticks! Sliced! Not these — these *chunks! *Who the hell do you think you're preparing food for? Bugs Bunny? We're serving the most powerful people on the planet! Slice the damned carrots thin!"

O'Grady spun to glare at Derek. "Who the fuck are you?"

"Maintenance. I understand you've —"

"Oh, so now you decide to show up! This kitchen is a goddamned disaster area!"

Derek didn't think so. It was huge, gleaming stainless steel, dozens of ranges and ovens and work areas. Chef O'Grady had a white-coated staff of well over a dozen to berate, belittle, and bark at, with plenty of room to maneuver. The air smelled delicious — roast chicken, baked fish, succulent beef. Derek understood the initial menu included prime rib and mahimahi and garlic mashed potatoes. He had slim hopes that he'd get to sample some of it in the kitchen during dinner. Steam filled the air, making the area feel like a sauna. The air conditioning couldn't keep up. Derek said, "What's the *biggest* problem?"

"If you people were doing your job, there wouldn't be a problem! What kind of incompetents are you? Why is my kitchen such a disaster area?"

Derek waited, unruffled by O'Grady's tantrums. "What needs fixing first?"

"You shouldn't have to fix anything! It should have been working properly! If you would —"

Derek glanced pointedly at his watch. "What's *first*?"

"The gas ranges, three and four. They're always on high. How can we cook if we can't turn down the heat? Have you ever heard of simmer? Have you ever heard of low? Have you —"

Derek pushed past O'Grady and walked over to where a handful of cooks were struggling with a dozen saucepans. "Which ones are three and four?"

One of the cooks, a round-faced kid with hazel eyes and a shock of thick brown hair, said, "These two. Can't turn 'em down."

"Yeah? Probably the switch contacts are shorted shut. We'll need to close it down, then I can fix them in no time."

"Hurry!" screamed O'Grady.

Derek rolled his eyes. "Let's get it shut off, dude, so I can get you back to work."

He patted the poor cook on the shoulder and headed out into the hallway to retrieve his toolbox, feeling guilty for the amount of verbal abuse the guy was receiving. Derek had sabotaged the ranges and the freezer the day before so he would be in the building when the summit began. He didn't want to leave it to chance that something might go down in one building while he was stuck in another. As much as possible, events were proceeding the way he had intended.

CHAPTER 16

Secretary Mandalevo stared at the computer screen, reading through all the documents and conclusions Akron had e-mailed him. Fingering the computer keyboard, he gazed out the window of Air Force One, noticing a broad expanse of river below them. Probably the Mississippi, he thought.

A heavyset blond guy appeared in front of him. "Secretary Mandalevo?"

Mandalevo quickly snapped the computer screen shut. "Yes?"

The guy stuck out a pudgy hand. "Frank Arlen. *Washington Post.* Mind if I sit down?"

Before Mandalevo could say anything, Arlen flopped into the seat across from him. Arlen flipped open a notepad. "Thought I'd just get some notes before we hit Colorado. Naughty, naughty, the way you've got all the press segregated from the summit."

Mandalevo shrugged. "I'm not part of those arrangements."

Arlen swept a greasy lock of blond hair off his forehead and fumbled in his coat until he found a pen. "Just want to confirm a few things. You started your career with the State Department, right?"

Mandalevo stared at the reporter. He did not like dealing with the press. He never had, and in his recent position as National Intelligence Director he liked it even less. He was a career bureaucrat. He started as an intern at the State Department, worked his way up to a series of postings around the world at U.S. embassies including Greece, England, Germany, Saudi Arabia, Kenya, Russia, and Argentina. He spent three years at the Central Intelligence Agency in the Intelligence Directorate, four years with the United Nations, then was made ambassador to Spain, then ambassador to the U.N.

"Are you writing a profile on me?"

"No, no. Just background."

Mandalevo cocked his head. "How about instead of dancing around like this you just come out and ask me whatever it is you planned on asking me after you asked all the stuff you already know."

Arlen gave an aw-shucks shake of his head that didn't even come near being sincere. "Hey, ya got me. What I want to know is whether or not you think the creation of the Office of the National Intelligence Directorate actually did what it was created to do. I mean, it's supposed to be nonpolitical."

Although not a politician, Mandalevo understood the use of political capital and the way in which information was coin of the realm and a tool. The NID was definitely political and no, it probably wasn't doing what it was designed to do. And if he said that his career in government would be over. He said, "Is there a question in there, Mr. Arlen?"

"Never mind. Know you're not going to answer that one. How about this one, then? What is the NID's current data on Richard Coffee and The Fallen Angels?"

Mandalevo returned a flat stare. "It's classified."

"I have a source that claims Coffee might do something at the summit."

Mandalevo didn't respond to that. Arlen poised, pen in hand. "Do you have a comment, Secretary Mandalevo?"

"I do not."

Arlen scribbled something down. He glanced up and said, "What's your take on the president's current erratic behavior?"

"I find nothing erratic about the president's behavior. And if this is where your so-called interview is going, it's terminated. Goodbye, Mr. Arlen."

"Hey, let's not —"

"I have work to do. Please leave."

Arlen, a smile on his face, got up and walked back to the press section of the plane. Trying to put that encounter out of his mind, Mandalevo reopened his laptop and studied the files more closely. There was little new information on Richard Coffee and The Fallen Angels. He had been fully and appropriately briefed over the last year on what little was known about their remaining members and Richard Coffee. It was useful information, but probably not as political currency.

Confirming that Derek Stillwater was alive, on the other hand, if used in the proper way, could be political dynamite.

During the first U.S. encounter with The Fallen Angels, Derek Stillwater had been directly involved in a number of deaths and illegal procedures. After the conclusion of the crisis, Stillwater was placed on leave from the Department of Homeland Security pending a Justice Department and congressional investigation.

Those investigations had been ongoing when Stillwater was called in to investigate a series of domestic terror attacks in Detroit. During the resolution of the case, Stillwater was reported to have died.

Mandalevo considered the implications of Stillwater's fake death. He gave James Johnston credit for pulling off an intelligence coup. Stillwater was undoubtedly a talented troubleshooter, though he wasn't one to color inside the lines. But if given the correct slant, it looked as if Johnston — with the full cooperation of President Langston — had faked the death of a government agent in order to end an FBI and congressional investigation. Stillwater's death had conveniently ended the investigations.

Stillwater was a bureaucratic problem. Although gifted in a crisis, he was an impossible political liability the rest of the time, unwilling to play by the rules.

In a lot of ways, Mandelevo didn't really care. As the director of national intelligence he was involved in a power battle for funding and control of intelligence with the Central Intelligence Agency, the Defense Department, the National Security Agency, and the Department of Homeland Security.

He knew members of Congress who would be very interested in knowing about this — members of Congress who controlled funding for the U.S. intelligence apparatus and who were not necessarily friends of James Johnston. So, how to make good use of this information?

Mandalevo opened his laptop and began writing a carefully worded briefing to several members of the Senate Intelligence Committee.

CHAPTER 17

Carl Smith strode to the middle of the parking lot of Discovery Park in Colorado Springs. This part of the park was dominated by soccer fields, their goal zone nets empty. Beyond were forested foothills crisscrossed with hiking trails and tempting views of the Rocky Mountains just above the tree line. The air smelled of coffee and donuts and mountain air and pine.

A good-sized crowd milled about, swigging coffee from biodegradable paper cups and chatting. A few early birds had lit up joints, but in general the crowd was a sober pack of free-worlders determined to save the planet from democracy, capitalism, and free trade. Quite a few eyes followed Smith's movements, and when he raised the bullhorn to his lips, there was a swell of murmurings, then applause.

"Good morning." Carl's voice boomed across the parking lot. "How is everybody today?"

A cheer rose from the crowd. Dozens of people raised signs with slogans painted on them in vibrant bloody colors. Smith liked this crowd. He liked how easily manipulated they were. All they needed was a shove in the right direction and they would do the rest. The signs read things like:

> G8 with a circular slash through it.
> G8=PROFITS OVER PEOPLE!
> DOWN WITH ECONOMIC TYRANNY!
> LANGSTON IS A WARMONGER!
> U.S. OUT OF MIDDLE EAST!!

Half the crowd had brought plastic mop buckets and wooden spoons and banged the buckets like drums. At first it was an unorganized thud and clatter, slowly gaining momentum into a low, primitive heartbeat.

Smith noted with satisfaction that half a dozen TV cameras were taking it all in.

Smith, voice magnified by the bullhorn, said, "Are you ready for the world to hear our voices?"

"Yes!!!"

"Are you ready to show the G8 the power of the people?"

"Yes!!!"

"Are you ready to show the G8 where the *real* power is?"

"Yes!!!"

"ON THE BUSES!!!"

Four battered yellow school buses were lined up in the parking lot. The crowd swarmed toward them like sheep toward a slaughter chute. It took a few minutes to fill them, the TV reporters squeezing on to catch all the action — a good demonstration, violent or otherwise, was much better news than a bunch of politicians massaging each other's egos for three days. The buses pulled out of Discovery Park and headed toward the Cheyenne Hills Resort.

In the lead bus, Carl Smith, whose given name was Carlos Santos, hung onto the shiny stainless steel pole by the door and shouted to the riders, "What do we do at the checkpoint?"

Somebody shouted, "We fuck 'em!"

"We march!" Santos shouted. "We march! They can't stop us! We have the right to be heard! ONE VOICE!!"

A handful in the bus shouted, "ONE VOICE!"

Louder, Santos shouted, "ONE VOICE!"

Everybody this time: "ONE VOICE!"

"ONE VOICE!"

"ONE VOICE!!!"

The chant in the bus was deafening. Santos raised his fist in the air. "REVOLUTION!!!!"

The crowd roared: "REVOLUTION!!!"

CHAPTER 18

Tobias Leeman watched Air Force One touch down at Peterson Air Force Base, which shared landing strips with the Colorado Springs International Airport. It was a picture-perfect landing on a clear, warm June day. When the jet slowed to a halt, six black limousines sped across the tarmac toward the plane. The airport had been shut down to commercial traffic. Only a handful of the press had been allowed in to watch the transfer. The area had been completely shut down to the public, who could not get closer than the outer perimeter.

Secret Service Agent Marilyn Ashland said, "Mr. Leeman? Ready?"

Tobias Leeman was a tall, lanky, bald man. His perpetual scowl was masked with a thick dark beard. His official title was the White House deputy national security advisor. His official title for the summit was Sherpa. Each country represented at the G8 Summit had a Sherpa, whose job it was to organize the activities of their leader. During critical negotiations, the president of the United States was only accompanied by his Sherpa and an interpreter.

Leeman would be able to communicate with his staff using the most cutting-edge tablet computers and Groove software. His task, besides organizing the event, was as the principal policy analyst. Directly beneath him was a pair of sous-Sherpas, one representing the U.S. interests in finance and the other in foreign affairs. In this case, the secretary of commerce and the deputy secretary of state.

Leeman chewed on his lower lip. "Give them a few minutes." He glanced over to where the press waited like jackals at a watering hole. He slapped his cellular phone to his ear and growled, "Ed? How're we doing?"

Edward Fanconi was the deputy United States chief of protocol, and it was his duty to welcome the leaders of the other countries, perform an arrival ceremony, and shepherd the leaders to a brief ceremony led by President Langston.

Fanconi's deep, careful voice boomed through the telephone. "It's a fucking nightmare, Tobey. The goddamned Saudi contingent refuses to land after the Israeli contingent and the Israelis, good God, they —"

"AF1 just landed."

"Thank God. I'm juggling, trying to make everybody happy. I hope —"

"Gotta go, Ed. Balls to the wall."

Leeman hung up and cocked his head at Special Agent Ashland, a middle-aged woman with high cheekbones, pure white hair she wore to her shoulders, and a strong, determined jaw. "It's showtime."

Lauren McCullough knocked on the door to President Langston's quarters on Air Force One and stepped in. "Ready, Mr. President?"

President Langston, standing by his desk, flung on his coat and paused to take a deep breath. McCullough had seen him do this before. It was an interesting shift, from a normal man with more than just the burdens of the world's most powerful leadership on his shoulders, to the president of the United States of America. The man in private was different than the man who occupied the presidency. The private man was aging at an accelerated rate due to personal tragedies and the pressures of the job. He was often preoccupied, indecisive, and malleable. The man who was the president was none of those things. He was vigorous, focused, and decisive.

Like everybody else who had close contact with the president, McCullough recognized that the president's personal personality was showing up more often where the presidential personality should have been. More than anyone else, she was worried. It was part of her job to make sure he was able to do his job. She just wasn't sure he was.

"Ready." He strode past her, announced in a loud voice, "Let's go change the world, folks!" and headed for his Secret Service contingent and the plane's hatch.

Three agents inside the plane escorted him to the ramp, then nodded. "Down the steps, Mr. President."

"Press?"

"A few."

"Very good."

Langston stepped through the hatch, pausing at the top to turn to the small contingent of media. He raised a hand and waved, expression grave and confident. Then he moved down the steps and was enfolded in the embrace of another set of Secret Service agents who ushered him into the back of a limousine, where Leeman awaited him.

"Good morning, Mr. President."

"Not so far, Tobey. How's it going?"

"Ed seems to have everything under control."

President Langston glanced at McCullough. "Well, there's a first time for everything."

McCullough said, "Ed's good at this. He just acts hysterical while he's doing it. It'll be fine. Things holding up with Israel and the Saudis?"

"Not according to Ed."

Langston rolled his eyes. "Bad idea. We've been inviting the Saudis for years and they always turn us down. We invite Israel, and the next thing you know, the Saudis insist they attend. Are we on schedule?"

"Perfect," Leeman said.

"Well, at least one thing's going okay."

In moments the limo arrived at the Peterson Air & Space Museum. They pulled up in front of the peculiar building, roughly the shape of a B on its side, the curved humps of the B facing forward, all done in white. They escorted the president toward the main entrance.

Leeman nodded. "Mr. President, I'd like you to meet Brigadier General Stephen Newman, base commander."

Newman was a hard, bald man with skin the color of charcoal. He saluted. "Welcome to Peterson Air Force Base, Mr. President."

"Thank you, General. A pleasure to meet you." As they shook hands the staff photographer snapped away.

"The other leaders are on their way, sir," Newman said. "You have time to meet my staff before they arrive?"

"Of course. My pleasure."

They strode into the interior of the museum. Several dozen military men and women stood at attention, awaiting their commander-in-chief's presence. Slowly, with great ceremony, President Langston made a few remarks, then shook hands with each person in the building.

Lauren McCullough watched from the sidelines, pleased how

Langston was doing. Beside her, Leeman checked his e-mail on the tablet computer. He said, "He seems preoccupied."

"He's always preoccupied."

"More than usual."

McCullough frowned. "Tobey, you do your job, okay? I'll do mine. He'll be fine."

"They say these things are casual, but you and I know better. You don't put the world's top eight leaders around a table with twelve others observing from the sidelines without everybody scrambling for position. He needs to be at the top of his game."

She stabbed him with her sharp gaze. "You worry too much."

"You're not going to be at the table alone with him."

"I said he'll be fine."

Leeman glanced around the room, focusing for a moment on President Langston's words. "—this emblem of our country's courage in the face of sacrifice—"

Voice low, Leeman said, "He hasn't been fine since the terrorist attacks. We all would have been happier if Richard Coffee had been caught before this summit. It's what's on his mind, isn't it? That The Fallen Angels are going to somehow make a run at him again."

"This summit is the most secure place in the world for the next three days, Tobey. Let Coffee take his best shot."

Leeman glanced sharply at her. "Don't tempt fate." He tapped his tablet PC and groaned. "Hollenbeck's plane just landed. Here we go. The British are coming, the British are coming—"

CHAPTER 19

Secret Service Agent Lee Padillo was in the International Center's basement security office when FBI Agent Sarah Macklin stepped through the door. Padillo was lead agent for this event, in charge of all security. Macklin was the bureau's point agent. Padillo, lean, swarthy, intense, sat back in an Aeron chair and stared intently at a computer screen in front of him, listening on an earpiece to an update from Peterson Air Force Base.

"Yes, everything's ready here. All assets in place?"

His agent at Peterson Air Force Base said, "Finally got things settled down between the Saudis and Israel enough to let them land. There's some quibbling over who rides with whom that should have been settled before now, but we're on top of it."

"ETA?"

"Thirty minutes. Wheels up in ten."

"Affirmative."

Padillo clicked off and spun in the chair to face Macklin. "Everybody's gathered at Peterson and are loading onto the choppers as we speak. ETA thirty minutes."

Macklin nodded. Slender, tall, athletic, she wore her auburn hair cropped just below her ears. Her navy blue suit was tailored to emphasize her broad shoulders, which made her appear more willowy than she actually was. She came off as determined because of a square jaw that she tended to lead with, and her habit of speaking through clenched teeth. "I need a minute in private."

Padillo frowned. "Can it wait?"

She shook her head.

He waved her over to a private office and kicked out the agent who was using it. It was a utilitarian box, a few photos of mountain vistas on the wall, a large metal desk, three chairs, and a computer. It was a temporary office used by whatever visiting security agent was running a particular security event. The resort's security director, a former FBI agent, had a much nicer office down the hall.

Macklin shut the door and said, "I just got a phone call from Director Bray. Something's going on. It's political, but it has some security implications. Are you familiar with a DHS troubleshooter by the name of Derek Stillwater?"

Padillo searched his memory and shrugged. "Name rings a bell, but I don't know why."

"He retrieved Chimera during last year's —"

"Yeah, yeah, yeah. Right. He's dead, though."

"So we were led to believe."

Padillo arched his eyebrows. "Meaning what?"

"Director Bray just received a phone call from Senator Weschel, head of the Senate Intelligence Committee. Weschel claims that Derek Stillwater isn't actually dead, and that he's here at the summit. Undercover."

Padillo blinked. "Undercover."

Macklin nodded.

"We weren't informed of this. Not at all. He didn't turn up on any background checks. Do we know what his cover is?"

"No," said Macklin. "And we haven't confirmed any of this."

"Who's Weschel's source?"

"No idea."

Padillo swallowed. Hard. The Secret Service was under the blanket of the Department of Homeland Security now. If Stillwater was really here, an undercover asset, he should have been informed.

"I don't —" He stopped, not wanting to make it appear he was out of the loop or that he didn't know how to handle this situation. "I see," he said. "I'll look into it. Thank you."

Macklin cocked her head. "Look, Lee. It's not completely clear if Stillwater's one of the good guys or not. We were investigating him. There were hints he was involved with The Fallen Angels. When he *died* it got set aside. This smells like a cover-up."

Padillo leaned back in his chair, hands up in a surrender gesture.

"All right. Thank you. I get your point. I want a couple people looking for him. Once they find him, we want him locked up. We can deal with the particulars after the summit's over. Take care of it. He's your baby. Work for you?"

Macklin shot him a thumbs-up. "Absolutely."

CHAPTER 20

Derek finished fixing the two sabotaged stoves under the harangues of Chef O'Grady. They fell off him the way water flowed off a rock. Derek wondered whatever would possess a man to scream at someone holding tools in his hand — an overwhelming desire to have a wrench jammed up his ass?

"Finally," O'Grady said. "You took long enough."

Derek stood up and turned to the chef, expression flat. He held a screwdriver pointed at O'Grady's swelling midsection. "It took as long as it took," he said. Something in his tone of voice and the look on his face must have gotten through to the chef, because he lapsed into silence for a moment.

Derek nodded. "Unless there's something else out here, I'll get to work on the walk-in."

"No," O'Grady said with a shake of his head. "That's it for here."

Derek collected his tools and walked away with a wink at one of the cooks. It was a short-lived respite. As soon as he was out of the area he heard O'Grady screaming: "Those are supposed to be *carmelized! Not fried! Carmelized!* We want the sugars! We're not doing Cajun here! Nothing's blackened! Where did you learn to cook? McDonald's?"

CHAPTER 21

Richard Coffee and *El Tiburón* closed the ceiling panel by the entrance to the main banquet hall and stepped off the ladder. Coffee tapped his earpiece, listened for a moment, then said to *El Tiburón*, "Wheels up at Peterson. ETA twenty minutes."

They pushed the now-empty dolly back into a storage area. Silently they stripped off their windbreakers and donned the white coats of the catering staff. Coffee spoke into his throat mic. "On schedule. I repeat, on schedule."

The two men shared a satisfied glance. Everything was going according to plan. *El Tiburón* said, "This seems too easy."

Coffee smiled. "Sometimes things *go* according to plan. But we're not through yet. Are you ready?"

"I'm ready."

The Fallen clamped a hand on the man's shoulder. "A pleasure working with you."

Without seeming to hurry, they separated. They exited the storage area, moving into the banquet room. *El Tiburón* headed toward one of the tables loaded with liquor, his job to mix in with the waitstaff. Coffee moved through on his way to the kitchen, where he would help deliver food to the banquet area.

Coffee checked his watch again. ETA: twelve minutes.

CHAPTER 22

Agent Sarah Macklin sat at her computer in the FBI command center in the resort's main building. It was a conference room with no windows, and they had brought in a dozen folding tables and loaded up the room with computers, telephones, and radio equipment. Eight or nine agents were monitoring the computers and talking on the phones, keeping tabs on various aspects of the security event.

Macklin compared the headshot of Derek Stillwater she had pulled off the bureau database with the headshots of male employees at the Cheyenne Hills Resort. She was able to winnow it down to about seven hundred faces just by eliminating the women. She started with last names beginning with the letters *A* through *I*. One of her agents, Bill Creff, looked at *J* through *S*. Joe Snyder sifted *T* through *Z*.

"Check this out," Snyder said.

She and Creff glanced over at Snyder's computer, peering at the face on the screen. Angular face, dark wavy hair, age thirty-five to fifty. The name was Stanley Federov and the file indicated he worked in the golf shop. They studied the image.

"Close, but not quite. Keep him on the list, though."

They went back to their computers.

Macklin's radio buzzed in her ear. She clicked it on. "Macklin."

"This is Padillo. POTUS is on his way. ETA four minutes."

"Understood."

She clicked past the face on the screen, an African-American. The next up on the resort's security database was a headshot of a guy on the resort's maintenance staff. His name was Michael Gabriel.

She pulled up Derek Stillwater's headshot and placed it alongside the one of Michael Gabriel that had been taken for his security badge.

The hair was different—much shorter and lighter in color, and he'd grown a goatee, but it was clearly the same man. "Bingo!" she said.

Snyder and Creff took a look. Creff said, "Been working here eight months. Timing's right."

"Good cover, too," said Macklin. "Complete access to the facility."

Macklin picked up the phone and dialed Steve Planchette, head of maintenance. When he answered, she said, "This is FBI Special-Agent-in-Charge Sarah Macklin. Is your employee Michael Gabriel working today?"

"Sure."

"Where is he right now?"

"In the kitchen, I think. There a problem?"

"No, sir. No problem. Thank you."

She hung up and looked at her partners. "Okay, gentlemen. Let's go pick up this guy."

CHAPTER 23

Derek Stillwater was working inside the walk-in freezer. The Cheyenne Center's kitchen area was large enough to support one walk-in freezer and two walk-in refrigerators. The refrigerators were convenient to the cooking areas, but the freezer was tucked away in a cul-de-sac near a service hallway, which was partly why Derek had chosen to sabotage it.

It was cold, so he propped the door open. For some reason known only to the contractors who custom made and installed it, the controls were inside the freezer instead of outside. The compressor was beneath the structure. The walk-in was large, easily twenty-five feet deep, seven feet high, and fifteen feet wide. Shelves ran along the walls and were jammed with frozen produce.

He had purposely created a short in the controls that would be relatively easy to fix. Still, it was a pain in the ass. In order to open the control panel all the way he had to shove aside a stainless steel shelf piled high with what looked like frozen turkeys — dozens of them. Then, jammed into the corner, he used his screwdriver to open the control panel, shut down the power so he didn't fry himself, then reconnected the wires.

Derek was in a very awkward position when a broad-shouldered woman in a dark suit stepped into the freezer, followed by two other men. Derek recognized the woman.

Sarah Macklin, the bureau's lead agent during the summit. Like most of the staffers at the resort, he had sat through a few briefings she had run on what to expect. He was not encouraged by her presence.

"Michael Gabriel?"

He nodded. "Yeah? Who're you?"

She held up her identification. "Will you please step out of there?"

"Uh, sure. Wait a second, I'm almost —"

"Now, Mr. Gabriel."

Taking his time, he joined the wires, closed the panel, turned on the power, and looked at the indicators. The power came back on. With it he heard the whir of the compressor kick in.

"Mr. Gabriel —"

"Just finishing this up," he said, "or we're going to lose a few thousand pounds of meat." He flashed Macklin a wry grin. "Wouldn't want to give all the leaders of the free world a case of salmonella poisoning, now, would we?" He screwed the panel shut.

"What's this all about?" he asked, squeezing out from behind the shelving. "Hey, one of you guys help me shove this —"

Macklin's gun was out, as were Creff's and Snyder's. "Dr. Derek Stillwater, please drop your tools and tool belt and place your hands on top of your head."

Oh shit.

"Hey, I don't —"

"Do it!"

Damn.

He cautiously slipped the screwdriver into his tool belt and held out his hands. "I'm going to unbuckle this, all right? I'm not going to do anything crazy. Okay? Ease down. Easy. I'm reaching down to unbuckle the belt."

He slowly dropped his hands to the buckle of his tool belt and unlatched it. The belt with a few of his tools slid away. He held it up in his right hand. "I'm going to put this right here next to my toolbox. Okay? Right here. Everything's cool."

Slowly he let the belt down.

"I'm coming forward. Slowly."

He did, hands held up.

"On your head."

He placed his hands on top of his head. Stepping backward, Macklin said, "Creff, pat him down."

Creff holstered his sidearm and deftly searched Derek. Creff pulled out Derek's wallet and flipped through it. "Michael Gabriel, it says."

"He's Derek Stillwater. Dr. Stillwater, you're supposed to be dead. Hands behind your back. Creff, cuffs, please."

"Hey, this isn't nece —"

Creff jerked Derek's arms behind his back and slapped handcuffs tightly around his wrists.

Derek protested. "Take it easy! I'm one of the good guys."

"That remains to be seen," Macklin said. "Now, step outside."

"I want you to make a call to Secretary James Johnston. His personal cell phone number is —"

"Can it, Stillwater." She stepped out of the freezer. Creff gave him a shove so he followed her out into the corner of the kitchen area. The freezer was near the service walkway that ran beside the kitchen. Derek stumbled out of the freezer and into the hallway, dropping momentarily to his knees.

"Hey, go easy!"

Creff stepped up, caught him beneath his armpits and boosted him to his feet. "'Hey' yourself, asshole!"

Derek turned to face Creff and froze. Standing behind Creff was Richard Coffee. Coffee recognized him at the same time.

"That's Coffee! Hey, look —"

Coffee recovered fast, hand slipping inside his white catering jacket. He pulled out a matte black semiautomatic with a slender, cylindrical silencer on the muzzle. With an eerie calm, he fired the gun.

There was a pop, not loud, and Creff's head snapped back and he fell to the floor.

Another pop, and Snyder went down.

Agent Macklin was struggling for her gun, eyes wide, when Coffee shot her in the face.

Derek, arms cuffed behind his back, tried to turn and run, but Coffee was on him in an instant. Squinting, Coffee spun him around, flung open the freezer door and shoved him in. He followed the move by smashing the barrel of his gun against Derek's head.

Derek's world exploded into sizzling reds and blacks and golds, but he didn't lose consciousness. He struggled to sit up, but everything seemed to be happening in slow motion. The freezer door closed. When it reopened, Coffee dragged Macklin's body in, followed shortly afterward by the bodies of Bill Creff and Joe Snyder.

Coffee disappeared for a moment. Derek's vision doubled, tripled, then returned to normal, though his skull throbbed and blood leaked down his forehead. Not as bad as Macklin, he thought, and turned away from the sight of her obliterated features.

Suddenly the door swung open and Coffee stepped through again. He reached down and hauled Derek to his feet. He slammed him against the stainless steel door and pressed the barrel of the gun under his chin.

"Not dead after all."

Derek didn't reply.

"Are you frightened, Derek? Knees shaky? Is this how Nadia felt when you tortured her to death? Helpless?"

Derek's mind raced. The still-hot barrel of the silenced gun burned into his jaw. "She's — not — dead."

Coffee's face twisted in unexpected shock. He smashed the butt of the gun against Derek's jaw. *"What did you say?"*

Stumbling to the cold metal floor, Derek tried to suck air into his lungs. His pulse hammered in his ears, blood roaring through his veins. "She's not dead," he said, wondering if the blow had broken his jaw. His speech seemed a little slurred. "They have her. The FBI."

"She's dead! You murdered her!"

Coffee was in his face. The icy control he so casually wore was only a thin veneer over insanity. Derek stared up at him, feeling calmer. "She's not dead, Richard. She's at Guantanamo with the rest of The Fallen Angels we captured in Alexandria."

"You lie!" The gun rose and fell again. This time Derek slumped to the floor, his vision blurring, unable to get up with his arms behind his back.

"You lie!"

Derek shook his head and instantly regretted the movement. "No," he grunted out. "She's alive. Just like I am."

Coffee spun in circles like a child unsure which direction to go. He flexed his arms in frustration, staring down at Derek at his feet. He raised the gun, aimed it —

He glanced at his watch and seemed to reconsider. "Fucker!" he coughed. "I'll be back for you later! You *will* tell me the truth about Nadia." Coffee reached down and ripped Derek's Iridium phone off his belt, dropped it to the floor and stomped it into pieces.

And Coffee was gone, the metal door of the freezer slamming shut behind him. Derek heard a metallic clank, then nothing.

Nadia Kosov, thought Derek. *We really do get punished for our sins.* Nadia Kosov had been Richard Coffee's common-law wife. She had tried to first recruit Derek to The Fallen Angels, and when that didn't work, tried to kill him. Derek had overpowered her and interrogated her — that was the official word for what amounted to torture — only she had accidentally died before revealing what she knew.

Derek was using this knowledge to keep Coffee at bay. He was using what must be a last desperate hope in Coffee's diseased brain to barter for his life.

If Coffee knew the truth, if he abandoned all hope that Nadia might be alive in a maximum-security prison cell somewhere, then he would put a bullet in Derek's head without blinking an eye.

Derek had some slim hope that their old friendship would at least make Coffee hesitate to kill him. But it was a hope as slim and as fragile as swamp grass and just as likely to bend, break, or pull from the muck as it was to hold. It was not something Derek wanted to wager his life on.

He stared at the pile of corpses, wondering which one had the keys to the handcuffs. Ignoring the lightning bolts of pain jolting through his skull, he squirmed toward the agent who had cuffed him.

CHAPTER 24

Irina Khournikova stood outside the entrance to the International Center with one of her fellow FSB security agents, Ivan Petrovitch. Coming toward the resort was a fleet of Sikorsky VH-3D helicopters painted green and white. She counted ten. These were Marine Helicopter Squadron-1, the personal helicopter transport for the White House, which were being used to fly the summit leaders from Peterson Air Force Base to the resort.

Ivan brushed back his thinning gray hair with a large hand and said, "It feels a bit like a show of power."

"Fairly standard transportation at these summits. And easier to control than limousines."

"*Da*. I suppose." Ivan was in his late fifties, a grizzled old veteran of the FSB, and before that the KGB, and unlike many in the bureau, Irina trusted him.

Irina checked her watch, noting that everything was proceeding right on schedule. That was good. It made everybody's life in the security detail easier. Still, she felt uneasy. She thought about Derek Stillwater, undercover. She had spent much of the last eight months studying what her government knew about the DHS troubleshooter.

If Stillwater was to be trusted, and she suspected he was, he had good reasons to want Richard Coffee either dead or behind bars. Not nearly as good as her own reasons. Her lover, Lt. Col. Sergei Dobrovnik, had been assassinated in Chechnya by Coffee, who had then been known as Surkho Andarbek.

It had been her job to root out the Chechen assassin, but it had become personal. And when it was discovered that Andarbek was actually a CIA agent — a rogue CIA agent, it was believed — the matter had become ever so much more complicated. She had spent years trying to track the mysterious Andarbek, who had moved in and out of Russia, Chechnya, and Georgia with ease. She had become an expert—as big an expert as anybody on the planet, she supposed—on The Fallen Angels, the name of Andarbek's group of operators. They headquartered in the Georgian mountains, bought or stole weapons, sold them to whoever needed or wanted them.

Over time they evolved into something else, a weird cultlike group of apocalyptic terrorists.

The first of the helicopters—Marine One—that carried the president of the United States and his staff, settled onto the expanse of lawn in front of the Cheyennne Center. A marine honor guard stood at attention, and a small military band played "Hail to the Chief" as President Langston deplaned, waving to a small contingent of the press.

Irina glanced upward at the roofs of the buildings, mentally checking off the Secret Service sharpshooters she saw at different points of the compass. She shifted her gaze to the Secret Service guards who walked alongside the president in their dark suits, eyes covered with sunglasses, bodies stiff with the focus of their attention.

President Langston stood listening to "Hail to the Chief," and when it was finally finished, he saluted and led the U.S. contingent through the entrance of the Cheyenne Center.

Another helicopter landed, then another, and another.

Inside the Cheyenne Center, she knew, the president would be preparing for a short speech in the main banquet hall. There would be a few other speeches, then the leaders, their translators, and Sherpas would move to the International Center's private room for a smaller, intimate series of meetings.

If she were The Fallen Angel, that is where she would make her move. She didn't think a man with the tactical experience—even brilliance—of Richard Coffee would try something at the main gathering of the leaders, with seven hundred people in a banquet hall and dozens of security experts. It was too large and unwieldy a group to try and control, unless Coffee had something else in mind, like a bombing.

Ivan turned and said, "Here is our leader," and stiffened his posture.

The fifth helicopter landed and Russian President Pieter Vakhach descended the stairs, waving at the press. Vakhach was a blade-thin hawk of a man, balding, and elegant. The U.S. military band broke into a version of the Hymn of the Russian Federation. It was a slow, but rousing march and Vakhach stood at attention as the band played.

Ivan said, "Ahhh. The old cold warrior in me gets chills hearing a U.S. military band playing our national anthem."

"Maybe you're coming down with the flu, Ivan."

He laughed. "*Da*. Perhaps. Well, things have begun, have they not? The world's leaders will talk for hours and accomplish nothing, and money better spent on other things will be wasted on security and endless chatter. Dull, boring, and routine."

"Let us hope, Ivan. Let us hope."

As they turned to go back inside the International Center, Irina happened to note the expression of Mikhail Alexandrov, the lead FSB agent who would be escorting Vakhach into the Cheyenne Center. She had been discussing things with him when she ran into Stillwater. Alexandrov was an odd one, a throwback to the KGB, a brutal, but efficient, security technocrat. With his cheap suits, bad English, and square head, he had a nickname throughout the FSB — Charlie Brown. Charlie Brown after the cartoon character who was always called a "blockhead." But nobody in the FSB had the balls to call Charlie Brown a blockhead. To be caught like that might not just end your career, but probably your life, gutted like a deer and floating down the Moscow River past the Vorobievy Hills.

In all the years she had worked for Mikhail Alexandrov, she had never seen him smile. But he was smiling now, as he led President Pieter Vakhach toward the doors of the Cheyenne Center.

PART II
ARCHANGEL

CHAPTER 25

President Langston appeared at the podium on the stage at the front of the main banquet hall of the Cheyenne Center. Standing in a row on either side of him were the eight leaders of the Group of Eight, plus the president of the European Union. The banquet hall was filled, nearly seven hundred government leaders and administrators from twenty countries. Seated at the front tables closest to the stage were an additional thirteen leaders and their Sherpas from countries with a vested interest in the summit.

The crowd was surprisingly supportive of President Langston, in large part because of the loss of his wife and children in a terrorist attack months before. They rose to their feet in a wave of applause.

Langston nodded, waited a moment for the applause to die down, and raised his hands. "Thank you, my friends. Thank you. Good morning and welcome to the Group of Eight Summit. I hope everybody had comfortable and safe trips here to this beautiful spot in Colorado, my home state. I hope you enjoy your accommodations and will enjoy your stay here. I know I'm looking forward to a good round of golf, and my friend Prime Minister Hollenbeck has promised to help me with my putting."

The crowd laughed.

Langston continued. "As you know, we come together every year in these informal settings to address major issues of concern to the world. This year our top priorities are counterterrorism, world poverty, and the Middle East. I am certain that—"

Standing behind a long table, *El Tiburón* looked around the banquet hall, making certain that everything was in place. He had been concerned when The Fallen was late from his trip to the kitchen area. Everything had been precisely on schedule up to that point, but The

Fallen had been nearly ten minutes late in returning to the banquet hall, slipping in just as the room was filling, nodding to *El Tiburón*, and taking up his post next to the storage room door.

El Tiburón respected The Fallen. He admired him. But unlike the rest of The Fallen Angels, he was not swept up in the man's charisma. Perhaps that was why he was now the second-in-command. *El Tiburón*, like most of The Fallen Angels, had a background in the military or intelligence. In his case he had grown up with the Colombian AUC, the *Autodefensas Unedas de Colombia* or United Self-Defense Forces of Colombia, a paramilitary organization that sprang up in opposition to the two major terrorist groups working Colombia—the National Liberation Army, or ELN, and the Revolutionary Armed Forces of Colombia or FARC—both communist groups that worked hand in hand with the drug traffickers to overthrow the Colombian government.

Although the Colombian government largely viewed the AUC as another terrorist organization, *El Tiburón* thought of them as performing the actions the government was too weak to perform itself. But AUC itself was not strong, and it was The Fallen who had inspired *El Tiburón* with his vision and ambition. It was possible to topple the Colombian government—all governments—and all it would take was a daring enough leader.

El Tiburón wanted a smoke. He had to have the discipline not to light up. This was not the time or place for it. But they were on the cusp of announcing themselves to the planet and the craving for tobacco was strong.

He glanced across the room at The Fallen. The Fallen's eyes were on the president of the United States, but for all his concentration and intensity, *El Tiburón* thought something was wrong. Whatever had happened in those ten minutes was distracting the man. That worried him. This mission was too complicated to allow for distractions.

El Tiburón glanced at his watch. Almost time, if everything went as planned.

President Langston was saying: "—and so I hope that we can put aside our politics—" the president cracked the crooked grin that had garnered him so many votes. "—well, some of the politics, anyway—"

The crowd laughed.

" — and make changes that will improve life not just for the Group of Eight or the twenty countries represented here today, but for the entire planet. So with that out of the way, let's get to work."

The crowded room again rose to its feet and applauded.

El Tiburón waited for the signal, his right hand in his coat pocket on the transmitter button.

CHAPTER 26

The buses carrying the protestors barreled down the road toward the first National Guard checkpoint. Carlos Santos leaned over toward the driver of the lead bus and said, "Punch it!"

The driver glanced at Santos in the long, interior rearview mirror at the top of the windshield. "SOP, right?"

"Do it!"

The driver grinned. "Fuck yeah!" and stomped on the gas pedal.

In the front seat, the TV cameraman looked up from where he had been taping the protestors inside the bus. To Santos he said, "Are you crazy?"

Santos flashed him a bright smile. "Welcome to the revolution, man."

The National Guard unit had their Humvee off to the side of the road. They had put up a barricade, but it was a pro forma type of structure, a wooden barrier that could be swung aside. The four guardsmen were spread across different points of the road, waiting.

"CRASH THE BARRIER!" chanted Santos into the bullhorn, inciting the protestors.

"CRASH THE BARRIER! CRASH THE BARRIER!"

The cameraman swung his camera toward the windshield, trying to catch it all. Next to him the reporter was talking into her tape recorder, narrating: "In an unexpected turn of events, the protestors are going to crash through the barricade on their way toward the Cheyenne Hills Resort, where the G8 Summit is just beginning."

The school bus picked up speed, rocketing and rattling toward the barrier. The guardsmen seemed to realize at the last moment that the bus wasn't going to stop. They scattered.

With a crash the bus slammed through the wooden barrier. The three buses behind them followed. They could hear the sound of weapons firing. Santos was certain the guardsmen were firing in the air. Their procedure would be to radio on ahead to the last checkpoint, where a more effective roadblock would be put in place.

And a minute later, he saw that this was the case. Not only had the guardsmen rolled their Humvee into the road, but they had reinforced the barricade with concrete blocks. They stood on each side of the road, weapons raised and ready. In the distance he heard sirens. The first checkpoint had sicced the cops on them. That was good.

The driver slowed. "What now?"

"Get close and stop," Santos said. He turned to face the protestors. "Are you ready?"

"YES!" they shouted.

"When we stop, we rush the barricade! DOWN WITH ECONOMIC TYRANNY!"

"DOWN WITH ECONOMIC TYRANNY!"

The bus came to a halt. The driver glanced at Santos, who nodded. With a flick of the handle, the door cranked open.

"OUT! OUT! OUT!" Santos shouted.

The first out were the TV people, who set up just off to the side of the road. Santos noted that the reporter was standing with her back to the barricade, so the cameraman got a good shot with her in the foreground.

Like a panicked herd of cattle, the protestors rushed out of the bus, bottlenecked at the door, then spread out onto the road, their placards raised. They were joined by the protestors from the other three buses, easily a hundred people. The protestors with makeshift drums began to thump out a heartbeat rhythm. Someone began a chant. "G8 NOT! G8 NOT! G8 NOT!"

Cautiously, standing just inside the bus, leaning out, one hand on the pole so he was higher than the crowd, Santos shouted, "WHO ARE WE?"

"WE ARE THE PEOPLE!"

"WHO?"

"THE PEOPLE!"

"GOOOOOO!"

The crowd surged toward the four armed Colorado National Guardsmen. Santos watched as the mob rushed The Fallen Angels who had taken over the guardsmen's checkpoint. To the driver he murmured, "Might want to take cover."

The driver glanced in the mirror. "Uh-oh." Behind them appeared three Colorado State Police patrol cars, sirens blaring, lights flashing.

The cameramen swung around to capture the police cars arriving. And then the first shot rang out.

The four terrorists dressed as guardsmen fired on the crowd. Screams lifted into the thin mountain air. As bodies fell, some of the protestors tried to reach the guardsmen, but were methodically gunned down. Others ran for cover. Behind the bus, the patrol cars skidded to a halt, blocking the road. The state troopers piled out, guns drawn, taking up positions behind their vehicles.

Santos noted with satisfaction that the troopers were on their radios. And the TV camera was rolling. He hoped they made it back to their satellite truck as soon as possible.

He pulled out a handheld radio and said, "*El Chacal* here. Phase two on schedule. Proceed."

The voice of The Fallen came over the radio. "Confirmed."

CHAPTER 27

President Langston was acknowledging the applause when his Sherpa, Tobias Leeman, walked across the stage and leaned toward the president's ear. From where *El Tiburón* stood he could not hear, but he had a good idea what was being said.

Langston cocked his head, then glanced out at the audience and raised his hand to wave. Leaning away from the microphone, he exchanged words with Leeman, nodded, and turned back to the microphone.

President Langston raised his hands for silence. "Ladies and Gentlemen, I'm afraid we've got a problem. We will be going into a temporary security lockdown. It appears there has been an altercation between the National Guard troops and some protestors at one of the security checkpoints outside the resort. This may require a change of schedule. For the time being, everybody will remain in the ballroom here, and we'll get you updated as soon as we have more information. Now then, our next scheduled speaker is Prime Minister James Hollenbeck." He turned to gesture toward the British leader.

"It is my great honor and privilege to introduce everybody to Prime Minister Hollenbeck. As you know, he and I go back a long ways. James, due to the security lockdown, you now have all the time in the world —"

All around Cheyenne Hall, emergency security lockdown was taking place. The doors to the banquet hall locked with magnetic clicks. The exterior doors to the building also closed and could not be opened until overridden from the security center. Steel security gates rolled shut over the main doors, running from floor to ceiling. In the basement levels, steel security gates dropped into place, locking down with a clank.

Not only was Cheyenne Hall secured from outside access, nobody inside would be able to get out.

Through his earpiece, *El Tiburón* heard The Fallen whisper, "Begin."

El Tiburón, heart racing, clicked the button of the remote control.

CHAPTER 28

Secret Service Agent Lee Padillo scowled at the monitors in the International Center's security office. He had sent Sarah Macklin and two of her agents off to track down Derek Stillwater and nothing had been heard from her. He tried radioing her and got nothing. Where the hell had they gone?

And now all hell had broken loose out at Checkpoint Delta. That should not have happened.

Punching channels on the console, he was able to pick up radio chatter from throughout the entire National Security Event, listening in on his own agents, the Bureau of State Security, the National Guard, and some of the media. It wasn't good. The press, all three thousand of them from around the world, were confined to the Phil Long Expo Center, where they could watch the summit via the six cameras set up in every room, allowing a 360-degree view of significant events. Confined there, that is, until news broke about the shooting. Then they all loaded up in their vehicles and headed this way, clogging the roads to the resort, threatening the state troopers and the National Guard, who were trying to get ambulances in to sort out the mess.

And now the Cheyenne Center was under security lockdown.

"This is a fucking hairball," said a voice behind him. Padillo turned to see Agent Vincent Silvedo stroll into the security center.

"What the hell are you doing here? You're supposed to be at the Cheyenne Center. We're in lockdown."

"Yeah, and I was outside when you went into lockdown."

Padillo rubbed his forehead and glanced over at the other three agents monitoring the radios and video screens. "Jesus! Silvedo, you weren't—what were you doing outside?"

"What do you think? Having a smoke. Then all of a sudden the doors come down and the entire building gets locked up tight."

"Get your ass back there."

Silvedo shrugged, then walked back toward the door. "Oh, Padillo, one more thing."

"What's that?"

Padillo's eyes widened in shock as Silvedo tossed a flash grenade at him. The concussion knocked him flat. His eyes sizzled crimson. Padillo realized he was on his hands and knees, blind, dazed, confused, uncertain how much time had passed. Only seconds? What the —

He heard footsteps as if from a thousand miles away. Struggling to gain his footing, Padillo heard a gunshot, then another. And another. He was scrabbling for his own gun when everything went dead in a brilliant flash of pain.

CHAPTER 29

In his earpiece, *El Tiburón* heard Vincent Silvedo say, "The Fallen, this is Chameleon. I have taken over security. You are a go. I repeat, you are a go." *El Tiburón* tapped the button on the remote in his pocket. It sent out a signal to the 240 specially prepared bottles of champagne scattered around the banquet hall. At the bottom of each bottle was a tiny radio-controlled detonator that provided just enough pop to explode the bottles.

All throughout the room burst a startling *crack!* followed by the even larger explosion of the bottles themselves bursting in a spray of glass.

Prime Minister Hollenbeck, who had been rambling on about a lasting peace in the Middle East, stopped in mid-sentence, ducking automatically. Cries of alarm, screams, and the clatter of overturned chairs filled the room. At least half the crowd leapt to their feet. An even more seasoned percentage of the crowd flung themselves to the ground, hands on their heads.

Dozens of security officials from various countries reached for their weapons, spinning, looking for the problem.

Across the room *El Tiburón* saw The Fallen reach inside his jacket, pull out a lightweight gas mask, and pull it over his face. *El Tiburón* did the same, as did the other members of The Fallen Angels around the room.

When the bottles burst, the room quickly filled with a grayish vapor. The bottles were loaded with a Russian-made aerosolized derivative of the painkiller Fentanyl. A similar compound had been used by Russian Special Forces to immobilize Chechen rebels in 2002 who held seven hundred hostages in the House of Culture, a theater in Moscow.

It took less than a minute for everyone in the banquet hall to fall unconscious.

The Fallen, *El Tiburón* and his terrorists, all clad in gas masks, began to move around the hall. Three ducked into the storage room and immediately returned with crates filled with plastic explosives and detonators.

The Fallen shouted into his microphone, "Are the cameras shut off?"

Mikhail Alexandrov, the Russian FSB agent who was called "Charlie Brown" behind his back, stepped close to the six video cameras, and cut off the feeds. "*Da!* The cameras are down."

The three Angels with the plastic explosives set about wiring the doors. The Fallen and four other men calling themselves *El Escorpión, El Tigre, El Barrucuda,* and *El Jaguar*, drew out cloth vests strapped with plastic explosives and climbed up on the stage where the leaders of the twenty most powerful countries in the world were crumpled, unconscious. Working quickly with stilettos, they cut off the men's coats and pulled on the "suicide vests," which they secured with steel locks. They then used plasti-ties to secure the leaders' hands behind their backs.

Standing on the stage, The Fallen surveyed the room. The gas had an amazingly fast effect, but lasted only fifteen or twenty minutes at the longest. The banquet hall's ventilation system worked quickly to clear the air of the Fentanyl. Already he could see people stirring. Into his microphone he said, "Two minutes. Check in by the numbers."

"*Uno*, check."

"*Dos*, check."

"*Tres*, check."

"*Quatro*, check."

The Fallen stood on the stage, eyes on his watch, counting down the time while his men finished securing the banquet hall. Finally, *El Tiburón* moved up the aisle toward the front stage, an MP-5 clutched in one hand. He stopped at the TV cameras that supplied a 360-degree view of the banquet hall.

With a flourish, he pulled off his gas mask and dropped it to the floor. Inhaling, he flashed The Fallen an okay sign and said, "*Doce.* Check."

The Fallen nodded. "Proceed."

El Tiburón flicked the switch that controlled all six cameras. He gave The Fallen a thumbs-up.

The Fallen stood motionless at the front of the stage. After two beats, three, he slowly reached up and drew off the gas mask. Staring into the camera, he said in English, "I am The Fallen Angel. We — The Fallen Angels — have taken over the G8 Summit and have all of the world's leaders as hostages. But first, we want you to understand what is at stake here."

He waved his hand at his men. As one, The Fallen Angels spread out across the room and stood over various individuals sprawled on the floor.

The Fallen Angel said, "These people are members of the security staff for the twenty countries present here today. There are fifty-three of them. They are members of the United States Secret Service, Federal Bureau of Investigation, and Bureau of Diplomatic Security. There are also members of the Israeli Mossad and ISF, the Russian FSB, and many, many others. We have identified every single one of them."

At a wave of his hand, The Fallen Angels fired their assault rifles on full automatic into the bodies of the scattered security experts. The bodies jumped as blood and tissue misted upward. The guns roared and cordite drifted into the air.

The Fallen gestured again and the guns fell silent.

He waited. "The Fallen Angels have arrived," he said. He made a slashing gesture across his throat and Mikhail Alexandrov, who was closest to the cameras, cut off the feed.

CHAPTER 30

Derek paused, gasping for breath. Nearly blinding pain blasted through his head from Coffee's blows, and blood seeped from inside his mouth. He didn't think Coffee had broken his jaw, but he'd definitely done some damage to a couple of teeth. Probing with his tongue, he was pretty sure a couple of molars had either been shattered or knocked out. They felt jagged, the gum swollen and raw.

The body nearest him was the female Secret Service agent, Sarah Macklin. She was crumpled halfway beneath the third agent, Joe Snyder, and he couldn't get to her pockets without a lot of work.

Blinking sweat out of his eyes, he tried to see exactly how the bodies were scattered. Coffee had shut off the lights when he left, and the only light in the freezer was what filtered through the small window in the door.

Agent Bill Creff had cuffed Derek's hands behind his back. Creff was farthest away.

Oh screw it, Derek thought, and rolled onto his knees, then awkwardly struggled to his feet. Over by the door he used his shoulder to click on the light. Blinking against the sudden illumination, he tried to push his way out of the door, but wasn't surprised when it didn't budge. He thought Coffee had locked the door. It was possible to lock the freezer door from the outside with a padlock. Coffee apparently had done so.

First, get the damned cuffs off, Derek thought. He stepped over the bodies of Sarah Macklin and Joe Snyder until he stood next to Creff. With a sigh, he dropped to his knees beside Creff's body.

"This isn't any fun for me, buddy," he murmured, and rolled to a sitting position so his hands were closest to Creff. He started with the agent's jacket pocket, which revealed only a wad of pink Kleenex. Further contortions got him into Creff's pants pocket.

Another wad of Kleenex.

Stumbling to his feet, he stared at the body. Creff was wedged against the shelving units. Getting into the other pockets —

Back down on his knees, he proceeded to roll on top of the stiffening corpse. Derek squirmed until he was lying with his hands near Creff's right-hand pocket, lying on top of the dead man. Staring up at the ceiling for a moment, he cursed every decision he had ever made in his life leading him to this situation. By scooting toward Creff's feet he was able to get the fingers of one hand into Creff's pants pocket.

His fingers wrapped around a set of keys. Clutching them, he then scooted upward and rolled off Creff's body. He found himself face to face with Sarah Macklin, green eyes glazed and empty. She had been attractive once, but death mocked beauty.

Sitting up, he felt like his head was going to explode. He sucked in deep breaths of frigid air, trying to get his body back under control. For a moment, spots danced in front of his eyes and he wondered if he would pass out.

Concussion. He was sure of it. What he really needed was rest. And maybe a skull X-ray. Or a CT scan.

His vision blurred for a moment, doubled, then shifted back to single focus. He didn't like that. He'd been cracked in the head and punched around a bit. The headache wasn't unexpected. The double vision, on the other hand, could indicate a serious problem.

His fingers fumbled with the keys. The cold made his fingers numb and he couldn't tell which key he needed by touch. Cursing, he dropped the keys on the floor and shifted around so he was lying with his nose inches from the keys in front of his face. He studied the key fob. It looked like a mountain climber's carabiner, but it said FBI in white letters on it. Derek saw that it was actually a miniature flashlight. Eight keys hung from it. One of them was the tiny handcuff key.

Using his tongue, he shifted and separated the keys until the handcuff key stood out alone. The metallic taste of the keys didn't go well with the blood trickling down the back of his throat. For a moment he thought he was going to vomit, but swallowed back the bile and got himself under control.

"Here we go again." Derek rolled again, twisted, and got the keys into his hands. After a moment's fumbling, the left cuff was off. With a sigh, he flexed his shoulders, stretched his arms, and unlocked the right cuff.

Derek stood against the door trying to think. Coffee had trashed his phone. He needed to get out of here. He studied the bodies of the three agents. Creff wore a communication unit around his waist, as did the other two agents. He quickly stripped Creff of the radio and plugged the earpiece into his ear.

"— Security Center, do you copy? I repeat, Security Center, do you copy?" The voice sounded stressed. "Goddammit, Padillo! Answer your fucking radio!"

Uh-oh, thought Derek. Not good. Lee Padillo was the head Secret Service guy. He was running the show. Why wasn't he responding?

He shifted frequencies. Another voice: "— the Cheyenne is under total lockdown. I repeat, total lockdown. No response from the —" The channel broke up in a burst of static, the words fading in and out. "— fuckin' firefight — National Guard — body — hostages —"

A chill ripped through Derek's body. It sounded like all hell had broken loose. Then another voice broke in and he realized just how accurate that assessment had been.

"This is Secret Service Agent Lawrence Swenson. I repeat, this is Agent Lawrence Swenson. I am now in charge of summit security due to the suspected death of Lee Padillo. A terrorist organization calling itself The Fallen Angels has taken over the Cheyenne Center, murdered the on-site security personnel, and is holding the G20 leaders and other members of the G20 delegations hostage. From this point forward we will maintain radio silence until I can get a sit-rep. I repeat, we will maintain radio silence from this point forward."

Derek changed frequencies, but came up with silence. His heart thudded in his chest and he closed his eyes, willing this mess away. Opening his eyes, he leaned down and picked up his tool belt, plucked out a screwdriver and studied the walls and the ceiling of the freezer, deciding what his best point of exit would be.

Gritting his teeth, he shoved aside the food on the shelves, climbed up until he was close to the ceiling, and started working on the screws that held together one of the stainless steel panels.

CHAPTER 31

El Tiburón thought it would have been more effective if they had waited for everybody to wake up. Killing the security people in front of all the bureaucrats would have had a controlling effect.

He worried about controlling the crowd. The Fallen Angels were an experienced, ruthless group. They were heavily armed, they had set up precautions all around the facility, they were in control. Still, they were outnumbered from within nearly six to one. And, although they had surprises set up outside the facility, he knew it wouldn't be long before the Cheyenne Center became the focus of a massive law enforcement and military operation.

El Tiburón wondered if The Fallen had made his first miscalculation.

Then he thought: *What difference does it make? We all have to die sometime. If we take them with us, what does it matter in the end?*

Around them, the bureaucrats were waking up. He wondered if they would all awaken. When the Russian FSB used the gas in the Moscow Theater, a lot of people had died. Of course, they had been severely underfed and dehydrated over three days, and many were children and the aged.

There were no children here. But not all of the G20 bureaucrats were young and healthy.

El Tiburón let a small smile flash across his face before settling back into his usual watchful calculations. He hoped many would die. It would make this operation easier.

At the front of the stage, several of the Angels had set up a row of chairs. One by one, they dragged a semiconscious world leader forward and propped him in a chair.

Around him, people began to stir, sitting up. Several vomited. The stink filled the air.

Near him, a tall, thin, bald man sat up, looked around, eyes widening in recognition. *El Tiburón* watched the man with interest. He expected the man to panic, to show anger or fear. Instead the man seemed to take in the scene instantly, understand exactly what was going on, and clamp down on his emotions. A neutral, calm mask was all he showed the world. He glanced up at *El Tiburón*. Their eyes locked. The man said, "Who are you?"

The man was with the American delegation, *El Tiburón* knew that much. But exactly who he was, he didn't know. He was slightly surprised that the man remained sitting on the floor. Around the room, dozens of people were waking, and often rising to their feet or sitting back in their chairs. Some were checking the people around them, trying to offer rudimentary first aid or assurance.

El Tiburón said, "We are The Fallen Angels."

The man merely nodded. He said, "May I stand?"

"*Sí.*"

The man studied him thoughtfully for a moment before climbing to his feet. He was taller than *El Tiburón* expected, slightly over six feet. The man scanned the room before focusing on the main stage where the leaders were starting to awaken.

Close to where *El Tiburón* stood, a man jumped to his feet, looking around wildly. *El Tiburón* wasn't sure, but thought he was with the German delegation. The man was short, with thick blond hair, pink cheeks, and a whispy mustache. There was something childlike about him. His blue eyes widened in alarm. "*Mein Gott! Mein Gott! Was machts? Scheisse!*"

The little German shouted something else unintelligible and sprinted for a doorway. The tall American reached for him, but was keeping an eye on his surroundings — keeping an eye on *El Tiburón*. Without hesitation *El Tiburón* raised his weapon and fired a single burst. The little German sprawled forward on his face and lay still. A few people screamed. More stared in horrified silence.

Raising his voice, he shouted to be heard. "I am *El Tiburón*. The shark. The Angel of Death. If you behave, you may survive this. If you do not, we will kill you without mercy. Without hesitation. Without regret."

He turned. The tall thin man watched him closely. It bothered him that the man did not seem afraid. The man seemed to be studying him as if gathering information.

El Tiburón stalked toward the man, who now did not meet his gaze, but shifted his body into a less confrontational posture, relaxing, turning his eyes away.

"Who are you?" *El Tiburón* demanded. "What is your name?"

"My name," the man said slowly, "is Robert Mandalevo."

El Tiburón turned the barrel of his MP-5 so it was aimed directly at Robert Mandalevo's chest. "Do you fear the Angel of Death, Robert Mandalevo? Do you believe I would kill you without hesitation?"

"Yes. I believe you would kill without hesitation." Mandalevo still did not meet his gaze.

"Believe it," *El Tiburón* said. "And I would enjoy doing it. Who are you? You are an American?"

Mandalevo nodded.

El Tiburón prodded him with the assault rifle. "Your position. Tell me. What is your title? What do you do for *El Presidente* Langston?"

Without blinking, without hesitation, Mandalevo said, "I'm the assistant deputy political advisor."

El Tiburón grimaced and instantly dismissed the man who was a minor bureaucrat in the White House administration. Without warning he slammed the butt of the rifle into Mandalevo's skull, who crumpled to the floor, hands trying to stanch the flow of blood from a gash in his scalp.

El Tiburón turned his back away from Mandalevo and strode toward the cameras. It was almost time for The Fallen to address the world.

CHAPTER 32

The two-foot-square stainless steel plate came loose and Derek slid it out and set it aside. Above the plate was yellow fiberglass insulation, which he also removed. Above that was a ceiling panel made of thick fiberboard and screwed into place. The typical walk-in freezer was custom built for each space, but there needed to be room for the compressor and wiring. The compressor in this particular freezer was set into an opening at the back of the freezer beneath the flooring. Above him, however, was a four-foot-high crawl space filled with electrical wires, heating and cooling ducts, and gas and water pipes, as well as fiber-optic lines.

A spasm ripped through his head. Wincing, he almost dropped the screwdriver, then as quickly as it came it was gone.

Not good, he thought. Working efficiently, he unscrewed the panel and set it aside, too. Above was darkness. He had been through the crawl space before as part of his maintenance duties. There were steel mesh walkways, I-beams, and in some cases precious little space to maneuver. The crawl spaces were dusty, moldy, and unpleasant.

He dropped back down to the ground and checked to see if any of the dead agents were still carrying their firearms. A quick search revealed that they were not. Coffee must have taken them.

Derek thought for a moment. Because he had known that his tool-box would be searched periodically as he tried to work, he had not kept a gun in it. Instead, over the eight months he was here he had stashed three weapons in each of the main buildings. The problem, he reflected, was he was currently in the Cheyenne Center. He had strapped a Sig Sauer P226R tactical combat handgun to a corner of the underside of the ballroom stage and camouflaged it beneath a matching wooden box.

He was a long ways from that gun. And even farther from the other two guns he had hidden in the other two buildings.

Derek pawed through his toolbox, settled on a lug wrench, a screwdriver, and his flashlight. There was also the flashlight on the keychain he had lifted from Agent Creff. Wishing that he had stowed some Tylenol, or even better, Percocet, in his toolbox, he clambered up through the hole into the crawl space. Carefully he set the panel and insulation back in place, plunging the space into nearly perfect darkness.

Derek turned on the flashlight and checked out the new terrain. He stood on a narrow, steel-mesh catwalk, about two feet wide. Although it ran straight into the distance, he couldn't remain on it because the contractors and engineers had placed the ductwork, pipes and wiring every which way, crisscrossing the catwalk, thoroughly blocking the path.

Metal hangers were bolted into overhead subfloor, maintaining a steel framework for the dropped ceiling. He knew from experience that they would maintain his weight, but for how long was always the question. They weren't designed to hold the weight of a 185-pound man.

Orienting himself, he quietly paced down the catwalk, stepping over wires and conduits until he noted that he had to climb over part of a wall. It wasn't a support wall so it didn't run to the ceiling above him, but there was only about two feet of clearance. Less, actually, he saw, because somebody had run thick insulated electrical cables over the wall at the nexus of the catwalk.

Derek flashed the beam around, looking for a safer alternative. He saw nothing. With a silent sigh he approached the wall and studied the electrical cables. They looked completely insulated. If they weren't, this would be the shortest terrorism counteroffensive in history.

He straddled the wall, slipping over the cables, trying not to touch them, but finding it inevitable. His back pressed against the rough concrete of the crawl space ceiling above him. He was squeezed against the cables.

Then he was over, balancing again on the catwalk. If he was right he was now above the kitchen area. Murmured voices wafted up from below.

Derek sprawled on the catwalk and tried to peer through the cracks to see down below. He could see nothing. He considered that problem for a moment, retrieved the Phillips screwdriver from his tool belt, leaned over and slowly began to drive a tiny hole into the plasterboard ceiling square.

He took his time, not wanting to create any noise or pop through suddenly. After a minute he felt the material give and he gently pushed the screwdriver through and pulled it back out. A pencil-sized beam of light shot upward past him.

Leaning precariously off the catwalk he pressed his eye against the tiny hole.

His range wasn't so hot, but he could see more than he expected to. He was directly above the part of the kitchen where the catering staff was gathered. Apparently they were all being held in one area. Most of the crowd was sitting on the floor in their white smocks and black pants, looking toward someone. A handful were standing. He recognized Maria instantly. She didn't look happy. She stood facing someone, her expression fierce, her posture defiant. She rattled off something in Spanish that was entirely too fast for Derek's limited Spanish skills. He recognized the tone and he recognized the word *jódale*, which he knew meant "fuck you."

Easy, Maria. Don't screw with —

A man in dark clothes appeared in his line of vision. He seemed familiar. Derek thought he was somebody on the catering staff. The man still wore the black shoes and pants, but he had removed the white smock to reveal a black turtleneck. Swarthy, with short dark hair, he now carried an assault rifle. From the looks of the collapsible stock Derek thought it was an MP-5. In guttural Spanish the man snarled, "*¡Cierre la boca, la ramera!*"

Derek wasn't sure what that meant, but he thought it was along the lines of, "Shut your mouth, bitch!"

And then the terrorist backhanded her, knocking her to the ground. Blood trickled from her mouth, and she stared at him in a mixture of fear and defiance.

The terrorist raised the MP-5 and aimed it at Maria.

Derek grabbed his wrench, lurched to his feet on the catwalk and jumped onto the ceiling panel. With a crash the panel exploded into fiberboard splinters, and Derek dropped straight through toward the ground.

CHAPTER 33

Secretary James Johnston sat around the long maple table in the White House Presidential Emergency Operations Center (PEOC) located in the basement beneath the East Wing. He wasn't alone. The vice president was there along with the national security advisor, the director of the FBI, the attorney general, the director of the Secret Service, the director of the CIA, and the chairman of the Joint Chiefs. All eyes were on a live feed from the Cheyenne Center, which was currently blank. All ears were attuned to a secure line from Colorado.

Secret Service agent Lawrence Swenson, now running the show in Colorado, was providing a calm and clear update that didn't quite mask that Swenson was the ad hoc leader in charge of the biggest terrorist cluster fuck in U.S. history.

"— thirty-five dead at Checkpoint Delta at last count, mostly protestors. We're still trying to figure out exactly what happened, but Brigadier General Cole is dealing with that. The rumor is that the shooters weren't real Colorado National Guard, but we haven't — Hang on."

Johnston looked at Attorney General Norris Penderton, a sinewy bit of a Texan who always wore sunglasses when he wasn't on camera. He wore them now in the gloomy PEOC, chewing hard on a wad of nicotine gum, sun-weathered face a study in intensity. Penderton leaned over and muttered, "Can't decide if Veep Newman's scared shitless or happy as a pig in shit."

Alexander Newman was the vice president, and Johnston wasn't sure either. Newman had been a senator from Alabama prior to election, and he wasn't considered a particularly viable candidate for president in the next election, even though the party would almost have to support him. A competent enough administrator, the guy lacked charisma, was stiff and wooden on camera. He was as ambitious as any other D.C.

pol — which is to say he'd fuck a snake and kill his mother, or vice versa, if it would get him elected president of the United States — but he wasn't a man who instilled confidence in the people around him, which went double for the professional crisis managers who were currently sharing the stage with him.

Swenson came back on the secure line. "We've got confirmation. The four Colorado National Guardsmen originally assigned to Checkpoint Delta have been found dead. Their bodies were in the Humvee, and initial impressions are they've been dead for some time."

Johnston said, "Agent Swenson, this is Secretary Johnston."

"Yes sir."

"What happened to Agent Lee Padillo?"

Static crackled across the line. Swenson said, "We're not sure, sir."

"Why is that?"

"Sir, Padillo was in the Security Center in the International Center. We have lost contact with Padillo and with the Security Center overall. All three buildings in the complex have been isolated from each other. The Security Center is locked down, and we're still trying to access the International Center's security system. There appear to be new codes to the security overrides."

"Do you think Padillo is part of this terrorist attack?" Johnston asked.

"Sir . . . Sir, I honestly don't know, sir. We're still — sir, the feed's coming back on."

The cameras from the Cheyenne Center ballroom clicked back on. Vice President Newman said, "Oh my God!"

On the screen they saw the twenty major world leaders propped in chairs, explosive devices strapped to their chests. For a moment the screen was blocked by a tall, dark-haired man moving away from the cameras toward the terrorist they knew as The Fallen Angel.

FBI Director Sean O'Malley said, "I want information on every single terrorist we see. We know who Coffee is, but who's that guy?"

CIA Director Lynn Ballard had a phone to his ear. "We're on it." He glanced at the screen and said, "Holy shit!"

Everyone's attention turned to him. Ballard pointed a finger. "That's Mikhail Alexandrov! He's with the FSB! He's with The Fallen Angels?"

Johnston's voice was low. "Coffee was noted for recruiting from within the ranks of intelligence agencies worldwide."

"But Alexandrov? I know him! I —" Ballard trailed off, expression stunned.

On the screen they watched the dark-haired man talk to Coffee, then walk away. Johnston murmured, "Whoever he is, he acts like the second in command."

Coffee moved toward the cameras until his image filled the screen.

"I am The Fallen Angel. This is our first demand." He paused. Silence stretched like taffy, tension increasing as every second ticked by. Finally: "It is exactly 11:00 A.M. Mountain Time. The United States government has twenty-three of my fellow Angels in custody at Guantanamo Bay, Cuba. All twenty-three of them must be released by noon, 12:00 CMT. They are to be given two fully fueled Pave Hawk HH-60 helicopters with filled auxiliary fuel tanks. They are to be released by noon with clear passage across the Gulf of Mexico into Colombian airspace. Several of The Fallen Angels are capable of piloting the Pave Hawk. At exactly 12:00 CMT I must receive a telephone call from one of the Angels, specifically Nadia Kosov, confirming that they are free. This is not negotiable. I will place a telephone call in the next five minutes directly to CIA Director Lynn Ballard to give him the appropriate number to call. If Nadia Kosov does not call me in one hour I will kill one of the leaders on the stage."

Coffee made a slashing gesture across his neck and the video feed was cut.

"We don't negotiate with terrorists," blurted the vice president. "The United States has a policy of not negotiating with terrorists." He was trying to sound strong and decisive, but there was a bit of a question in his words.

Johnston clutched at the table. His stomach roiled, eyes wide. Nobody noticed his reaction as everybody in the room started talking about what they should do to respond to The Fallen Angels' demands.

"We've got a problem," he said.

Nobody heard him. The vice president said, "We're going to need to coordinate with —"

"Lynn," said O'Malley, "get the NSA and NRO on the line and tell them we need some recon ASAP of the Cheyenne Resort. We need to know what's going on —"

General Viteras Puskorius, chairman of the Joint Chiefs, said, "I can mobilize Delta Force ASAP, start a —"

"We have to contact the leadership," said the national security advisor, "to make sure the G20 don't initiate their own —"

Johnston slammed his fist down on the table and roared, "*Shut up!*"

Everybody stopped talking and turned toward Johnston. "We're fucked," he said. "Even if we wanted to, we can't meet those demands. Nadia Kosov is dead. And the reason Coffee wants her specifically is because she was his common-law wife."

CHAPTER 34

Derek crashed through the ceiling almost on top of the terrorist. The man spun, startled, eyes wide. As Derek fell he saw the terrorist raise his MP-5 toward him almost as if in slow motion. Striking out with the wrench Derek made contact with the barrel of the assault rifle just as he slammed to the floor.

The MP-5 swung wide and down and the Angel squeezed the trigger. A burst of gunfire ripped up the tile floor. Bullets whistled and ricocheted off steel tables and cast-iron cooking surfaces. The kitchen staff screamed, some covering their heads, others diving to the floor.

Derek, having performed more than a few HALO parachute jumps in his military career, hit the floor hard, knees bent, dropped, and rolled. He came up swinging the wrench.

The Angel, eyes squinted in hard, angry slashes, tried to raise the MP-5 again, but the wrench came down on his hand. With a guttural howl he dropped the weapon with a clatter.

Derek moved in, still swinging.

"Bastardo loco!" The man launched himself at Derek, arms and legs flailing. The terrorist was a skilled, experienced fighter. He liked to fight inside, grappling with Derek, limiting the wrench as a useful weapon. His elbows slammed into Derek's ribs. Derek narrowly dodged a fist to his jaw.

Derek rotated his grip on the wrench, not holding it like a club but like a clumsy knife. The hesitation cost him dearly. The Angel wrapped his hands around Derek's throat. Squeezed.

Within seconds Derek weakened, a cloudy veil dropping over his vision.

With a short, hard thrust, Derek slammed the handle of the wrench into the man's belly, just inches above his crotch. With a groan the Angel dropped to his knees. Derek spun the wrench around —

"Michael, watch out!"

The Angel lunged out of the crouch with a stiletto in his hand, a battle-lust shriek tearing the air. Derek brought the wrench down on the blade — not quite fast enough. It caught him alongside his ribs. A ribbon of pain lanced through his side.

The terrorist grinned, laughing low and nasty. He thrust the knife again.

Derek, ready, stepped sideways and back, bringing the Angel along with him, using his momentum against him. Again the knife clipped his ribs, but as the terrorist tumbled forward, Derek slammed his knee into the man's crotch. When the man groaned and leaned forward, Derek smashed his elbow onto the back of the man's head, following with a savage swing of the wrench to the base of the skull.

With a visceral crunch the man collapsed to the ground and didn't move.

Cautiously Derek checked the terrorist's vital signs. There were none. The terrorist's neck canted at an odd angle, a trickle of blood leaking from his nose, the back of his skull crushed.

Derek looked up at the crowd. "One down. Now —"

Maria, eyes wide, picked up the MP-5, aimed it toward Derek and pulled the trigger.

CHAPTER 35

Robert Mandalevo sat in a chair in the ballroom, slouched forward, hands in his jacket pocket. It was a pose held by many in the ballroom — those alive. Clearly, the gas the terrorists had used had killed some people. This was, in general, a group of politicians and bureaucrats experienced with crisis behavior. Many had military training. Many of the diplomats and bureaucrats in this room were from countries with a long and active history of terrorism attacks.

In Mandalevo's right coat pocket was his PDA, a sophisticated bit of handheld computer technology that allowed him to browse the Internet, check and send e-mail, keep track of dates, and use it as a cellular phone. It was also secure and encrypted.

Before sitting he had taken a peek to make sure his fingers were on the right buttons, then he slumped into the chair, just another frightened and demoralized bureaucrat.

But his fingers carefully moved on the tiny PDA keyboard. When he had the text message written, he clicked on SEND.

CHAPTER 36

Bullets ripped the air by Derek's side. Something took a nip at his hip, like a bee sting, and then he was moving, hurling himself to the floor.

As he came rolling to his feet, he noted that Maria wasn't looking at him. Her intense gaze was focused across the room. The gun was too much for her. As she fired, hands clutching the stock, the barrel jerked upward.

Jumping toward her, Derek knocked the weapon from her grasp. Gasping, she bent over, hands over her stomach. "*God!* What have I done? Oh, Michael! I shot you!" Her trembling finger pointed toward his hip. His shirt and pants were now soaked with blood. The ribs hurt like hell, a jagged arc of electric pain. The hip just felt sedated, a dull ache.

Without comment he turned and, holding the weapon ready, approached Maria's intended target. Another black-clad man carrying an MP-5. He was blond, broad-shouldered, and dead. The 10-mm rounds had started at his stomach and stitched upward, obliterating his chest, neck, and face.

Limping slightly back to Maria and the kitchen staff, he said, "Two down. But this might bring some attention. I've got to get you the hell out of here."

"Who are you?" somebody asked.

"I'm one of the good guys."

A red-haired woman in the black skirt and white blouse of the wait-staff, said, "We can't get out of the building. There are more of them and they've rigged explosives on the doors and the gate's come down over the window."

He considered. "I've got an idea. Everybody, follow me!"

He moved away, leading them toward a doorway at the end of the kitchen through which the now-dead blond had apparently arrived.

Standing by the door he listened intently, crouched down, ignoring the sudden sharp pain in his side, and peeked out. This was an entry area that led to the loading dock. There was an emergency exit and beyond that another set of double doors and a utility hallway. The area was empty.

He pushed the door open, held a hand to his lips and waved for everybody to enter. To his mind they were entirely too slow and noisy, but in only a few seconds everybody was crowded into the anteroom.

Derek studied the emergency door. There were small packets of Semtex plastic explosives attached to it. Small didn't mean harmless. Less than a pound brought down Flight 103 over Lockerbie, Scotland. The wiring to the detonators wasn't straightforward. They appeared to have been booby-trapped. The wide double doors leading to the loading dock seemed unmined. But Derek didn't trust his eyes. He had no clue what was on the other side of the doors. The doors to the utility hallway, on the other hand, were definitely booby-trapped. A tangle of wires, Semtex, and a radio receiver with a red light, suggesting The Fallen Angels could turn them on or off at will. Or blow them from a distance.

"Okay," he said, "nobody tries to leave using these two doorways. I can't tell if this one is rigged or —"

"We can't just stand here!" yelled one of the cooks in a panicky voice. He was a blocky man with a shaved skull, skin tanned and smooth. His eyes were wide, face stretched taut in fear. "I can't stand it. They're going to come after us. We can't just stand here. We'll be sitting ducks. All that shooting —"

He lunged toward the doors to the loading dock.

Derek spun, hand outstretched, a cry of, "Don't —"

The cook slammed into the doors with his considerable bulk, meaty forearms crashing down on the door levers.

Derek, heart hammering in his chest, turned, caught Maria in his arms, and leapt toward the entryway. They were almost there when an explosion blasted into the crowded anteroom.

A pressure wave moving over 30,000 feet per second slammed into Derek, driving him and Maria through the doorway and back into the kitchen, followed by a rain of debris — shards of steel, brick, wood, lathe — and human flesh.

It took a few moments for Derek to come to his senses. He was lying sprawled on top of Maria, whose eyes were closed. She seemed to be mumbling to herself.

Wincing, Derek rolled off and gently shook her. "Maria, are you okay?"

She opened her eyes. "Am I dead?"

"No. Are you hurt?"

"My ears hurt."

Derek smiled slightly. "Yeah. Mine too." He turned to look back toward the doorway. There was nothing there. A pile of rubble, shredded metal and wood. There were no screams or cries or moans. He and Maria had been farthest from the blast on the opposite side of approximately twenty people who had taken the full force of the explosion — saving their lives, but the others losing theirs.

Dimly, he heard the thump of feet and shouts in what he thought was Spanish coming from the opposite end of the kitchen. He quickly scrambled to the dead terrorist and flung open his black jacket. Around his waist was a communication kit, the cords trailing to his ears and a throat microphone. Deftly Derek unbuckled it, snatched up the knife the terrorist had wielded, glanced around, and dragged a steel table beneath the ceiling tile he had crashed through.

Maria was now on her feet, tears streaming down her face. He caught her by the arm and dragged her to the table. "Up you go."

"Who are you?"

"Derek Stillwater, Department of Homeland Security. You first."

Slowly she climbed up on the table. He boosted her through the hole, then handed her the MP-5 and the communication kit. Then he reached up, caught hold of the frame, and with a groan, hauled himself through the hole.

Below him he heard a door clang open and two of Coffee's Fallen Angels rushed into the kitchen. Derek paused, brought the MP-5 up to his shoulder and waited.

As the men appeared before him he squeezed the trigger.

There was a loud, heart-stopping click! In the gloom Derek raised the gun to stare at the translucent magazine. Empty.

The two Fallen Angels below heard the click, stared upward, and raised their weapons. One shouted in Spanish.

Maria whispered in his ear, "'*Surrender now.*'"

"No damned way," he said, gripped her arm and dragged her as fast as he could along the catwalk.

Gunfire shrieked beneath them, chewing through the ceiling tiles.

CHAPTER 37

CIA Director Ballard held his phone in front of him as if it were a writhing rattlesnake, waiting for it to buzz.

FBI Director O'Malley was on his own phone, voice firing like a machine gun, "—we want a lock on that, get the NSA on the number—"

Attorney General Penderton leaned over toward Johnston and said, "He really thinks we need the NSA to pinpoint Coffee's cell phone location? We all know where the fuck he is. I can tell him precisely where the sonofabitch—"

Vice President Newman stood up and in a loud voice said, "I think we need to invoke the Twenty-fifth."

The room fell silent. Not a word from anybody. Newman wanted to invoke the Twenty-fifth Amendment of the Constitution, which stated clearly in Section 1: "In case of the removal of the President from office or of his death or resignation, the Vice President shall become President."

Penderton slowly shifted aside to study Vice President Newman. He cleared his throat, tucking his nicotine gum into one cheek. "Well now, Mr. Vice President, bringing that up certainly makes some sense now, but—"

The door to the PEOC burst open and Lt. General William Akron, deputy director of the National Intelligence Directorate stepped in. He ran a long-fingered hand through his shock of gray hair, expression tense, but under control. He paused, searching the room.

Secretary Johnston said, "Oh hell, Bill. Robert's there, isn't he? We should have called you in immediately. Thank God you're—"

Akron waved him off. "I need to wi-fi my laptop in. Where's the—" He bustled over to the table, set up his laptop and tapped some keys. In a few seconds one of the wall-mounted plasma screen monitors brought up the desktop of Akron's computer screen. A few more key taps and he had his e-mail in-box on the screen.

"I just got this a few minutes ago—"

Director Ballard's phone buzzed. Everyone froze. Ballard picked it up and said, "Director Ballard, Central Intelligence, here."

He listened for a moment, nodded. "Now, Mr. Coffee, you have to understand that this is not a winnable situation—"

He looked at the phone. "He hung up. He recited the phone number and then hung up." Ballard recited the number and everybody jotted it down, wondering exactly what good that was going to do them.

Vice President Newman, still on his feet, said, "Gentlemen, we really need to discuss invoking the Twenty-fifth."

"Yes, Mr. Vice President," said Secretary Johnston. "In a moment, with your permission. Bill, what's up?"

Akron pointed to the computer monitor. "I got an e-mail from Director Mandalevo. He's inside the ballroom. He's got his PDA with him and he's—look."

They all studied the screen. The message read:

> BA—Xspt 12 bogie internal. RC. Adrov&Xman rt hand. Recog 3. Aryeh. Dorf. Christo. C4?on doors/G8. FM remote. Warn SS. DS in/out? Keep posted RM

"Now what the hell does that mean?" snapped Vice President Newman. Still on his feet, he sounded more and more petulant as time went on.

Secretary Johnston, voice low, whispered, "Jesus. He's got balls."

"Mr. Vice President," Akron said, "Secretary Mandalevo is feeding us intel. The BA is me—Bill Akron. Xspot means he's at the X spot—inside the ballroom. But what's important—"

"Secretary Mandalevo is inside the ballroom with all the other terrorists?" asked Vice President Newman. Johnston wondered about Newman's limited grasp of the actual logistics of the crisis. He wasn't surprised by Newman's focus on who was in charge, but he wished that Newman would get a quicker grasp of the big picture. If they were to do anything, they needed to organize information fast and get moving. They had to be proactive, not reactive.

"Yes, sir," said Akron.

General Puskorius said, "What else? What's after Xspt?"

Akron said, "RC. I think that's Richard Coffee. The Fallen Angel. Then Androv&Xman rt hand. We have a list of the intelligence agents working the ballroom from other countries. I took a look. The head of the Russian security forces is Mikhail Alexandrov. I think Bob's telling us that Coffee's top people — his right-hand men — are Mikhail Alexandrov and this Xman."

"Does that correspond with anybody?" Johnston asked.

"Not that I can see. I think Xman means Bob doesn't recognize him."

Johnston studied the screen. "Recog. Means recognize?"

"Yes, I think so. Recog 3 means he recognizes three of the terrorists. Aryeh, Dorf, and Christo. By comparing to the list, I think they're Didier Christophe from the DGSE and—"

Vice President Newman asked, "Who?"

"*General de la Securite Exterieure*," said Akron impatiently. "French Secret Service. Franz Dorfmann with the *Abwehr*." He glanced at Vice President Newman and said, "German Secret Service. And Amnon Aryeh with Mossad." Again, he glanced at Newman and said, "Israel."

"Okay," said General Puskorius. "'C4?ondoors/G8.' I think I can figure that out. Plastic explosives on the doors and on the leaders of the G8. We knew about the G8, we could see it. That's useful information. 'FM remote?'"

Akron hesitated. "I can't be certain, but I think he's saying that they have the plastic explosive detonators set to go off with radio remote control. And 'Warn SS' means warn the Secret Service."

"'And DS in/out?'" said Puskorius. "What's that mean?"

Again Akron hesitated. "I'm not —"

Johnston growled, "Yes, you damn well are sure. Yes. The answer is yes. I'd stake my life on it."

"What the hell are you talking about?" demanded Director O'Malley. "What does 'DS in/out?' mean? Jim? Out with it."

"I think he's asking if Derek Stillwater is in or out. If he's with The Fallen Angels or if he's on our side." Secretary Johnston waited, knowing a blowup was coming.

Akron nodded. "Yes, I think that's what it means."

"Derek Stillwater?" asked the vice president. "That renegade agent of yours? What, he's involved — He can't be, he's dead."

Johnston leaned forward and rested his elbows on the table. "Derek Stillwater isn't dead. We faked his death and placed him undercover at the resort because of a fragment of intelligence we picked up suggesting Coffee was back in the U.S. and might be interested in the G8 Summit."

Attorney General Penderton slammed his fist down on the table. When he shouted, his nicotine gum flew from his mouth and landed in the middle of the table. "Goddammit, Jim! That bastard was under investigation by me and the bureau. Are you crazy? You want to end up in Leavenworth or Guantanamo? He was in cahoots with Coffee and these Fallen Angels."

"Oh bullshit!"

Vice President Newman shouted, "Hold it, hold it. Why wasn't I advised of this?"

"Because you didn't need to know," Johnston said, voice cold. "It was only known to me, President Langston, and two or three key people —"

"How did Mandalevo find out?" Penderton snapped. "How long has he known?"

"He found out this morning during the intelligence briefing with the president. President Langston let slip that I had an undercover asset in place. Bob confronted me about it, but —"

"He asked for a follow-up records check after that meeting to determine if Stillwater was actually dead," Akron said. "It didn't take long to find out he was still alive. You just had to know where to look."

Penderton said, "I cannot fucking believe this! It's bad enough we've got enemies on the outside, but, Jim, you can't go running ops like this. It'll look like a fucking cover-up. DHS faking an agent's death to avoid investigation by another branch of the government. The media get this you'll be —"

Johnston glared at the AG. "Oh put a sock in it, Norris. You were feeding the media all sorts of bullshit about Derek to keep your face on the news. You've read all the files, classified and not. There's no hint besides that fake e-mail that Stillwater was involved with Coffee. And now is not the time for politics."

"Exactly," said Vice President Newman. "We need to create a plan. We need to start with —"

Akron said, "Excuse me, Mr. Vice President. Should I e-mail Bob back telling him DS is in?"

"Yes," said Johnston. "But we don't know where Derek is or if he's even alive. He has a sat phone, but I haven't been able to reach him."

General Puskorius climbed to his feet. "That's it, then. Let Swenson know what we've got. I'm pulling in my D-boys to see if they can plan an op."

"I'm in charge here," said Vice President Newman. "I haven't approved any rescue operation. D-boys? I suppose you mean Delta Force."

Puskorius stared at him. "Yes, Delta Force. We've got to at least get them to within striking distance. As for who's in charge, Mr. Vice President, that's a political decision that has to be made by your cabinet. I'll be back once I get this op going." He turned to FBI Director O'Malley and CIA Director Lynn Ballard. "I'll need Lynn and Sean on this. And Jim, it would be helpful if I had some idea of what your boy Stillwater might be capable of."

"I'll get you his file ASAP."

Puskorius nodded. "If I remember correctly, he was Army Special Forces."

"Yes."

"And if he's still alive, he might be somewhere in that building."

"I hope so."

"So do I, Jim. I really do. Let's see if we can give this poor bastard some backup." And with that, he stepped out of the PEOC.

CHAPTER 38

El Tiburón paced around the ballroom. He spied somebody trying to make a call on a cell phone. He stepped over and jabbed the barrel of his assault rifle into the man's ear. Trembling, the man turned to him. His large brown eyes filled with tears, his pointed chin trembling beneath a Van Dyke beard. One of the Spaniards, thought *El Tiburón*. It would be tempting to kill the man. They had discussed cell phones and PDAs while planning this mission, but had decided that dealing with five hundred or more phones and PDAs would be a waste of time. Threats would be just as effective. He held out his hand.

Timidly, the Spaniard dropped the phone into his palm. *"Gracias,"* *El Tiberón* said with a grin.

He turned and held up the phone. In heavily accented English he shouted, "No cell phones. No PDAs. No communication with the outside world. *Comprende*? I will shoot the next person I see trying to use his phone." He raised his weapon and aimed it at the Spaniard.

The Spaniard cowered in fear, hiding his head behind his hands.

"Comprende, amigo?" He nudged the Spaniard with the gun.

"Sí! Sí, comprende!"

"Or—bang!"

The Spaniard gave out a high-pitched shriek when *El Tiburón* made the shooting noise. *El Tiburón* laughed and moved on, in better spirits than he had been while listening to The Fallen's initial ransom demands. Thinking about that now he strode toward the front of the stage.

President Jack Langston, as well as the other leaders, watched him closely. President Langston called out, "Who are you? Hello, you there. Who are you?"

Coffee raised his rifle and pointed it at Langston. "You will speak when spoken to."

Langston scowled. "Or what? You'll kill me? Isn't that what you plan to do, Coffee? Let me ask you something, Mr. Coffee. Didn't you sign an oath to —"

Coffee fired off a burst of gunfire just over the president's head. President Langston barely flinched, although other leaders cried out or tried to cower in their seats. Coffee turned away from the leaders to meet *El Tiburón's* gaze. *El Tiburón* saw that the confident The Fallen was back, that the hesitant man of only moments ago was gone. Still, things were not right.

The Fallen raised his hand in a stop gesture, and lifted his phone to his ear. "CIA Director Ballard?" He read off his cell phone number and clicked off. "*Si?*"

El Tiburón stood close. Voice low, he said, "You varied the plan. Who is this Nadia Kosov?"

Coffee's jaw grew taut. "It is not your concern. Things are going as planned."

"No," *El Tiburón* insisted. "No. Already you made a change. First request, release your *compadres. Si*, I understand. But you put an extra stipulation on it. Who is Nadia Kosov?"

"As I said." Coffee's voice was soft, but it carried real menace. "It is none of your —"

Muffled gunfire broke out from somewhere outside the ballroom. Coffee turned toward the sound, an expression of interest on his face. Into his throat mic he said, "Perimeter three report in by the numbers. I repeat, perimeter three, report in by the numbers."

There was long silence. Finally, "*Numero dos, numero uno* is not responding. I will check.

"*Tres*, status clear."

"*Quattro*, status clear. Request —"

More gunfire vibrated in the air. Coffee met *El Tiburón's* gaze.

Many of the people in the ballroom were rising to their feet. The noise level increased as they began to babble among themselves.

"Report in," Coffee said. "*Dos*, report."

Radio silence. *El Tiburón* murmured, "*Pastinaca* and *Serpiente*."

Coffee nodded. "*Tres* and *Quattro*. Check on *Pastinaca* and *Serpiente*. Check them."

El Tiburón said, "This would be early for a counteroffensive."

"And not large enough. We'll know a counteroffensive when it happens. I wonder—"

An explosion shook the building. Screams filled the air as the ballroom trembled. Coffee unhooked a PDA from his belt, clicked it on, and studied the readout. "The loading dock. Somebody set off the explosives."

Into his microphone, he rattled off numbers in Spanish. "Status?"

After a moment of static-filled radio silence, their voices came on. "On our way. Repeat, we are okay and on our way. There appears to be a large explosion at the loading dock entrance."

"Check for survivors," said Coffee. "And look in the kitchen area to see what you see. Report in. Over."

He turned to *El Tiburón*. His face was untroubled. "*El Tigre* and *El Oso* are on top of things."

El Tiburón's eyes glittered. "That won't help *Pastinaca* and *Serpiente*, will it?"

The Fallen met his gaze, unflinching. "We all have our roles to play, *El Tiburón*. We all have our duty to perform. Both you and I. Go back to your post."

El Tiburón stopped himself from a harsh retort, but instead spun on his heels and stalked back toward the television cameras. A man in a gray suit, one of the German delegates, said, "What is going on? What was the explosion?"

Without hesitation *El Tiburón* backhanded the man, who staggered away, hands to his face, blood spurting from his broken nose. *El Tiburón* followed after the German. He stepped in and slammed the butt of his MP-5 into the man's face once, twice, knocking him to the ground. He brought the MP-5 around so the barrel was aimed at the man cowering on the floor. "*No questions!*" he screamed. "*No questions! Comprende? Do not talk to me! You are expendable. You are like ants on the ground beneath my boot. No questions!*"

He kicked the German twice in the ribs before returning to the television cameras, people shifting nervously away from him as he walked by, eyes down, not meeting his gaze, not daring to draw his attention or rage. "*My duty*," he raged. "*My duty is to my people! I know my duty!*"

CHAPTER 39

Derek and Maria rushed through the darkness along the narrow catwalk in a crouch, bullets buzzing around them like a swarm of bees. Maria moaned in a high-pitched hum as she ran. Derek shoved her forward — smack into the dividing wall. She cried out, but not for long. Derek picked her up and flung her over. She fell with a harsh cry onto the catwalk on the other side. Derek dived after her.

Below him the two terrorists spoke to each other in Spanish. He grabbed Maria and whispered in her ear, "What are they saying?"

She listened and whispered back, "They're not sure what to do. They came up against a wall. They're going to come up here and check on us."

Derek squinted through the gloom, thinking. He studied the bit of wall they had climbed over. Reaching into his belt, he pulled out the stiletto. This, he thought, is suicidal.

Approaching the wall with the electrical lines snaking over it he waited a moment for his eyes to adjust to the gloom, then used the knife to carefully peel the insulating rubber from the cables, exposing the electrical wiring. Not far away he could hear the men clambering up into the crawl space. He didn't have much time. Taking a deep breath, he stripped off one more piece of rubber, snapped on the mini-flashlight he had taken off Agent Creff, and tossed it so its light aimed away from the wall.

Another searing pain tore through his head and he staggered for a moment, fireworks bursting before his eyes. Sucking in air, he crept toward Maria who was huddled on the catwalk. He gently reached down, took hold of her high-heeled shoes and slipped them off her feet. "It'll be easier for now. Follow me," he said, took her hand, and began to sneak deeper into the bowels of the crawl space, shuffling along beams, over heating and cooling ducts, edging along the framework for the drop ceiling. Finally, they stopped at a juncture, solid wall at their backs, perched on a support beam.

Behind them the two terrorists approached the dividing wall. Derek paused, crouching on a rusty beam, his fingers against Maria's lips. They were only twenty or thirty feet away, barely concealed in the shadows.

A moment. Two—

A deathly scream echoed through the crawl space, followed by a thud and a crash as one of their pursuers grabbed hold of the bare electrical wires, then fell through the ceiling tiles to the floor below. Derek hoped he'd gotten a lethal shock. He waited, uncertain what the second terrorist would do.

Derek heard murmurs, again in Spanish. Maria gripped his hand, whispered in his ear, "He's on a radio, I think."

Derek still held the radio pack he had taken off the terrorist. He searched for the earphone jack, put it in his ear and fumbled with the switches.

"—alguien se defiende—él saboteó el crawl space—"

Derek yanked out the earpiece and handed it to Maria. "Translate."

She stuffed it into her ear and listened for a moment. In a whisper she said, "Someone—someone, The Fallen Angel? The Fallen Angel is telling him to go to the walk-in freezer in the kitchen. To open it and get back with him. They—"

The remaining terrorist shuffled away and they distinctly heard him drop back to the floor below.

Derek hissed, "Keep listening. Come on." He spidered his way back across the cables and conduits to the catwalk, and raced toward the walk-in freezer where he had begun.

Maria kept up, sticking close to him, fear radiating off her like heat waves. She kept one hand on his shirt, not letting go.

Finally, Derek stopped, listening. Below him came the rattle and clank of keys on a padlock. The door to the freezer opened with a shushing sound. Instantly Derek dropped off the catwalk onto the tiles, crashing to the ground below. He slammed his shoulder against the freezer door, clicked the padlock shut, and flung himself to the floor out of the way. A moment went by. The muffled sound of gunfire escaped from the freezer as the terrorist tried to shoot his way out. The glass window shattered. Then silence.

From his position on the floor, Derek studied the freezer door. A couple bullets had punctured through, but clearly not all. Firing a gun inside a stainless steel box was not the brightest thing to do. At least one of the bullets — maybe more — would have bounced around off steel shelves, walls, and flooring. Derek had no desire to place his head against the small window and see if a ricochet had killed the guy. It could be a ruse, but he doubted it. At least one of the terrorists was a moron. Hopefully a dead moron. He doubted if many of the others would be as stupid.

Without thinking about it, he clutched at a St. Sebastian's medal he wore around his neck with a steel four-leaf clover and ju-ju beads. He wasn't superstitious — not exactly; but he believed in luck, good and bad. You never knew when the good luck was going to come. It was horribly unpredictable that way. But one thing was for sure — you could always count on bad luck. It was always just around the corner. So was good luck, for that matter, but you couldn't depend on it.

Pulling over another chair, he poked his head up into the crawl space. "Come on down for a bit." Maria was pressed against a steel I-beam that ran straight up and down through the building, trying to be as small as possible. She crawled toward him and he helped her down.

"I'm really glad you're alive." He studied her for a moment then held out his hand. "Hi, I'm Derek Stillwater."

She clenched his hand for a moment before pointing. "You're bleeding. I . . . I shot you."

He touched his ribs and pulled away blood. "Okay. Right. Stay right here." He found a basket of the catering staff's clean linens. He plucked several clean napkins out of the pile and headed back toward Maria, stopping to grab a bottle of unopened sherry.

Pain radiated from his ribs and his knee and his head, and for a moment exhaustion — the adrenaline rush fading — swept over him. Gathering his reserve, he handed her the bottle of sherry and peeled his shirt off.

"I could use a drink," she said, just a hint of mischief in her voice.

"We get out of here, I'll buy you one."

"I'd like that."

"Maybe somewhere warm," he said. "Without terrorists."

"I'd like that even better."

She pulled open the sherry and held it up. "What's this for?"

He handed her one of the napkins. "Soak this with sherry."

She did. The smell of the alcohol filled his nose. He took one of the other napkins, folded it repeatedly and said, "Now, I need you to gently clean off my ribs." He took the folded napkin, stuffed it in his mouth and bit down.

Maria dabbed at the wounds in his side. As soon as the alcohol touched the knife and bullet wounds Derek went rigid, moaning into the cloth, hands balled into white fists. Sweat beaded up on his entire body. He shivered.

"I'm sorry."

Yeah, me too, he thought.

The linen came away with rust-colored blood and brighter scarlet. Still bleeding, but clotting. He'd been grazed, but deep. Taking several of the napkins he formed a makeshift bandage and pressed them against his ribs. He pulled his blood-soaked shirt back on.

He looked at the bottle of sherry for a second then said, "Go grab a couple of bottles of these, okay?"

While she gathered the sherry, he crossed over to the electrocuted terrorist, who was lying on the floor, body lifeless and rigid on top of one of the stoves. Derek picked up his MP-5, studied the magazine. Half empty. Searching the man, he found a pack of cigarettes, a lighter, two more full magazines for the MP-5, the radio kit, which he co-opted for himself, and a knife. Derek hefted the knife, studying it. It wasn't just any knife. It was an Emerson CQC-7, an absolutely amazing work of art. Seven inches long with a razor-sharp blade and serrated edge. It could cut through steel if he needed it to. He attached it to his belt and felt significantly more optimistic about their likelihood of surviving the day intact.

Derek took a minute to absorb their surroundings. The abandoned kitchen, the dead terrorists, the pile of rubble and debris at one end. Everything was coated with a fresh layer of gray dust. It still hung in the air like fog. The acrid odor of blood, cordite, and the distinctive stench of detonated Semtex.

Maria showed up with six bottles of sherry and a bottle of vodka. "We having a party?"

Derek nodded, opening all of the bottles. "Yes. A cocktail party. A Molotov cocktail party." He poured a quarter of the booze down a sink.

Using the knife he stripped linens and forced them into the bottles. Looking around, he found a cloth bag that held potatoes. He dumped the potatoes and carefully placed the sherry and vodka bottles in the bag.

"You've got a job now," he said, and tapped the radio kit. "Let's get this on you. I want you to listen and translate." He helped her put the kit around her waist and adjust it. Then he disconnected the microphone so she wouldn't inadvertently click it on. "Tell me everything you hear. Okay?"

"I . . . I don't know if I can do this."

He held her by both arms. "You saved my life. Honey, you can do anything. You have to do this. There's nowhere else to go. If I could get you out of here, I would. I need you. Hell, Maria. The whole world needs you."

Her eyes went wide. She had been trembling before, but receiving instructions — doing something — seemed to calm her a little bit. She took a deep breath. "What are we going to do?"

Derek grinned. "I heard them use a word on the radio, a Spanish word. *Saboteó*. What does that mean?"

"Sabotage. Or booby-trap."

"Yeah, that's what I thought. That's what we're going to do, honey. I'm going to make their life miserable, even it if kills me." He took her hand. "Come on, let's go." Carrying the MP-5 and the bag of Molotov cocktails, he led Maria over to the chair and helped boost her back into the crawl space. "Let's hunt some Fallen Angels."

CHAPTER 40

Secret Service Agent Lawrence Swenson leaned over a computer termi-
nal in the Mobile Command Unit, essentially a bus stripped of seats and
redone as a high-tech communications center. Six agents monitored radios and computers. Swenson was a broad, burly man with graying hair
and a thick black beard. His eyes blazed as he studied the computer monitor. Into his microphone he said, "I want a heads-up when you're ready
to breach the security center. Do you think anybody's in there?"

"Negative. Can't tell."

"Keep me posted."

"Agent Swenson?"

Swenson turned to glare at the speaker, one of the Russian security
people. He searched his memory for a name, but came up blank. "Who
are you?"

Holding up identification, she said, "Russian FSB. I'm Agent Irina
Khournikova. May I have a moment?"

"Look, lady. Every country represented wants a piece of my time.
Why don't you get in line."

Khournikova stepped closer, keeping her voice low. "I have information that might be of use to you."

He studied her for a moment before waving for her to follow him
into a tiny office that should have been in use by Lee Padillo. Swenson
didn't have a good feeling about Padillo's disappearance. He was pretty
sure Padillo was dead.

The office had just about enough space for a computer, desk, and
two chairs. He crunched into the chair behind the desk, fingers subtly
dancing on the keyboard as he sat.

"Sit. Khournikova, right? Name rings a bell. We met, but —"

Khournikova, still standing, tapped the computer monitor. "What does your computer say, Agent Swenson?"

Swenson shot her a bland look then dropped his gaze to the computer. "Huh. So you're the one. Tell you what, Agent Khournikova. You're either an expert on Richard Coffee and these Fallen Angels, or you're some sort of collaborator. Give me one good reason why I shouldn't have my people lock you up until this whole cluster fuck is a bad memory."

"Because I can provide you with information that might help end this sooner rather than later."

Swenson made a come-on gesture with his left hand. His right hand never strayed too far from the semiautomatic on his hip. "I'm all ears. Have a seat."

Khournikova sat. "One of my security people is apparently one of The Fallen Angels."

"Mikhail Alexandrov," Swenson said. "We know."

Khournikova remained expressionless. "Very good, Agent Swenson. I'm reasonably impressed. May I ask a question?"

Swenson shrugged.

"What language are they using to communicate with each other?"

Swenson cocked his head, interested. "Spanish. Coffee's fluent in about eight languages."

"At least," Khournikova said. "But he has not been long in Central and South America. Probably twelve months or so."

"Yes," Swenson said. "Probably. Seeing as how he slipped away from you in D.C. around then. That wasn't long after you escaped from an FBI interview room, now, was it?"

Khournikova sighed. "'Escape,' is an interesting choice of words, seeing as how one of your FBI agents was intent on assassinating me under the nose of your own people."

"Yeah," Swenson said. "I guess it's all a matter of interpretation. You got a point about this Spanish-language thing?"

"The Fallen Angels are international. They are made up of —"

"I've read the file," Swenson interrupted. "In fact, only recently."

"They started in the Republic of Georgia. Coffee — calling himself Surkho Andarbek — recruited his members from intelligence agencies around the world."

"Yeah, disgraced and otherwise 'fallen' spies. '*Traitors*' is another word for them."

Khournikova nodded in agreement. "I dedicated years to studying Andarbek and The Fallen Angels. To the best of my knowledge they recruited no one from South or Central America. They undoubtedly have some assets there, but I do not believe that the core of The Fallen Angels comes from the Americas. They are Russian, Eastern European, and Asian. Most of those are in, how do you say it? Gitmo."

Swenson sat up, fingers twisting at his beard. "How reliable do you think your insights into The Fallen Angels are, Agent Khournikova?"

"I haven't caught him yet, so they are flawed. I believe, however, that there is only one other person on the planet with more insight into Richard Coffee."

"Yeah? Who would that be?"

She cocked an eyebrow. "You don't know?"

"I'd like to hear it straight from the horse's mouth." He flashed her a sardonic grin. "No offense intended."

"None taken, Agent Swenson. I believe you must know of Dr. Derek Stillwater."

Swenson thumped his fingers on his thigh for a moment. "I, um, mighta heard of Derek Stillwater. You know, of course, that there were suspicions that you and he were in cahoots with Coffee."

"Do you believe that?"

Swenson shrugged. "I'm not privy to every bit of information on the events of last year. All in all, I would have to say no. But Stillwater's dead, right?"

She paused before answering. "I do not believe you think so, Agent Swenson. Perhaps he has been in touch?"

"From beyond the grave?"

She shook her head. "You are . . . bullshitting me. Testing me. You must know that he's alive and he's here."

"Must I?"

She nodded.

Swenson kept his gaze on her for a long moment. "Let's back away from Stillwater for a moment, Ms. Khournikova. Just for a second. You were talking about these Spanish speakers and The Fallen Angels being relatively new to Central and South America."

She nodded.

Swenson splayed his fingers. "So?"

"If he has Spanish speakers — and it appears he is working with a team of them, correct? — then they are not part of the original Fallen Angels. They are some sort of cabal he has recruited or, perhaps, collaborated with, in order to meet his — and their — goals. If he is working with people from the Americas, I suspect they're from Colombia, El Salvador, Nicaragua, or perhaps some of the Mexican provinces, such as Chiapas."

Swanson craned his neck backward and stared at the ceiling of the tiny office for a moment, thinking. "Okay, Ms. Khournikova. I've got a tiny bit of intel for you. For a while there the NSA hacked in on their communications before they went into a scramble mode. They're still working on it, but in my experience with Radio Shack encryption technology, we're shit out of luck on breaking through in anything resembling a useful amount of time. But in that brief — *fucking brief* — window of opportunity, they picked up three or four people talking in Spanish. The NSA — you know who they are, right?"

"Yes."

"Right. You would. The NSA turned it over to some analysts in the CIA and they're pretty sure that the accents and syntax mean these guys are from Colombia."

"As I suspected."

"Great. What does that mean?"

Khournikova leaned forward. "What is in Colombia, Agent Swenson?"

"Cocaine and a bunch of paramilitary and terrorist screwballs. Not much else except carnations and coffee beans."

"These are not drug traffickers."

"That wouldn't have been my guess."

"So they either come from inside the Colombian government, which I doubt, or they come from antigovernment organizations. Knowing who the anti-Colombian government organizations are will get us a long way toward knowing more about this group, who I would not call The Fallen Angels, despite being led by Richard Coffee."

"And," Swenson said slowly, "if we can figure out who they are, maybe we can figure out what they really want. And try to anticipate it."

Khournikova nodded. "Yes. I think that would be a good approach."

Swenson said, "All right, *Agent* Khournikova. You're on my team. You stay here. Right here. By my side."

"You don't trust me?"

Swenson stood up. "Let's just say I'm keeping my mind open. Now, you had something to say about Derek Stillwater?"

"He is here. He was undercover. If he's still alive, he may be of use to us."

"How do you know all that?" Suspicion was back in Swenson's voice.

"I ran into him earlier this morning. He was dressed as a . . . mmm, janitor. He was on a work elevator, how do you say it —"

"Freight elevator."

"Right. Freight elevator. We saw each other. It was an accident. I cornered him shortly afterward and we decided to try and trust each other."

Swenson nodded. "Okay, Agent Khournikova. Here's what I know about Derek Stillwater." He raised his fingers. "One: he was undercover. Two: when this went down, we think he was in the kitchen area at the Cheyenne Center. Three: three of my agents went to pick him up and bring him back and keep him out of the way. Four: shortly afterward, they went off the grid. Shortly after that everything went to hell." He stood, hands on hips, glaring at her.

"So we don't know if he's one of the good guys or not. We don't know if he's alive. I've received a brief communication from my boss saying that if Stillwater is alive, he's one of the good guys. I'm not going to take that at face value because as everything else here has shown today, there aren't a hell of a lot of people you can trust. On the surface, it looks like Still-water was in cahoots with Coffee and offed a couple of my agents. That's what the facts seem to indicate. If you have any other *facts*, I'd like to hear them."

"No other facts. Can you explain the explosion and the gunfire?"

Swenson shook his head and suddenly looked very tired. "No, I cannot. Can you?"

"I hope it is Derek Stillwater running his own guerilla war against Richard Coffee."

"I hope it is, too, Agent Khournikova. But I have no evidence of that whatsoever. Zero. And until I do, he's going to be treated like an enemy asset. I have informed my people to treat him as such. Barring other evidence, they are to shoot him down as if he is a member of The Fallen Angels."

CHAPTER 41

Derek and Maria sat on the catwalk in the crawl space, taking a breather. Maria whispered, "We should have grabbed a couple water bottles. I'm thirsty."

He nodded, agreeing with her, but didn't comment. Instead he held a finger to his lips, and returned to studying the disaster in front of them. For what he had in mind he needed to figure out where Coffee had his men laid out. He was pretty sure he knew. Clearly, inside the main ballroom were the main group of terrorists. But arrayed throughout the facility — in the service hallways, in the kitchen, probably in the lobby — he would have also posted men.

The Cheyenne Center in many ways was a building inside a building. The center was the ballroom, a large open space. Around it were hallways. On the opposite side of those hallways were storage rooms, kitchen and utility areas, and the outer wall of the building. When the Cheyenne Center went into security lockdown, the open lobby areas and various exits were covered by a steel-mesh gate that dropped from the ceiling or rolled out from the walls.

Derek knew that the lobby was a problematic area for Coffee. It angled from the southeast corner of the building all the way along most of the front. Eight glass double doors and assorted windows presented a tactical hole in Coffee's plan. The steel mesh would keep an assault force out — at least for a while — but it was wide open for sharpshooters. That is, if Coffee's men hadn't somehow managed to block out the windows, which he suspected they had. But he doubted that Coffee would leave that space unguarded.

There had been two men in the kitchen. Apparently, there had been two more in the eastern utility hallway. Derek figured at least two and possibly more manning the lobby area, which was very large. That was where he and Maria were headed. If they could get there.

They crouched on the catwalk, but in front of them was what looked like a pile of rubble — bricks, torn and twisted metal, shredded plaster, and sheetrock. They were near where the explosion had been. Derek wondered if there was another way.

Maria tapped him on the shoulder, pointing at her ears. He turned on his radio and listened to Richard Coffee talking to people he gave numbers to: *cinco, seis, siete, ocho.* Numbers five, six, seven, and eight. He and Maria had managed to eliminate four. He wondered how many more there were.

She listened, expression intense. She hunched her shoulders over, frowning.

"What?" he asked.

"He's telling them to stay sharp. To keep an eye out for Derek Stillwater. That you're dressed like a maintenance guy and you're really dangerous and to kill you on sight."

Derek smiled. "Anything else?"

"No. He told them to stay in — border — maybe perimeter three, zone one. I think he meant perimeter. Now there's silence."

Derek studied the tangled maze of metal. "Ready? We've got to be careful."

Derek clicked off the radio. He was relying on Maria to monitor the radio chatter, but he wanted to concentrate on any sounds around them.

He crept forward slowly. Whenever he made a move, he tested to make sure it would carry his weight. The explosion had kicked up a cloud of dust and mold that still hung in the air like smog. He felt a tickle at the back of his throat and in his nose, blinking as particles irritated his eyes.

The catwalk came to an abrupt end, dangling into space. Below them was a pile of rubble. They were still over the hallway outside the kitchen area.

Reaching up, Derek grasped a metal heating duct. It was about two feet wide and maybe nine inches high. It was suspended from the ceiling by metal braces bolted into the roofing. Slowly he shifted his full weight onto the duct. It held with a metallic shiver and groan.

Maria whispered, "I am not getting inside that thing."

"Too small," Derek said. "On top, though —"

He stood up and slithered on top of the duct. It was tight. There were only about eighteen inches between the top of the duct and the ceiling. He crawled forward.

Behind him he heard a muttered curse, then Maria was behind him. Inch by inch, they wriggled along the ductwork, desperately trying not to make noise.

Derek felt a vibration. He froze. Maria bumped into him.

The duct dropped half an inch with a shudder.

Maria let out a little cry.

More vibration. Gripping the flashlight, Derek aimed it around. From here they had two choices. Keep going or drop a dozen feet onto a pile of shattered bricks, concrete, and jutting steel rebar.

"Move," he hissed, and pressed onward.

The ductwork twitched. He picked up his pace. The MP-5 on his back scraped against the rough concrete above him.

Another jolt. Bigger. A chuffing sound, as of metal bolts tearing slowly from concrete.

"*Michael!*"

Derek lunged forward, faster, scurrying.

Maria: "Wait!"

"Hurry!"

Faster. More vibration. The ductwork was starting a regular rattling rhythm.

"Ooooh!"

The ductwork twisted, shifting a good three inches on the right side. Derek felt himself sliding off, and with a grunt, lunged off the duct toward a steel I-beam. He slammed into it with an "ooooph!" and angled himself to a better position. Twisting around, he saw Maria scrabbling at the ductwork as she slid sideways, long nails clicking on the metal.

Reaching out, he caught her around the waist and hauled her toward him. With a cry, she flailed about, snagging his arms.

"A little help here!" With her full weight suddenly on him, Derek was afraid they were both going to fall off the I-beam. He felt a tearing sensation in his side and sheets of pain blasted through his ribs. Almost dropping her, he groaned and leaned back, drawing her upward.

Feet kicking wildly, she boosted herself next to him on the beam.

Derek flashed the light on the ductwork. Now that their weight was off it, it had ceased tilting and was only vibrating softly.

"I could really use a *drink*," Maria whispered fiercely.

Derek reached into his bag and pulled out the bottle of vodka. "One sip," he said, and handed it to her.

She pulled the soaked rag out, took a hit and handed it back to him. He took a sip, winced, then shoved the rag back in.

"Where are we?" she asked.

Derek flashed the light around. "Above the east utility hallway. We can edge along this beam for a bit then get back on the catwalk."

She clung to the beam, eyes wide, face covered with grime. "I called you Michael. I guess you're really Derek."

"Yes."

"I liked Michael."

"You'll probably like Derek, too. Take a breather, then we should keep moving."

Maria was quiet. "Maybe I should just hole up here and you go do whatever you need to do."

Derek tried to relax, but it was almost impossible balanced on the I-beam, the rough metal cutting into his thighs and hands. "I need you."

She didn't say anything for a long time. Finally, "One more sip?"

He handed her the vodka. She took a swallow and handed it back.

He placed it carefully back in the bag and checked his watch. He didn't know if there was a clock ticking down somewhere. It was 11:43 a.m.

Taking a deep breath, he whispered, "Let's go," and began a slow, awkward crawl along the I-beam. His knee ached, his back screamed with pain, and his head throbbed. The instances of double vision were increasing. A wave of vertigo washed over him, like clinging to a tilting planet. He froze, sucking in air, forcing himself to focus. After a moment his equilibrium returned to normal. *Not good*, he thought, and continued forward.

Finally, after five minutes, he stretched off the I-beam onto the catwalk. Holding a hand out, he helped Maria over. They were above the utility hallway on the east side of the Cheyenne Center. It looked like they had a clear shot from here to where he knew there was a set of service stairs and an elevator. He glanced at his watch again.

11:50 a.m.

They hurried along the catwalk, stepping over pipes and wires, but running into no more obstacles. They moved carefully so as not to make noise. Derek periodically popped on his flashlight to check the way, but tried to keep its use to a minimum.

11:53 a.m.

They came to an abrupt stop at a half-wall. On the other side of the wall was what appeared to be a smooth cement block structure. Derek knew it housed an elevator. Near the catwalk, at about waist height, was a metal hatch cut into the wall. It allowed access to the elevator shaft.

Derek shone the light over the half-wall, the elevator unit, and the utility hallway. He knew a doorway built into the half-wall divided the elevator lobby from the utility hallway. Across the structure ran several thin wires, like fishing line.

He clicked off the flashlight.

Three red lights burned in the darkness.

He flicked on the light again.

"What is that?" Maria asked.

"The wall, the doorway, and the hatch to the elevator unit are all wired with explosives," he said.

The only sound was the sharp intake of breath as Maria took in that information. "What do we do?"

Derek looked at his watch again, feeling an urgency he couldn't quite explain. "I don't know," he said. "I'm thinking."

Suddenly she tapped him on the shoulder. She pointed to her ears. He clicked on the radio and listened to Coffee rattling away in Spanish.

He shot Maria a questioning look. "*Madre de Dios,*" she whispered. "What?"

"He's telling all his people to be on extra alert, because he doesn't believe they will meet his first ransom demand at noon and he will have to kill one of the G8. He says to prepare for a possible counterattack."

CHAPTER 42

Richard Coffee crossed the ballroom to speak with Mikhail Alexandrov and Amron Aryeh. Seeing them talking, *El Tiburón* joined them. Although he was technically The Fallen's second in command, he understood that Coffee's relationship with the Russian and the Israeli went back much further than his own, that they were, in some peculiar way, members of the original Fallen Angels.

The Fallen nodded to him in greeting, but addressed Alexandrov and Aryeh. "I don't like what's going on out there. I want you two to go out there and take out whoever is causing problems."

El Tiburón said, "Why don't you tell us who it is who is causing the problems."

Without warning Coffee snapped a fist into *El Tiburón's* face. The blow sent him reeling, stumbling to the ground. In a flash he was back on his feet, reaching for his gun. Before he could even swing the barrel around, Coffee had his Glock aimed in his face. The Fallen said nothing. He waited, expression neutral.

El Tiburón held his hands up in a surrender gesture. His jaw throbbed, but it was not overwhelming. It was certainly not as painful as the humiliation. "No disrespect, Fallen."

Coffee still didn't say anything. The gun didn't dip or waver.

El Tiburón bowed his head, breaking eye contact. "I'm sorry, Fallen. I meant no disrespect."

The air felt heavy with anticipation. Every single one of the captives —and their captors—watched in breathless silence. *El Tiburón* waited, coiled within himself, body and *life* balanced as if on a blade.

Coffee nodded and plunged the Glock back into its holster. His attention refocused on the Russian and the Israeli. "I'll let you out the east door. Come on."

The three men moved through the crowd, which shrank away from them. *El Tiburón* returned to the TV controls. Blood filled his mouth. He spit it on the floor. He liked the taste of blood in his mouth. He was a shark. He was *El Tiburón*. His gaze lingered on The Fallen and a blossom of rage grew in his gut. *Not grew*, he thought. *Just came out of hiding*.

He watched The Fallen pull out his PDA and tap keys, disarming the explosives on that particular door. Aryeh, slim, wiry, with short curly hair, and Alexandrov, with his big square head and flat Slavic features made for an odd-looking pair, except *El Tiburón* knew they were stone killers. They both held their MP-5s at the ready. When The Fallen gave the signal, they slipped through the door. As soon as the door was shut, Fallen tapped a key on the PDA, rearming the door's explosives.

Richard Coffee turned and stared at him from across the ballroom. He jerked his hand and thumb in an upward gesture, meaning, "Turn on the TVs."

El Tiburón flicked on the TV cameras.

The Fallen strode across the room and up onto the stage to loom over the leaders in their chairs, their suicide vests grisly reminders of their helplessness. The Fallen pulled up another chair, spun it around next to the U.S. president and straddled it. *El Tiburón* moved the camera in for a close-up of the The Fallen in his black fatigues, his burning eyes, and square jaw, and the haggard, pale president of the United States, tied immobile in a chair. The Fallen spoke into a wireless microphone taken from the podium.

"So, Mr. President. It is only minutes until the first deadline. Do you think your government will release my people from Guantanamo Bay?"

President Langston, eyes locked on the camera, said in a strong, clear voice, "The United States does not negotiate with terrorists."

The Fallen smiled. "That means no. I was very clear in my demands. If I do not receive a phone call from Nadia Kosov stating the condition of —"

He was interrupted by his phone ringing. *El Tiburón* noted the look of eager anticipation — even surprise — on The Fallen's face. The Fallen jerked out the cell phone and put it to his ear. "Nadia?"

Who was Nadia? *El Tiburón* wondered, that so much hope would fill The Fallen's heart?

The Fallen listened for a moment. "Stop now," he said, voice harsh. "I was very clear on this." He clicked off the phone and dropped it into a pocket. To President Langston he said, "You are quite correct, Mr. President. They will not negotiate. Yet. As promised, I am going to kill one of the leaders here. But who shall it be? You decide. Tell me, Mr. President, what world leader will pay for your country's stubbornness?"

President Langston said, "I will not negotiate with you either."

The Fallen laughed and climbed to his feet.

El Tiburón pulled back so all of the leaders were in the picture.

"Mr. President," The Fallen said, "this is not a negotiation. One of them will die. You will eventually die. But our life is built upon the choices we make, is it not? Who will you choose? Will it be your friend, Prime Minister Hollenbeck? U.S. and British relations will survive you choosing his death. President Waldenstrom? Eh? The head of the European Union? No, what do Europeans care of the EU president? Merely a bureaucrat, no nationalist pride there."

He strode down the line of leaders. "Crown Prince Talal? Will the U.S. oil imports survive your fingering the Saudi leader? Hmmm. There's potential there."

The Fallen paused, body erect, clearly conscious of the eyes of the world on him. "Perhaps it's time to restart the Cold War. Perhaps President Vakhach?"

President Langston said, "If I must choose, then I choose myself. Kill me in exchange for the end of this situation."

The Fallen burst out laughing. "Playing for the cameras, Mr. President? This isn't an election year. You can't even run for office again! How noble and self-sacrificing. But no, I don't think so. That would be too simple and easy for you. I think there's a lot to be said about a new Cold War."

He walked behind the line of leaders and stood at an angle to Russian President Pieter Vakhach. Vakhach was a slim, balding man with sharp features and piercing dark eyes. There was something vulpine about the man, something that always gave the impression of an untrustworthy predator plotting an ambush.

Vakhach sat straight, not looking backward. His voice steady, he said in Russian, "I am prepared to die. I love my wife, Sasha, and my children, Ivan and Boris. I hope you will remember me with warmth and love. I hope Mother Russia will continue to grow and prosper. Farewell."

"Yes, yes," said The Fallen. "Very nice. Farewell to you, too." He raised the gun, aimed, and squeezed the trigger.

CHAPTER 43

Crouched on the catwalk, Derek felt a slight vibration beneath his feet. He reached over and gently touched Maria's wrist, hoping to communicate that he wanted her to stay very still and be very quiet.

Somewhere below and behind them a door opened. A moment later the door shut with a soft click. There was almost no sound of people below, yet Derek sensed the presence of at least one person, possibly more.

Leaning toward Maria he brought his lips to her ear and in a barely audible voice said, "Don't make a sound." Carefully adjusting the MP-5 and sack of Molotov cocktails, he slid to the catwalk until he was lying bellydown. Again, he wasn't able to see anything.

Reaching for his screwdriver, he was preparing to drill another tiny hole in the drop ceiling when a low voice spoke in heavily accented English, "Nothing."

The voice was almost directly beneath them. A different voice, this one also accented, but a much different accent and a higher-pitched voice, said, "Fallen, this is *León*. East hallway, perimeter three, is clear. I repeat, east hallway is clear."

Definitely two men, Derek thought.

Maria tapped him on the shoulder and pointed to the radio. He clicked on his radio to hear Coffee saying in English, "What's the status at the loading dock?"

The higher-pitched voice said, "A big pile of rubble. You can't get through that way. No one but a rat could get through that."

The other voice, in what sounded like a Russian accent: "Somebody blew themselves up."

Coffee: "*Tigre. Oso.* Status?"

Two separate voices, clearly Spanish accented, identified themselves: "*Tigre* here. Clear."

"*Oso* here. Clear."

Coffee: "*León* and *Puma*. Is the east hallway secure?"

The one called *León* said, "Secure. No one can get in here from the kitchen and the other entrance is totally wired."

"*Da*," said *Puma*. "It is secure."

"Then come on back. I need you more in here. Radio me when you get to the door."

"Affirmative," said *Puma*.

Derek swallowed. He leaned toward Maria and whispered, "Take the cocktails down the catwalk as far as you can go, light one, kick through the ceiling tile and drop it, then run! Now! Hurry!" He shoved the lighter into her trembling hand.

He sensed hesitation then felt the catwalk vibrating as Maria did as he told her to.

Bringing the MP-5 around, double-checking it was loaded, the safety off, he crouched in place, ready.

A click and the lighter flashed in the darkness. Maria crouched a good twenty yards away, shaking hand holding one of the bottles of sherry, flame quivering as she tried to get the wick to ignite.

Below: "What's that? Someone above us? Move!"

Dammit!

Gunfire roared from below. Each bullet hole through the ceiling let in light that acted like a laser beam in the crawl space, skewering the dust. They were everywhere, simultaneously moving toward Maria and himself.

Maria seemed frozen in place. The wick didn't want to light. The needles of light raced along toward her position.

The wick lit, then went out.

Derek kept his eyes on the beams of light as they zigzagged back and forth. Part of the firing stopped. It was followed by a clatter then a metallic sound as another magazine was slammed home.

Come on, Maria. Come on.

Her hands shook so badly it looked like a dancing firefly from Derek's viewpoint. Then the torch lit.

Maria leaned over, slammed her foot through the ceiling, and tossed the Molotov cocktail through the hole.

"Jump!" Derek followed his own advice and stepped off the catwalk onto the dropped ceiling tile, which disintegrated around him. As he fell, he fired the MP-5.

He was firing at nothing.

In the direction he was facing there was only a burning pool of alcohol amidst broken glass.

He hit the ground hard, dropped, and rolled. Behind him were the two terrorists. One, a blocky, square-headed Slavic guy was pressed against one wall. The other, slim, wiry, looked Middle Eastern, was sprawled on the floor, gun held ready.

Derek continued to fire. He hit the Russian, who jerked spasmodically, dropping to his knees, stumbling sideways on top of the Israeli. Derek, continuing to roll, fired. The body of the Russian jumped and thumped and twitched as Derek's 10-mm rounds tore the body to shreds.

The Israeli struggled to get out from behind the Russian's corpse, finally using his body as a blockade.

Derek continued to roll. He tried to take careful aim on the Israeli, but the man was on the move as well. Bullets whined past Derek's head, ricocheting off the walls.

He squeezed the trigger.

Nothing.

The MP-5 magazine held sixty rounds, and on full automatic, it took only seconds to empty the weapon.

It was empty.

And the Israeli knew it. He shoved aside the Russian and climbed to his feet. He brought up his own MP-5 and sighted on Derek. "A walking dead man. Say good-bye, whoever you are."

Derek tensed, waiting for his death. His luck had finally run out. He was too far from the man to go after him. He was in a straight hallway with nothing to hide behind.

He heard something like breaking glass. Derek had just long enough to think, "Maria?" before the hallway was filled with a wall of fire and debris. He was slammed off his feet by the force of the explosion.

Everything went black.

CHAPTER 44

El Tiburón moved the camera in for a close-up as The Fallen squeezed the trigger. He wanted the world to see the assassination of the Russian leader in all its bloody reality. This is power, he thought.

A rattle of gunfire sounded from outside the ballroom. On the monitor, Pieter Vakhach flinched, then settled into a frozen, watchful calm. The crowd, tensely watching the drama, shrieked and screamed at the unexplained noise. *El Tiburón,* through the cameras, saw The Fallen's expression — saw his distraction.

"Shoot him," *El Tiburón* hissed. "What are you waiting for?"

The gunfire continued. On the stage, The Fallen turned toward the east doors, waiting.

Silence. The gunfire ended. The Fallen turned back toward Vakhach and raised his weapon.

An explosion rocked the building. The floor shook. More screams. The tremors were so strong that for a moment The Fallen staggered, then righted himself. He tapped his throat mic so the entire network could hear. "*León. Puma.* Report in. What is your status?"

Silence.

"*Tigre. Oso.* Report in. What is your status?"

After a moment of confused rustling and static, a voice came on: "*Tigre* here. The elevator lobby and the doors between the lobby and the east hallway just blew. I have no idea what set them off. Uh — I'm fine and —"

Another voice, "*Oso* here. I'm — I'll live. I was a little close to the explosion. I'll — I'll be all right."

"Can you access the east hallway?"

Oso: "Negative, Fallen. Area completely blocked."

"Maintain positions."

Blood boiling, *El Tiburón* started toward the front of the ballroom. The Fallen spun and pointed at him. "Maintain position."

"Don't you get it? Someone is picking off our people one by one!" he shouted. "We're losing the third perimeter!"

The Fallen seemed to grow taller, his eyes blazing with anger. "Do your job! I know what I'm doing."

The Fallen strode back to Pieter Vakhach, raised his gun and pulled the trigger. The bullet tore through the back of the Russian leader's skull and exploded out his face, spraying blood and bone and brain. Vakhach slumped forward and toppled over to the floor. The gunshot faded away, lost in screams and shouts of outrage.

The Fallen turned so he gazed directly at the main camera. "You have exactly one hour to comply with our original demands or another leader will die." With a slashing gesture, he ordered *El Tiburón* to shut off the cameras.

CHAPTER 45

Derek came to abruptly, jerking to consciousness as if thrust through a plate-glass window. One second it was black, the next he was in the light lunging for his assault rifle. Everything hurt. There were sharp, needle-like jabs of pain all over his body, exclamation points in a general background ache. He felt pressure on his right leg.

Blinking, he looked down. The hallway was littered with debris — concrete and wood and wires and bits of metal. A large chunk of concrete rested on his leg.

He tried to sit up. Inside his skull it felt like a great weight was sliding on a greased surface. The weight smashed into the front of his head, right behind his eyes. Fireworks went off and the world grayed out again. Gasping for air, he twisted sideways and retched.

This time when he came to he noticed the body of the Israeli terrorist. The corpse was a dozen feet away, twisted in a way nature had never intended, dark eyes staring blankly into whatever level of hell was reserved for terrorists.

A hand gently touched his brow. Blinking, Derek looked up. Maria sat near him. Blood covered her face and oozed from a vicious gash in her forehead. She was completely coated in grime and soot, her clothing torn and scraped.

"Sit still," she said.

"Are you okay?" he croaked out.

Her smile appeared alabaster against the dirt. "I've had better days. Let's see if I can get that cement off your leg."

She staggered to her feet and stumbled over to him. Derek noted a deep cut in one of her thighs, blood running down her leg.

"We've got to take care of your leg," he said.

"Later," she muttered, and crouched down next to him, pain twisting her face. She gripped the cement block and with a grunt, shifted it a few inches. Derek thought he was screaming until his throat couldn't take it, slipping back into the darkness, but a moment later he looked up to see Maria crouched by his foot studying the concrete.

"Sorry," he said.

She turned to him, expression grim. "For what?"

"Uh, screaming."

"You didn't scream. You just passed out. That leg hurt?"

He started to shake his head, thought better of it, and said, "No. Yes. Never mind. Does your leg hurt?"

"Like a sonofabitch. Next time I decide to play commando, I don't want to be wearing a skirt."

"Next time."

"I can't lift this thing."

"We need a lever. Maybe one of the guns."

She looked around. "Okay, *amigo*. With the right lever you can move the world." She limped over and picked up the Israeli's MP-5. Walking back to Derek, she started to set the stock against the concrete block.

"Uh, Maria?" Derek's voice was soft but urgent. "Take the fucking magazine out and put the safety on before you shoot yourself in the head."

She plopped down on the floor, dropping the gun to the ground, put her face in her hands and began to sob. "*I . . . I can't do this! I can't!*"

Maria was out of reach, but he tried to touch her and reassure her. It wasn't easy twisting. Again, he felt the world gray around the edges, but by concentrating and sucking in deep breaths of air, he managed to stay conscious. "Maria," he said, "Maria, listen to me. I need you. I really need you right now. You can do this. In fact, you're amazing. I couldn't have gotten a better person to help me out here. Look at me."

She took her hands from her face. Now she looked like a raccoon, her tears creating clean circles under her eyes. He wanted to laugh, but didn't. "Okay, honey," he said, "hand me the gun."

Sniffling, she handed it to him. He removed the magazine, checked to make sure the barrel was clear, clicked on the safety, and handed it back to her. With a fierce look of concentration, she jammed the stock under the cement block.

"Ready?"

"When you are."

With a grunt she levered the block off his foot. The pain was intense, but not the worst he'd ever experienced. He slowly moved his leg and tried to rotate his ankle and flex his foot. More sparklers of pain, but not unbearable. He didn't know if he had broken anything. It was possible, and he thought the foot might be swelling. The worst thing he could do now was take the boot off. If he did, he'd never get it back on. Using the MP-5 as a crutch, he lurched to his feet and tried to take a step. Painful, but usable — barely. *A sprain*, he thought, *or maybe just bad bruising.*

"I'll help," Maria said, and slipped in under his arm. "Where do you want to go?"

"A beach in the Virgin Islands might be nice. How long do you think it would take to get there?"

She smiled. "Is that a proposition, *amante*?"

He smiled back. "Maria, let me tell you something. I own a sixty-foot cabin cruiser docked back in Baltimore. If we get out of this mess alive, you can join me and we'll take it down to the Caribbean for a few months."

"Promise?"

"Promise."

"I'll hold you to it. Now, where do you want to go?"

"Our dead friend over here." He pointed to the Israeli.

She helped him hobble over to the Israeli. The more he moved, the easier it got, although he knew these things were relative. He wouldn't be sprinting anywhere anytime soon, and if he had to jump again, he was totally screwed.

Awkwardly kneeling, Derek roughly searched the corpse, coming up with another knife, a radio receiver that appeared to have been damaged in the explosion, and nothing else. Using the knife, he started slicing the Israeli's shirt to pieces. When he had enough strips, he gestured for Maria to sit next to him. She did.

He wiped the blood on her leg, studying the wound. It was about two inches long and looked deep, but it was starting to coagulate. "That must hurt," he said.

"You think?"

He looked up at her. "I don't suppose you've got any of those bottles of sherry still around?"

"Sorry. No. I'd be drinking them if I did."

"How'd you get this cut?" He noticed that her legs and arms were bruised and scraped, but there were only the two cuts.

"The catwalk sort of collapsed after the explosion. I fell through the ceiling, and I think I got this from either the catwalk or those wire supports for the ceiling tiles."

"Okay," he said. "We'll just have to make do." He wadded up some cloth and wrapped a bandage around it, tying it tight. "It's going to get stiff."

"Better it than me." She sighed. "Michael—I mean, Derek." She smiled. "Why did you call yourself Michael Gabriel? Did you pick that name yourself?"

"The guy who's behind all this?" Derek dabbed at the cut on her forehead, decided it wasn't that bad and would be fine if he left it alone. "His name's Richard Coffee. He calls himself The Fallen Angel. You know, Lucifer. The Devil. Well, I was here to stop him in case he tried something. The only two angels with names mentioned in the Bible are Michael and Gabriel. They're both archangels. I thought it fitting."

Maria brightened. "So you are an archangel? A warrior angel of God?"

Derek shrugged. "Right about now I think I'm the luckiest guy on the planet. I thought this guy was going to take me out when the whole damn place exploded. Do you have any idea what happened?"

Maria colored slightly beneath the dirt on her face. "I did it."

He studied her. "Did what?"

"I saw what was going to happen. So I was, I don't know, twenty yards from all those explosives? So I grabbed one of those sherry bottles and threw it at the wall."

He raised his eyebrows. "And must have hit the tripwires."

"Must have, because the next thing I know—boom!"

"Must have been a hell of a throw."

She curled her bicep and said, "I used to play softball in high school. Pitcher."

"Excellent. And thanks. You saved my life." He studied the hallway. It was thoroughly blocked from both ends. There were two doors leading into the ballroom, but there was no way they should go in there. "We're going to have to go back up there."

Maria shivered. "And go after those two guys in the lobby? *Tigre* and *Oso*?"

Derek frowned. "What do you think?"

"Perhaps," she said, "we have been lucky enough for one day." She reached out and snagged his St. Sebastian's medal, four-leaf clover, and juju beads. "Even with these, you may be running out of luck."

He didn't say anything. He stared at his foot.

"Do you think we can do it, Derek?"

"I think I should. You're right. You may have already put yourself into enough harm's way. Maybe just getting you someplace safe would be a better idea."

She was silent a moment. "He killed somebody. One of the leaders."

"What?"

She tapped her earpiece. "Lucifer. The Fallen Angel. Whoever he is. Richard Coffee." She shivered. "It must be very black coffee, Derek. He killed one of the leaders. I think it was the Russian leader, what's-his-name, Vakhach? I heard it over the radio. He says he'll kill another one in less than an hour if his demands aren't met."

Derek glanced at his watch. 12:17. Much less than an hour.

"I . . . I have to stop him. I have to try."

She nodded. "You know him? He is — something to you?"

"A friend. An old friend."

"Okay, my archangel. I will help you. Let's go."

PART III
THE ANGEL OF DEATH

CHAPTER 46

Secretary Johnston and everybody else in the PEOC studied the text message on the screen. It read:

> 2 EXPL XSIDE — DS? GUESS 4 BGs DEAD. 10 IN-
> SIDE. XMan & RC FIGHT. RC — PDA 2 CTRL C4.
> JAM?

Johnston scratched his jaw, reached over and swallowed half a cup of coffee that had grown stale and bitter. He felt rather stale and bitter himself. His stomach was tight and acid reflux bit at his throat. He needed to focus on the problems at hand and not the emergency phone call he had gotten from his daughter, telling him about her mother's latest Alzheimer's episode — microwaving a bowl of oatmeal and an oven mitt for twenty minutes until it caught fire. Johnston shoved that dilemma to the side. "'EXPL'?" he said.

Lt. General Akron sighed. "I think that means explosion. *Two explosions outside.*"

FBI Director O'Malley said, "We know there's been two explosions. And they've been inside the building, but not in the main room. 'DS'? That means he thinks Derek Stillwater caused them?"

"Or he wonders if he did," Johnston said. He stretched back in his chair, listening to his spine pop, thinking, *Getting old and falling apart.*

"Let's hope it's him," O'Malley said. "Okay, Bill. 'GUESS 4 BGs DEAD.' Does that mean what I think it means?"

"I'm guessing, but I think Bob's saying he thinks four of the bad guys — BGs — are dead."

Akron looked pale and drained. Johnston thought they all did. The footage of Vakhach being executed had riveted the world, but now everybody knew what was at stake. Already governments were starting to point fingers, and almost all of them were working to take their kidnapped leaders out of the loop. It wasn't all that easy, though.

Vice President Newman had called a meeting in fifteen minutes to implement invoking the Twenty-fifth, which would require the vote of the cabinet. But two of the cabinet members — Robert Mandalevo and Joshua Babcock, the secretary of commerce — were kidnapped, and two others were out of the country. The secretary of transportation was on a trip to Canada and the secretary of state was in Indonesia.

Akron said, "And '10 Inside' suggests to me that at least two of the dead were from the twelve that were inside the ballroom. Something's going on. Somehow somebody is picking off these terrorists."

"Stillwater," Johnston said. "I'm convinced." His gut said it was true. He had a lot of faith in Derek. Maybe too much.

O'Malley grunted. "Good for you. I'm not."

Johnston let it go. O'Malley was pissed about Derek's faked death. "'Xman and RC fight.' Trouble in paradise? We saw the exchange between Coffee and the Hispanic guy, *El Tiburón.*"

CIA Director Ballard said, "We're working on identifying him. There's a Russian FSB agent working with Agent Swenson and her people to figure him out."

"Khournikova?" asked Johnston. He had been briefed by Swenson and wasn't sure he thought that was a good idea. He wasn't a huge believer that Khournikova was on their side. She definitely fell in the "undecided" column.

"Yes. And I know what you're thinking."

"Swenson wants her under his eye," Johnston said. "He's not sure he trusts her. Why should I?"

"I don't either, but she came up with a few good ideas. And if there's bad blood between this guy, the Shark, and Coffee, I'm all for it."

"Sure," Johnston agreed. He turned back to the screen. "Now, I'm confused. What's all this? 'RC — PDA 2 CTRL C4. JAM?'"

Akron licked his lips. "I think it means Richard Coffee's using a PDA to control the plastic explosives."

Director Ballard blurted, "He's suggesting we jam the signal? I've got to get the NSA on this — ASAP." Ballard was on his phone already.

Johnston glanced at O'Malley. "Puskorius needs to know about this." He glanced at his watch. "The op's about to begin."

O'Malley nodded. "Better call him yourself. Try to coordinate with the NSA. I hope this works."

Johnston nodded, thoughts on Derek Stillwater running around picking off Angels. *If* he was alive. *If* that's what he was doing. That thought did a little two-step with his thoughts about his wife's increasingly loopy behavior. He split up that pair and concentrated on the national crisis.

There had been no contact from Derek, and a call to his sat phone indicated he was off the grid. Johnston shot off a little prayer to whatever gods might be listening and stood up.

"I'm off to discuss invoking the Twenty-fifth. Keep me informed. I'll call Puskorius on the way."

CHAPTER 47

Richard Coffee stepped around the corpse of the Russian leader, jumped off the stage, and strode over to Franz Dorfmann. *El Tiburón* jogged over to where the two men stood near the front of the room. *What now?*

Coffee stopped talking for a moment to watch him approach, then nodded. "I need *Perro Loco* for a special op."

"Are you sending him to his death, too?" asked *El Tiburón*.

Coffee spun, gun up, but this time *El Tiburón* was ready. The two men stood in identical crouches, handguns aimed in each other's faces.

Franz Dorfmann, the Mad Dog, who had spent much of his career as an assassin for the German *Abwehr,* calmly reached out with both hands, gripped the men's wrists and forced them to lower their weapons. "*Nein.* Not now. Now is for discipline." He turned to *El Tiburón*, a merry expression on his sharp, angular features. "Is this not a suicide mission, comrade? A foolhardy mission by a small band of brilliant and audacious rebels? We all have to die someday. Why not today? It is a beautiful day, is it not? Today is a good day to die."

"Perhaps if The Fallen will tell us who is picking us off one by one. What angel of death is stalking us and cutting our numbers? He knows. It's time for him to share his secrets."

Coffee's expression was taut, rage and violence just below the surface of his skin like frigid water beneath black ice. "You will never know all my secrets. But, *Si, El Tiburón.* Who is the real Angel of Death here? Me? You? *Perro Loco?* Or is it this man who hunts us?" He turned away, but not before the icy expression turned to one of contempt. "*Perro Loco, El Tiburón* is correct. Someone stalks us. His name is Derek Stillwater. Unless things have changed, he is a troubleshooter for the American Department of Homeland Security."

"How do you know this?" *El Tiburón* demanded. He felt his heart rate accelerate. Finally, some truth from The Fallen.

"I ran into him in the kitchen just before the op started. I killed three Secret Service agents who were arresting him, and I locked him in a walk-in freezer in the kitchen."

"Why didn't you kill him?! You fool —"

This time Coffee was faster, his gun barrel inches from *El Tiburón's* eyes. "Do *not* think I won't kill you."

"Without me," *El Tiburón* hissed, "my men will not follow you to their graves."

The German interrupted, voice calm. "I need to know more about Derek Stillwater. Clearly he is a capable enemy."

Coffee lowered his weapon. "We were once partners. U.S. Army Special Forces. He's a specialist in biological and chemical warfare. He has a Ph.D. He's very, very smart. But don't let that specialty fool you. He was trained like I was — he's a killer, and his years out of the service haven't dulled his edge. It won't be easy taking him down."

"No problem." Dorfmann pulled out his handgun, double-checked it was loaded, a round in the chamber, the safety off. With a lightning fast flick of his hand he had his combat knife out of its sheath. Without any warning whatsoever the glittering black blade slashed across *El Tiburón's* shirt. It left a six-inch-long flap in the cloth, but didn't touch his skin. "I have a rather sharp edge myself."

"Games! Now is not the time for games!" spat *El Tiburón*.

Dorfmann — *Perro Loco* — laughed. "It's all a game, *El Tiburón*. You take yourself so seriously." He nodded to The Fallen and headed toward the doors.

Coffee called him back. "*Perro Loco!*"

Dorfmann turned back, eyebrows raised, expression mocking. "*Si, jefe?*"

"Don't underestimate Derek Stillwater. He's very creative. Very resourceful." Coffee hesitated. "He saved my life more than once. Brought me back from the dead. He's come back from the dead himself. He's very hard to kill. I've tried. You're going to have to stop him for good."

"My pleasure!" To *El Tiburón*: "*Auf wiedersehen, meiner Kleiner Fisch. Bis später.*"

Dorfmann paused at the door long enough for The Fallen to shut down the detonators, then slipped out like smoke and was gone.

El Tiburón locked eyes with The Fallen. "You talk about Stillwater as if he's still your friend. You should have killed him when you had the chance. It's not like you to show mercy. You left a trained killer alone in a walk-in freezer just before our op began. And now he's stalking us. You may have given *Perro Loco* his death sentence. And we need the numbers here."

Coffee did not flinch. "Be careful, *meiner Kleiner Fisch*, that I don't give you *your* death sentence." And he walked away.

CHAPTER 48

Maria helped Derek limp toward the end of the hallway. They paused for a moment at the body of the Russian. Derek performed a rough search, coming up with a fresh magazine for the MP-5. Otherwise, the man had nothing left to take. *I already took his life,* thought Derek. *What else was there?* He stood up and studied the field of rubble.

"I want to get to what's left of the elevator shaft," he said. "When they put these charges in place they were pretty clever. They could have put enough to take the whole building down. There's been plenty of damage, and both explosions have managed to shut down the hallways. I wonder if they planned it this way or if they had a lot of dumb luck."

Maria said nothing. Her arms were crossed over her chest. She stood, self-contained, shivering. Derek sighed, reached over, and held her. "You've been amazing," he said. "Absolutely amazing. You're one tough babe."

Voice muffled against his shirt, she said, "Mama didn't raise no wimps."

He didn't know whether to laugh or to cry. "No, she didn't. Smart, tough, and beautiful. But we can't stand here. Let's get going."

He nudged her forward, and together they picked their way over and around the debris field, finally clambering on top of a huge pile of brick, concrete, and steel.

Derek reached out and grasped the twisted remains of the catwalk. It seemed relatively secure, angling upward into a hole in the ceiling. "Follow me," he said, and began a laborious scramble upward into the darkness.

Struggling, his ankle throbbing, Derek thought he heard the whisper of a door opening and closing beneath and below them, farther down the hallway. He paused, ears straining to hear. Nothing. Doubt gnawing at his guts, he continued forward.

CHAPTER 49

Lieutenant Sam O'Shay, U.S. Army's 1st Special Forces Operational Detachment, Delta, checked his gear — the High Altitude Precision Parachute System (HAPPS) — for the tenth time, studied his altimeter, then double-checked his watch. He and his five-man insertion team were roaring at 20,000 feet over the Rocky Mountains toward the Cheyenne Resort. Operation Tagger had been put together just about as fast as any op could be put together.

"Okay, gentlemen," he said into his radio, the roar of the CASA C-212 Aviocar aircraft drowning out any other communication. "Operation Tagger. There are three, I repeat, three Secret Service snipers on the roofs of each building. We will be landing on the Cheyenne Center itself. The snipers have been made aware of this operation."

"Gee, you take all the fun out of it," said Santiago, smirking.

O'Shay knew Santiago made jokes to overcome his fear. He continued. "There are approximately six hundred hostages being held, at last count, by ten — I repeat, ten! — armed terrorists. The building has been wired with C4 or Semtex and the detonators are controlled via a PDA held by the terrorist leader. He doesn't have to turn them all on or off, he can control each individually. Also, the leaders of the world — including the president of the United States — are wired with C4 or Semtex and can presumably be detonated by hand. The Puzzle Palace is going to scramble the satellite signals and jam any radio signals starting in five minutes. Gentlemen, they will not be able to set off or turn off those explosives from this time forward. They will not be able to communicate with each other. But we will not be able to communicate with each other, either. Stay in visual communication and be careful. Let's hunt some bad guys." He looked at his watch then checked in with the pilot.

"T-minus four minutes, Lieutenant. Proceed with predrop."

They were going to perform HALO drops, or High Altitude Low Opening. They didn't know who The Fallen Angels had outside the facility watching. They didn't know what the communications were like. The NSA would be jamming all communications, but they didn't know if these guys had some sort of visual communication or not.

Lieutenant O'Shay thought their intel sucked, and had spoken freely to General Puskorius on that issue. The general had ordered him to proceed, which was the job of Delta Force, after all. To do the impossible. Antiterrorism, hostage rescue.

In O'Shay's ears the pilot said, "T-minus two minutes. We have a westerly wind at ten knots on the deck."

O'Shay studied a PDA attached to his wrist, part of his complicated drop-and-insert gear. He punched a key and brought up aerial photographs of the Cheyenne Center. To his team he said, "Note the layout of the buildings. Do NOT miss the Cheyenne Center. Do NOT confuse them."

Santiago said, "Looks to me like there's a Starbucks down the road. Maybe I'll drop in there for a Frappuccino."

"Santiago, we pull off Tagger and I'll buy the beer for the next month."

"Promises, promises."

"T-minus one minute."

"We're up," O'Shay said.

His team trotted toward the back of the C-212. With a punch of a switch, the rear hatch opened. Wind roared into and out of the plane.

"Let's go!" O'Shay rushed forward and threw himself out of the hatch, spread eagle. Even through his flight suit he could feel the bite of the cold at 20,000 feet. The oxygen through his mask tasted metallic and flat.

Down they plunged, gravity grabbing the team and dragging them toward earth at ever-increasing speeds.

O'Shay, into his radio, counted off his altimeter. "20,000. 18,000. 16,000 —"

Faster and faster. Finally, visual. He spotted the Cheyenne Resort just outside the suburban sprawl of Colorado Springs. The green open spaces of the golf course, the blue of the lake, the outline of the numerous buildings and parking lots.

They were right on target. He checked the GPS on his left wrist, noted the pilot had been accurate in their launch time. If they didn't encounter wind sheer on the ground, they shouldn't have a problem hitting their targets.

His team screamed downward at 260 feet per second.

4,000.

3,000.

2,000.

At 1,000 feet, his chute opened automatically with a ripping, popping sound. His entire body jerked at the deceleration, a snap to every bone and muscle in his body that he would feel for days afterward. His hands by his sides, he yoked the controls until he had the rectangular shape of the Cheyenne Center in his line of vision.

I hope to hell the snipers have been informed.

Around him he saw the rest of his team, parachutes open, flying toward their target.

800 feet.

700.

They were low enough they could now see details of the building. Black-topped roof. Red brick walls. The snipers weren't visible against it from this height. He noted the Mobile Control Unit. He noted the National Guard rolling down the roads, setting up perimeters — tanks and armored personnel carriers and Humvees.

400 feet.

Something caught his attention out of the corner of his eye. A splash of scarlet where there shouldn't be one.

Twisting around, he saw Santiago's jumpsuit covered with red. Santiago slumped unnaturally in his harness.

Another.

He swiveled his head. Franklin. A mist of red swirling into the updraft, a fog of blood escaping from a helmet that was barely there.

O'Shay went cold. There were snipers out there, taking out his team as they parachuted in.

Into his microphone: "Snipers. Take evasive action! I repeat, take—"

But the National Security Agency was jamming all radio and satellite communications in the area. They couldn't hear him. No one could.

O'Shay spun his chute in an erratic fashion, jinking, swerving, trying to avoid being an easy target. Another of his team went down, slumped in his harness, blood soaking his flight suit.

Where the hell were the snipers? Not the bureau snipers on the building. In the hills surrounding the resort?

"Goddammit, we didn't have enough —"

But Lieutenant O'Shay didn't have even enough time to finish his thought as a high velocity sniper round struck him in the chest as he crossed into the three hundred-feet range.

CHAPTER 50

Derek found the elevator structure to be relatively intact. The wall that had separated the hallway from the elevator was gone. Huge chunks of concrete and steel were piled six and seven feet high, some of them from the elevator infrastructure, most from the floor, wall, doors, and ceiling.

The catwalk was a twisted, unstable wreck. As they inched along, the catwalk wobbled and vibrated with every move they made. Finally, drenched in sweat, vision doubling, pain flashing through his head and leg, he made it to the wall. Instead of a steel hatchway crisscrossed with wires and Semtex, Derek found a ragged hole in the structure.

Derek hauled himself through and sprawled atop the elevator car. Maria slipped in beside him.

Gulping air, he studied their situation. They could drop into the elevator through the roof hatch, pry open the doors, and possibly make their way into the lobby, though he had suspicions that there was as much debris blocking that way as was blocking the route they had come.

In addition, it was almost certain that two of Coffee's Fallen Angels were patrolling the lobby, armed and in better shape than he and Maria.

He took the flashlight out and beamed it upward. His heart sank.

Some elevator companies placed steel rungs into the elevator shaft so maintenance workers could climb up and down the shaft as necessary. Most did not. Derek knew that most elevator workers just rode the elevator on the roof — elevator surfing — until they got to the motor and gears built into the rooftop elevator controls. That was apparently the situation here. There was no ladder or steps or steel rungs. What he saw were blank concrete walls and steel cables that ran upward past the limits of his flashlight beam.

Derek was intimately familiar with the Cheyenne Center. The elevator was built to ferry people from the basement to the first floor. It also had a secondary function: to move maintenance people to the ballroom attic or to the roof. The attic was actually another crawl space, about five feet tall, filled with a mass of electrical wiring and heating and cooling ducts for the main structure. If the crawl space between the first floor and superstructure was a complicated, tight mess of infrastructure materials, it was nothing compared to the one above the ballroom.

They could go down, he supposed. Access to the basement would give them hallways to move through, in and around the structure, possibly even out of the Cheyenne Center. That might be desirable. It was time to get Maria to safety.

It was just that he wasn't entirely sure how he was going to accomplish that. You couldn't slip beneath an elevator from inside the elevator. If he activated the elevator — there were override controls on the roof of the elevator — the two Angels in the lobby would be alerted to their presence.

"This is fun," said Maria. "But where to now?"

"I'm thinking."

"Well, don't hurt yourself —"

Derek held up his hand, suddenly tense. Maria started to protest, but he slapped his hand over her mouth. He thought he heard a noise.

He waited, ears tuned to every sound, no matter how small. He thought initially it must be the movements of the two Angels in the lobby. But what he heard was a slow, delicate, regular rhythm from below them, from where they had just come. The catwalk.

Slowly leaning toward the hole in the wall, he rested his hand on the remnants of the catwalk.

He could feel the tension in the wrecked metal. And the vibration. Tiny, regular, as if it were supporting somebody's weight.

A moment later, the metal vibrated harder as whoever was on the structure moved forward.

Derek jerked back inside and studied the elevator shaft. He put his lips to Maria's ear. "Can you climb ropes?"

"I don't know."

He studied the elevator cables. There were six thick metal cables, at least an inch in diameter, maybe even thicker. They were greasy, which was going to be a problem. He grabbed hold, testing them. The metal cables would rip their hands to shreds. There was no way they could climb these things.

He reached down and flipped open the hatch to the elevator. He pointed down. Maria clambered down. Derek followed.

With a shrug, Derek tapped the button for the basement. With a grinding sound, the elevator dropped downward.

With a clunk it stopped and the doors opened. Derek stood ready, the MP-5 aimed into the basement elevator lobby. No one. Good.

Taking Maria's hand, he rushed out of the elevator.

CHAPTER 51

Irina Khournikova followed Agent Swenson out of the Mobile Command Unit. The U.S. National Security Agency was jamming all phone, radio, and satellite transmissions in the area just as Operation Tagger began. The only way they would have to communicate with anybody for the next fifteen minutes was via landlines and e-mail, although Swenson had seemed unsure as to whether or not those would be available.

Irina didn't like the unknown quantities. She recognized an operation put together too quickly without enough intel, and she knew from personal experience how these ops tended to end — tragically. She kept her opinion to herself. She thought Swenson had too many balls in the air as it was.

Outside, they kept an eye on the sky. Irina said, "What of the Security Center?"

"No word."

"I'll go check."

Swenson reached over and snagged her arm. "I want you with me."

"Right where you can keep an eye on me."

"That's right. Ah, here they come."

She looked skyward. At first she saw nothing but birds. Then they grew larger and she realized the birds were human beings in free fall, growing larger and larger.

Then the blue parachutes blossomed above them, the canopies almost invisible against the Colorado sky.

"Your, how do you call it, Delta Force? The best of the best of the best?"

"Roughly equivalent to your *Spetsnaz*."

Irina nodded, hoping this worked. She counted five parachutes. She could only see them because she had known where to look. Something caught her attention.

"What was that?" she asked.

Swenson scowled. He had heard it, too. The sound of a gunshot from somewhere in the hills. "Dammit! What —"

He sprinted into the MCU and returned a moment later with a pair of binoculars. His posture as taut as a bowstring, he focused the binoculars on the incoming paratroopers. "Holy fuck!"

"What is it?" she asked.

He handed her the glasses and she located one of the plummeting soldiers. He was slumped in his parachute harness, blood streaming from his head, which appeared to be blown to pieces. "Sniper," she said. "In the surrounding hillside?"

Swenson raced back into the MCU, growling commands. "Get me General Cole on a land line *NOW!* Inform Puskorius that snipers are taking out the Delta team! Do it! *Do it!*" He spun around then rushed out of the MCU toward an FBI agent armed with an assault rifle and screamed, "There are hostile snipers in the hills. I want teams scouring for them right now! *Right now!* Get on it!"

The agent ran off. Swenson spun again, an expression of near panic on his grizzly face. He stared at Khournikova. "Are you armed?"

"No."

"Follow me." He raced back into the MCU. She followed him. He yanked open a locker door. It was filled with rifles and handguns. He gestured. "Arm yourself. Khournikova, pick a team of my people and go open up that motherfucking security center. Do it now!"

"Yes, sir," she said, reaching in and pulling out an MP-5 assault rifle and a Sig Sauer P229 handgun, grabbing magazines to go with them. "Communications?"

He tossed her a handset. "It's useless right now, but communications will be back up ASAP, fourteen minutes at the latest. I sent three people over there and haven't heard from them. Something's going on. Clean it up."

He took a breathless gulp of air and snarled, "You understand what I mean here, Khournikova?"

She nodded. She understood perfectly. She hesitated, then pointed to another locker. He followed her gaze. This locker held hand grenades, flash grenades, and other high-level ordinance. "That might be helpful."

They locked eyes. Swenson slowly nodded. "Go for it, Khournikova."

She grabbed a canvas shoulder bag and retrieved several flash grenades, carefully placing them in the bag. She said, "I can do this better alone."

He paused, thinking it over. "You can trust my people."

"Maybe," she said, "but I think I can only trust you. And I think *you* can only trust *me*."

He nodded. "You're Special K. Understand?" He held up his radio. "These channels are just for you and me. I'm Superman."

"With the S on his chest," she said. "For Swenson."

"Bingo."

"I'll be in touch." And the Russian agent sprinted out of the MCU toward the International Center. In the surrounding hillsides she heard the sound of gunfire as a firefight started between the enemy snipers, the snipers on top of the buildings, and the Colorado National Guard. Richard Coffee had thought of everything.

Except Derek Stillwater, she reflected. Maybe Coffee *hadn't* thought of everything.

CHAPTER 52

Derek took Maria's hand and pulled her into the hallway, which was lit up with fluorescent lights. He felt very exposed, but saw no one.

Maria tapped a finger to her ear. "That's weird."

He shot her a sharp look. "What is?"

"The radio's all staticky."

Derek flicked his radio on and listened to the static. "That's interesting," he said, and clicked it off. "I think it's being jammed."

"Jammed?"

"Yeah. They don't want anybody to communicate with each other."

"They? The Fallen Angels?"

"No," Derek said. "The good guys don't want The Fallen Angels to communicate with each other. The government's jamming communications. That usually means some sort of op is starting."

Behind him he heard a light thunk, as if someone were stepping onto the roof of the elevator.

Derek rushed toward the far hallway, his injured leg throbbing, causing him to lurch along like Frankenstein's monster. He stopped. The steel doors were shut, and they were wired with Semtex. He spun and raced in the other direction, if his stiff, lumbering shuffle could be considered racing. Here, too, the hallway doors were shut and wired with explosives.

"Are we trapped?"

Derek glanced nervously toward the entryway to the elevator lobby. Was there someone in there?

He lunged across the hallway into the open door of a meeting room. Carefully he closed the door except for a crack. He brought the MP-5 around and crouched down, waiting. Sweat beaded on his forehead, dripped into his eyes. His lungs burned, his stomach churned, and his ribs, head, neck, back, and leg hurt. He was a fucking mess, and he knew it.

He waited, ignoring his body's signals of pain and discomfort, his body telling him to take a break, to quit, to get help. He waited.

It only took a few seconds. A dark-clad man flitted into the hallway. He had an MP-5 raised and he moved like liquid silver, quick and silent. The man disappeared from view. Maria started to say something, but Derek placed fingers against her lips.

Bang!

She jumped, crying out.

The Angel was starting with the meeting room at the opposite end of the hallway.

Bang!

Derek, expression grim, shut the door, locked it, and limped to the opposite side of the room and struggled on top of a folding table. He lifted aside an acoustic tile, shined a flashlight around, then helped Maria up next to him. He caught her around the waist and lifted her into the crawl space. Reaching up, he hauled himself up, and shifted the tile back into position.

This crawl space was tighter than the previous one they had been in. Only about three feet high, with no catwalk. There were I-beams and supporting walls and heating ducts and electrical wires and fiber-optic cables. There was a metal rectangular gridwork that supported the lights and ceiling tiles. They weren't designed to support the weight of a man or even a slender woman.

Derek spidered along until he was balanced on an I-beam, Maria perched beside him.

Bang!

The third meeting room.

Derek studied the space, and pointed toward the far wall. In her ear he whispered, "One at a time. Very careful."

He edged out on the gridwork, which wobbled beneath him. Only about eight feet and he would be at an I-beam that ran parallel to where he was now. He knew it delineated the back wall of these meeting rooms. On the other side of the wall was another hallway bordering the building's power plant.

He was about four feet from the I-beam when —

Bang!

The terrorist was in the room they had just vacated.

Derek clicked off his light, balanced on the metal braces, an awk-ward, uncomfortable position, his gun strapped on his back where he couldn't reach it. The crawl space was plunged in darkness, lit only by slivers of light around the edges of the acoustic tiles and the fluorescent lights. Maria was a good five feet away from him.

Light footfalls drifted up from the room below.

Silence. Then the sound of movement.

Suddenly an acoustical tile exploded upward, the crawl space filled with light. The Angel burst upward into the space, MP-5 held aloft.

He was right in front of where Maria crouched.

Derek saw the MP-5 swing toward him. This was it, he thought. Nowhere to go. Maria brought a knife down in a vicious arc, slamming into the terrorist's shoulder. The man screamed, falling backward, the assault rifle rattling out a torrent of bullets that chewed up the ceiling tiles.

"Come on!" Derek screamed, reaching out his hand.

Maria scuttled across the tiles and caught his hand.

They leapt from wire to wire, a daddy longlegs dance, until they were on the I-beam.

Derek slammed an elbow through the fiberboard walls, once, twice, then kicking at it. Finally, in frustration, he took out the MP-5 and fired half a magazine until there was a large hole. He stuck his head through, saw empty hallway, grabbed Maria, and tossed her through it.

He turned to see the Angel clambering awkwardly up into the crawl space. Derek fired off a burst and dropped down next to Maria. His leg nearly collapsed beneath him. The pain of impact made him cry out, but he gritted his teeth, caught her arm, and rushed toward the door leading into the power plant of the Cheyenne Center. In a guttural, German-accented snarl, the Angel said, "Run away my little kitties. The Mad Dog is nipping at your heels. Run!"

CHAPTER 53

Secretary of the Treasury Donald Sloviak took off his horn-rimmed glasses, studied the paper in front of him, then looked back up at the table occupied by members of President Langston's cabinet. Sloviak was a stoop-shouldered, bow-tie wearing wonk, totally charisma-challenged, but for some reason Vice President Newman had asked him to chair the meeting.

Secretary Johnston glanced at his watch and growled, "For God sakes, Don. Just read it and get on with it. Or have the vice president read it."

Sloviak looked uncomfortable. He was balding with steel-gray hair that flaked dandruff onto his shoulders, his eyes were muddy, and he wore a perpetual puzzled expression on his face. He perched the glasses back on his nose and sighed. "It saddens me to —"

Vice President Newman cleared his throat. "Secretary Johnston, do you have an objection?"

"No. It's probably the appropriate course of action. But we're in the middle of crisis operations and protocol can drag on and get in the way of what we're trying to do. Come on, Don. Move it along."

Sloviak hesitated. "It saddens me to suggest that under Section Four of the Twenty-fifth Amendment to the Constitution, the cabinet needs to instate Vice President Alexander Newman as acting president until duly elected President Jack Langston can be reinstated to office."

Newman said, "Read Section Four, please."

Johnston sighed. Operation Tagger was underway. He really needed to get back to the PEOC.

Newman snapped, "Secretary Johnston, is there a problem?"

"Keep it moving, Mr. Vice President. We have an operation starting as we speak."

"Who authorized that?"

Johnston glared at the vice president. "I did."

Secretary of Defense Marlon Sandhill said, "As did I. Along with General Puskorius. We alerted your office. You weren't available."

Vice President Newman seemed momentarily speechless, the silence in the room as thick as Texas chili. Finally Newman said, "Mr. Sloviak, read Section 4."

In his reedy voice, Sloviak read:

> Section 4. Whenever the Vice President and a majority of either the principal officers of the executive departments or of such other body as Congress may by law provide, transmit to the President pro tempore of the Senate and the Speaker of the House of Representatives their written declaration that the President is unable to discharge the powers and duties of his office, the Vice President shall immediately assume the powers and duties of the office as Acting President.

"Very good," said Vice President Newman. "Because President Langston is currently incapacitated due to the terrorism crisis, I invoke the Twenty-fifth amendment of the United States Constitution under Section Four. Upon majority vote of this cabinet, I will assume the duties of the acting president. Let's us begin the vote." He looked to Secretary Sloviak.

"Do you vote to invoke the Twenty-fifth Amendment of the United States' Constitution?"

Sloviak swallowed. "Aye."

One by one the cabinet members present voted to turn control of the government over to Vice President Newman. The secretary of state and the secretary of transportation were patched in via teleconference. The final cabinet member to vote was Secretary Johnston. He hesitated before nodding. "Aye."

"So be it," said Vice President Newman. "We'll get the chief justice in here, send written notice to the speakers, and we'll get a press conference going as soon as —"

The door to the room opened and a tall, angular woman with gray hair to her shoulders hurried over to Secretary Johnston. She handed him a telephone. "It's Agent Swenson, sir."

"Johnston here." Johnston held up a hand to the group, asking them to wait. He listened for a moment then nodded. "Okay. Keep me informed." He hung up.

Everybody waited.

"Operation Tagger was a disaster," he said slowly. "The Fallen Angels had snipers up in the hills around the resort. When the Delta Force troopers parachuted in, the snipers took out every single one of them."

Vice President Newman, face slowly turning red, said, "This is your disaster, Jim. Yours!"

Johnston shrugged. No kidding, he thought. Homeland Security oversaw the Secret Service. Secret Service oversaw the summit security. He was screwed.

Now-President Newman said, "What else?"

Johnston said, "Several more Secret Service agents have gone missing trying to retake the security office in the International Center. There was an active firefight between the enemy snipers, the FBI, and the National Guard. They think there were four, and they've killed three. The fourth is fleeing into the mountains. Our people are in active pursuit."

He paused. "We've received intelligence that the numbers of terrorists inside the ballroom continues to drop, now to nine. Dorfman, the German, left to pursue the rogue agent who is picking off their people."

"What is your plan now?" President Newman demanded.

Johnston raised an eyebrow. "Plan?"

"You have a Plan B? A contingency plan?"

"We'll have to discuss it with General Puskorius and my people." He looked at his watch. "But the next deadline is coming up in less than twenty minutes. You need to make a decision whether or not we meet their demands, or at least as much of them as we possibly can."

"Me?"

"Yes — *Mr. President.*"

Newman seemed startled that along with the title came the responsibility of this decision. He frowned. He turned to Secretary of Defense Sandhill. "They wanted those people out of Gitmo and on a chopper headed toward Colombia. Make it happen."

Sandhill said, "Sir?"

"Do it."

"They wanted two choppers and clear passage into Colombian air space," Sandhill said. "We can't guarantee Colombian air space."

Newman grinned like a barracuda, all teeth and aggression. "We're buying time here. Give them their fucking helicopters. Let them fly out of there. Keep some F14s on their asses ready to blow them out of the air as soon we can. Got that?"

Secretary Johnston said, "We've still got the Nadia Kosov problem."

"Deal with it!" President Newman spun on his heels and walked out of the room.

Johnston looked over to Sandhill and Attorney General Norris Penderton. Penderton looked thoughtful. He said, "I hope he realizes that nobody seems to be negotiating with these guys. You think Coffee will give us some breathing room if we release his people?"

Johnston shook his head. "I think if we can't produce Nadia Kosov, nothing else matters."

CHAPTER 54

Derek had his keys in his fist as he and Maria approached the door to the power plant. Fumbling with the key ring, the first key didn't fit. He nearly dropped the entire ring. Maria caught his hand. "Steady," she whispered.

He nodded, took a split second to look at the number on the lock, then plucked a key out and slammed it home. With a turn of the key the door opened and they slipped inside just as he heard a thud. Derek glanced over his shoulder to see the terrorist dropping to the floor thirty feet away. He pushed Maria inside and followed, pulling the door closed and clacking the lock shut.

Furnaces and boilers roared. The temperature was a dozen degrees higher than it had been in the rest of the building. The metal flooring trembled beneath their feet. Maria stood just inside the power plant, chest heaving as she dragged in air. Her dark curly hair was a snarl of tangles, her face smeared with grime and blood, clothes torn, bloodied, and matted with dirt.

"You're beautiful," Derek said. "You know that?"

She giggled. "You know how to show a girl a good time, big boy."

"Yeah. Come on. It won't take him —"

A round of gunfire slammed into the door near them.

Maria screamed and turned to run. Derek caught her and brought her close. He pointed upward. The power plant was a large sunken part of the building. On their immediate level a four-foot wide walkway stretched in two directions. Four metal risers dropped down to the main floor. Bordering three sides was a four-foot catwalk of steel mesh, no railing. The main floor of the power plant was crammed with massive furnaces, air-conditioning units, and giant red-painted tanks for hot water. It was the trunk line for the heating, cooling, plumbing, and electrical — the space was crisscrossed with hot and cold air ducts.

He pointed upward. "I want you to go up there. See where that air duct is? You can hide behind it and he won't be able to see you."

"What about you?"

More shots into the doorway.

"Go!" He gave her a shove. Reluctantly, she limped toward the steel stairs leading up to the upper catwalk.

Derek frowned and hobbled down the metal steps and slipped into the shadows of the furnace. Heat came off the furnace in waves. He glanced around, spied Maria, and gave her a thumbs-up. In a moment she was gone.

He brought the MP-5 around, leaned against one of the boiler tanks, almost burning his arm on the hot metal. Shifting locations, he stood behind a round metal duct about three feet in diameter, covered with pink fiberglass insulation. He wasn't wild about it as a hiding place. Bullets would sheer right through it as if it were onionskin paper.

Another round of gunfire rattled into the door.

Followed by silence.

The guy, Mad Dog, was smarter than the other people who'd gone after him. Or he'd just learned his lesson.

Silence. And more silence.

From above Maria said, "Derek? What's going—"

Suddenly the lights clicked out. All of them. "Don't talk!" he called out. "Not a word!"

The generator still hummed. The furnace and air-conditioning units still roared. But the electrical lights were off. Like somebody had flicked a switch or closed a circuit.

He didn't like that one bit. The power plant had four doors. They were all supposed to be—

What was that sound? Shuffling?

In the darkness, Derek tried to focus on the sound, which seemed to be an echo of some sort. But from where? It stopped before he could pin it down.

He listened. Nothing. He couldn't hear Maria. He couldn't hear the sound, whatever it had been. All he could hear was the roar of the machinery in the room.

He disciplined himself to wait, hoping Maria would stay right where she was.

Creak.

Derek tensed. Somebody was moving. Maybe it was Maria.

Or maybe it was just metal adjusting to her weight or his weight or changes in the room's temperature.

A scream tore through the space. It was followed by the German-accented voice floating down from above.

"Well, *fraülein*. Aren't you a pretty little thing? So tell me, where is your boyfriend, eh? Come out, come out, wherever you are. *Herr Doktor* Stillwater? If you do not show yourself by the time I count to five, I will slit this pretty little lady's throat. *Eins.*"

"Run!" Maria shouted. "Run, Derek!"

"*Zwei.*"

Derek swallowed. If he stepped out, they were both dead. If he didn't step out, Maria was almost assuredly dead.

"*Drei.*"

His eyes had adjusted to the dim light. Mostly pilot lights that lit the gas furnace and hot water tanks, causing an eerie reddish glow.

"*Vier.*"

He studied the furnace next to him. Along the bottom was a ledge where a sheet of blue flame burned off the gas that fed the furnace. An idea came to him. A crazy, suicidal idea.

He called out, "Okay, okay. I'm coming."

CHAPTER 55

Irina Khournikova stood behind an oak tree thirty yards from the entrance to the International Center. The sounds of gunfire from the hillside were beginning to fade, the firefight coming to an end.

She studied the building, her gaze taking in the numerous closed-circuit cameras scattered around the grounds. She was convinced that the International Center's Security Center had been taken over by one or more members of The Fallen Angels and they were using the cameras to keep tabs on any counter-terror measures the Secret Service might take.

Using the tree trunk to lean against, she set the MP-5 on single fire, sighted in on one of the cameras, breathed in, out, then squeezed the trigger. The camera exploded with a satisfying pop!

Methodically, Khournikova shot out the seven cameras she identified on her side of the building. Three of them she hit on the first shot. The other four had required two or even three shots. She was a decent marksman, but worked much better in close and hand to hand. Still, she had accomplished what she wanted to accomplish.

She slipped from the cover of the oak and ran to a blue spruce closer to the building. She rolled to the ground and slipped beneath the boughs, lying flat on a mat of dried pine needles. The odor of spruce filled her nose. She waited, motionless, heart beating in her chest, a reassuring clockwork that she was still alive.

A minute ticked by. Two.

Gracefully, she rolled out from under the tree and sprinted to the entrance of the building. Two security cameras monitored the front entrance. Using the Sig Sauer, she blasted them to pieces and slipped through the door, keeping to the walls.

Whoever was in there would know she was coming. She studied the lobby. It was a long, wide entryway, complete with fountain and bronze sculpture of the world held on the fingertips of an extended hand. From the ceiling hung a glittering modern chandelier of lights and mirrors. Several full-grown sycamore trees grew from the main floor, branches extended in leafy abundance toward a pyramidal skylight. The floor was granite, steps leading up on either side of the fountain to the main level. More utilitarian steps led down to meeting rooms and the security center.

Irina went up.

She took out two more security cameras, comfortable that she had blinded the security center to her activities in this part of the International Center. Now it was time to play mind games.

Irina slipped into the men's bathroom on the upper level. She climbed up on a sink and unscrewed the fasteners holding an acoustic tile in place, and hoisted herself up into the ceiling area.

Irina shined her flashlight around, finding what she hoped to find. Fiber-optic cables. She followed the line of cables until they met another group and split off in several directions. Using her combat knife, she sliced the bundle of cables. She moved farther along the crawl space along an I-beam until she came to another line of fiber-optic cables. Again, she cut them.

Time to move back, she thought, and retraced her path to the men's bathroom. She dropped down on the sink, crept to the doorway, and slipped out. Back in the lobby, she climbed up into the branches of one of the sycamore trees that grew in the lobby and settled in to wait.

CHAPTER 56

Derek moved toward the stairs, arms held out in a gesture of surrender. "I don't know if you can see me, but I'm coming out. Let her go."

Above him he heard the sound of movement. The German-accented voice said, "Let there be light."

With a click a bank of lights flashed on, barely illuminating the power plant. Above him, at the top of the stairs, was the tall, broad-shouldered terrorist. The shoulder and right arm of his black clothes looked wet from blood that oozed from the wound where Maria had struck him with the knife.

The terrorist had his right arm around Maria, a wicked looking blade pressed against her throat. In his left arm he held an MP-5, which he had aimed down the stairs.

"Let her go," Derek said. "I'm the one you're after."

"*Ja, Herr Doktor* Derek Stillwater. It will be my pleasure to kill you. You have caused much trouble on this day, *nein*?"

"Let her go."

"Same old tune. But you still carry your weapon. Set it down on the ground."

When Derek hesitated, the terrorist flicked out with the knife. Maria gasped and a thin line of blood leaked out from a shallow cut in her throat.

Perro Loco snarled, "Do it!"

Derek shrugged off the MP-5 and held it out by the shoulder strap. "I'm setting it down. Right here." He dropped the assault rifle with a clatter.

"*Gut. Das ist gut!* You certainly make it easy." Dorfman brought the MP-5 around toward Derek.

Gunfire ripped through the power plant — repeated small explosions rattling around against metal.

Dorfman ducked, confused.

The 10mm bullets Derek had placed in the blue flame of the furnace pan had ignited.

Derek charged up the stairs, lunging to get hold of the knife held to Maria's throat.

Dorfman responded by swinging the MP-5 at Derek, striking him in the neck with the barrel.

Dazed, vision blurring, Derek stumbled, teetering on the metal stairs.

"She's dead!" shouted Dorfman. "She's —" He howled in pain as Maria grabbed his arm with both hands and sunk her teeth into his wrist.

Derek lurched forward and yanked the MP-5 from the terrorist's grip. Dorfman dropped the knife and slammed his free hand into the back of Maria's head. With a cry she tripped forward, tumbling down the stairs, knocking Derek down as she flailed past him. Derek snagged the rail, hand out for Maria, inches out of reach. She rolled past him with a cry. Twisting, he launched himself upward at the terrorist.

Dorfman fumbled for the assault rifle. Derek booted it away. Fast as a snake, Dorfman kicked out, catching Derek in the ribs. Derek fell again, skittering down the steps, grabbing the railing, and swinging to his feet as Dorfman snatched up the loose knife.

Derek leapt to the landing, pulling the knife he'd taken from one of the terrorists in the kitchen.

Dorfman laughed. "I love a knife fight. Bring it on *Herr* Green Beret. It's been a while since I gutted an American Special Operative."

Derek stayed in a crouch, knife in his right hand. He focused his attention on the blade in the terrorist's hands.

Dorfman feinted left, left, back, laughing the whole time. Derek didn't flinch or move. Pain ripped through his skull and his vision blurred. He worked to maintain his focus, to ignore the wave of vertigo.

Dorfman shifted the knife to his right hand, then his left, then his right again. "Come on, *Herr Doktor*! Show me how tough you —"

Dorfman stumbled backward as a blast of gunfire ripped into his chest. With a guttural gasp he fell backward to the metal catwalk.

Derek glanced down to where Maria was sitting at the base of the stairs, the MP-5 in her hands. He said, "I love you."

"You should, after that. Three times I've saved your butt. How long were you going to screw around with that asshole?"

"Thanks to you, I didn't have to."

He checked to make sure the German was dead before limping down the stairs to Maria. "Are you okay?"

She shook her head. Her leg bent at an awkward angle beneath her and sweat beaded her forehead. If possible, she was even paler than before. "I think it's broken."

He leaned over and kissed her. He felt her leg. "Not compound, I don't think. But you're not going anywhere. You are one tough chick, you know that? Let's get you comfortable."

In a janitor's closet filled with brooms, mops, buckets, and bottles of bleach, Derek found an old blanket and a box of rags. He grabbed a pair of brooms and some of the rags. He snapped one of the broom handles into two pieces and gently fashioned a splint on Maria's leg. She cried out, biting her lip when he moved her. Finally he got her into a comfortable position. He created a nest for her with the blanket and helped prop her against one wall. "I don't suppose you have some Tylenol, do you?" she asked.

"No. Sorry. How's the pain?"

"I've felt worse."

He didn't believe her. "Hang on." He limped back to the body of Dorfman and searched his pockets, coming up empty. Derek returned to Maria.

"Is he dead?" She gestured feebly with one hand.

"Definitely."

"Then I can stay here while you . . . you go do what you have to do."

He met her gaze. "I don't like the idea of leaving you here alone."

"I might be safer here than with you, *amante*."

"You've got a point. It hasn't been so safe being with me."

She was quiet and he saw she was crying. It was the first time he'd seen her cry. During everything she'd held on, been tough. Brave. He cupped her cheek and kissed her. "You've been fantastic today. I couldn't have done it without you."

"Go," she said. "Go. But kiss me. I'm afraid I'll never see you again."

"You'll see me again. And we've got a date for my boat. Right?"

She closed her eyes. "Go, *amante. Adiós.*"

Derek kissed her long and sweet then picked up his MP-5, made sure he had a full magazine, and quietly slipped out of the power plant.

CHAPTER 57

The sun was harsh and hot at Guantanamo Bay, Cuba, beating down on the tarmac of the naval base's runway. A team of naval guards marched the twenty-three captured members of The Fallen Angels toward two waiting Pave Hawk helicopters, their rotors already spinning.

Captain Sean Alexander stopped the group and said, "Who here are pilots?"

The group of terrorists stared at him, not responding.

Alexander took a step closer. His blue eyes were glittering and hard. He was a tall, lithe man, quick on his feet, a Naval Intelligence officer who was part of the Gitmo security team. He had short blond hair and a square jaw and a mind that whirred and spun as fast as any supercomputer. He held up a telephone. "This is an Iridium satellite phone. The number for Richard Coffee is already programmed in. Once you're in the air, you're to contact him and tell him where you are."

A wiry Asian, Moo Duk Kwan, stepped forward. Alexander knew Kwan was a former South Korean intelligence officer. He also knew that Kwan was one of four of The Fallen Angels qualified to fly the Pave Hawk. Kwan held his hand out. Alexander dropped the phone into it. Kwan remained where he was, gaze fixed on Alexander.

Alexander looked down at the Korean, feeling the waves of hatred and antagonism aimed at him. In a level voice he said, "You've been given clearance to fly to Colombia. The Colombian government has been alerted."

Kwan glanced at one of his companions. Alexander knew his name was Gregor Grünwald, a dropout from what had once been the East German *Stasi*. He had read his file provided by the German government. Grünwald was a scary, dangerous man. An assassin, soldier, pilot, computer expert, and probable sociopath.

Grünwald said, "Let's go." He turned without a second glance, and led the twenty-three terrorists toward the waiting helicopters.

They split into two groups without discussion and one by one climbed aboard, the hatches slamming shut. A moment later the rotors spun faster. The helicopters lifted off like giant locusts and headed south and west over the Gulf of Mexico.

Alexander watched until they were dark specks on the horizon. He turned and walked back to a waiting Humvee. What he had just done — releasing twenty-three terrorists under a ransom demand — made him feel like a coward, like somehow they had just lost a major battle. Knowing that F14s were tracking the choppers didn't make it any easier.

His second in command, Lieutenant Drew Stevens, was talking to someone on a telephone. He nodded and clicked off. Stevens said, "They made the call."

Alexander nodded. "What did Coffee have to say? They know?"

Stevens hesitated. "He asked about Kosov first."

"Not good. What did they tell him?"

"That she wasn't with them. And as far as they knew, she never had been. They thought she was dead."

"She is. What was Coffee's reaction?"

"He said something they thought was a code. He said —" Stevens checked a note. "'Delta, Delta, Bravo, Delta, Gamma, Alpha.' And the guy on the phone, that German prick, Grünwald, repeated it back to him."

Alexander clenched his jaw. "Sounds like code. Like they had some sort of plan for this."

Stevens shrugged. "We've been interrogating these guys unsuccessfully for almost a year. Does that surprise you?"

Alexander shook his head. Not much about The Fallen Angels surprised him anymore. They were more cult than terrorist organization. They were all highly trained intelligence officers who had abandoned their countries and their loyalties to give their lives to this guy, Richard Coffee.

Stevens studied his boss for a moment. "Sir, what are you thinking?"

Alexander glanced around. "You and I probably know more about these people than anybody else on the planet, don't we?"

"I think so, sir."

"So you tell me. Under what circumstances would it be a good idea to let these people loose?"

"None, sir. But they're going to kill the world leaders if we didn't."

Alexander cocked his head. "Letting them loose on the world is like dumping a school of barracuda into a kiddy pool. I think we should shoot those choppers out of the sky and let the hostages take their chances." He climbed into the Humvee. "And that was my recommendation to General Puskorius."

CHAPTER 58

Derek felt uneasy leaving Maria alone, but didn't see where he had any real choice. He'd end up getting her killed if he tried to bring her any farther, and he couldn't just stay with her while the hostage crisis played out above their heads. He slipped out of a doorway at the back of the power plant that led to the hydraulic pit. He walked down a dozen metal stairs and waited in the darkness.

The stage in the main ballroom — directly above him — could be raised and lowered depending on what use the room was going to be put: concerts or plays or speeches, or if they just needed more floor space for dining. The hydraulic pit was essentially a large open space beneath the stage filled with the machinery used to raise and lower the stage.

From here he could access the ballroom if he had to. At least in theory. Off to each side was a doorway leading to side entrances of the backstage area. He quickly checked them. From the hydraulic pit side, they appeared normal. But he found it difficult to believe they wouldn't be wired with explosives on the other side.

Toward the back of the stage was a trapdoor. Moving beneath it, he studied the square wooden entrance. It was about four feet by four feet, hinged on one side, and latched securely so there was no give when somebody walked on it. It was cleverly designed and tight — no light seeped around the edges.

So close — the G20 leaders were right above him — wired with explosives, guarded by armed maniacs.

He crept over to a corner of the stage where he had hidden a handgun. He opened the cleverly concealed wooden box and removed the weapon, made sure it was loaded, and slipped it into his belt.

Now what?

He tried to think of the various ways he could move around the building, and an idea occurred to him.

He approached yet another door, this one leading to a storage area at the very back of the building. It was very unlikely this door had been wired with explosives. At least he hoped so.

Derek took a deep breath, gripped the handle, and turned it.

Nothing. He pushed into the storage area. A large, dark room filled with tables, chairs, recording equipment, lighting equipment, boxes of linens, plumbing fixtures, and other detritus — the spare parts bin of the Cheyenne Center. Keeping the flashlight to the ground, he picked his way around the clutter toward the back corner of the room.

He flashed the light upward. *Yes,* he thought.

Twelve feet off the floor was a cold air intake vent. It was about three feet wide and eighteen inches tall.

Sweat beaded up on Derek's forehead as he thought about this. *Just do it,* he thought. *Don't think too much.*

Carefully he started to move boxes around under the cold air vent. *What I'd give for a ladder,* he thought.

Finally, after fifteen minutes of stealthy movements, he was able to climb up on the boxes so he was level with the vent. Using the screwdriver that he had been carrying since getting out of the walk-in freezer, he unscrewed the grille and set it aside.

With a sigh, he squeezed into the vent. It reminded him of every thriller movie he'd ever seen. Probably every thriller movie ever made. It was a joke, too. In those movies the air ducts were huge. This one wasn't. It was tight. Very tight. Eighteen inches was barely enough room for his body while lying flat. And even that was tight. He had to be careful not to make noise or display any light.

Derek squirmed forward and hit his first turn to the right. It took a lot of effort to make the turn, and in the process he scraped his ribs against the metal of the ductwork corner. Pain shot up and down his side, radiating throughout his body. He stuffed his fist into his mouth to muffle the groans. His vision grew dim and his breathing echoed harshly in the duct.

Derek's brain played little games — thoughts of getting stuck here, unable to move forward or back. The space seemed to get tighter and tighter around him, the air thinner and thinner. He willed himself to calm down, to not panic.

Breathe, dammit. Breathe!

Slowly the panic seeped away. Calmer, he inched forward toward a dim patch of light. It seemed to take him forever to get to a T-junction, even though it was probably only about a dozen feet away. If it had been the length of the building he knew he wouldn't have been able to do it.

Off to his right, the duct ended in a grille that glowed palely in the darkness. To his left the duct seemed to curve upward. He thought it probably did. He wanted to go up, but knew there was no way he could climb vertically in the duct. So he went right.

As he had suspected, the grille looked over an elevator shaft. This was a freight elevator on the opposite side of the building from the elevator he and Maria had taken to the basement. It would have to do.

It took longer than he had expected to remove the grille from the inside, but finally he was able to pop it off. He was five feet above the freight elevator. Squirming out, he thought he was going to pass out again. He wasn't a contortionist on a good day, and today was definitely not a good day.

Dangling out of the grille, hands reaching for the steel cables, he lost his balance.

With a stifled cry, he dropped onto the top of the freight elevator with a hard thunk that jarred every nerve in his body. Blackness. Slowly the world moved from black to gray to twilight, a world in fuzzy focus. Dirt. Grease. Dust. Shafts of dim light beaming from small holes way above. He lay on top of the elevator for a moment, catching his breath.

This, he thought, *isn't going to work. You're not up to this. Get real.*

He had to consider what he had been unwilling to do before — climb up the elevator cables. Forty feet up a rope would not have been difficult for him, even in his current battered condition. Forty feet up greasy metal cables with metal splinters ripping his flesh was a different story.

He studied the cables and the walls of the elevator shaft. He saw his goal. Near the top of the building was an elevator entryway that led to a workspace at the back of the stage near the roof of the Cheyenne Center. The freight elevator was the only way to enter this space, which was used to access the lighting board for the stage.

I could just ride the elevator up there, he thought. But Derek knew that it would instantly alert Coffee and his men to where he was and where he was going.

"Shit." He looked upward. Taking out the Emerson knife he had lifted from one of the Fallen Angels, he cut off his shirtsleeves. Removing his leather belt, he cut it into strips and wrapped the cloth from the shirt around the leather, then wrapped them around his hands, like cloth-covered leather gloves.

With a sigh, he gripped the cables and began a slow, arduous climb upward.

CHAPTER 59

From her awkward perch in the sycamore tree in the lobby of the International Center, Irina Khournikova thought she heard faint sounds from the lower level. She kept perfectly still, waiting, straining her ears to hear.

Yes, she thought after a moment. Someone is moving down below. Someone moving very quietly, very slowly, very deliberately.

She heard a clatter, focused on the source of the noise, and caught her breath.

Bouncing along the slate floor was a hand grenade.

The concussion wave nearly blasted her right out of the tree. Shrapnel bit at the limbs and peppered her side, though she was mostly protected by the sycamore. Stifling a cry, she clung to her branch, ears ringing from the concussion, which had torn a hole in the floor and thrown up a huge cloud of dust and debris. Blinking her eyes, she tried to focus. She saw a figure rush through the fallout toward the front entrance.

Swinging her rifle around to take aim, she watched the blocky figure spin and toss two more grenades, one toward the upper level, the other falling very close to the trunk of the tree she was in.

Desperate, rifle dropping away, she leapt toward the railing of the second level overhang just as both grenades exploded. With a crack, the tree collapsed as the shrapnel and concussion tore apart the trunk. Slowly, the tree began to fall toward the ground.

Irina slammed into the rail and dangled, feet flailing for purchase in the air, fingers coiled around the metal bars just as the grenade above exploded.

She lost her grip and fell fifteen feet into three feet of water in the fountain. It wasn't quite enough water to break her fall entirely. She smacked into the basin's concrete bottom with enough force to knock her breath out. Sputtering and coughing, she fought her way to the surface, gasping for air. She rolled over the ledge and fell to the ground, covered with chunks of wood, rock, dirt, and marble.

Glancing wildly around for the MP-5, she saw that the tree had landed directly on top of the assault rifle. She staggered to her feet, water streaming from her clothes, sodden hair clinging to her scalp. The world rolled and swooped and she found herself falling back to the ground, unable to keep her balance. Blinking grit from her eyes, she tried again. She knew the grenade's pressure wave had done damage to her ears. Not only was her hearing muffled, but she felt a swirl of vertigo every time she tried to stand.

She felt around until she located the walkie-talkie she'd been given. She clicked it on and pressed the talk button. "Superman, this is Special K. Superman, this is Special K. Do you read?"

Nothing. She checked the radio. She couldn't hear well enough to know if it was working, but she thought the fall, the water, and the concussions had disabled it. Or the NSA was still jamming communications. She tried to stand again, and this time, by gripping a tree branch, was able to stay on her feet. She gulped air and pulled herself hand over hand toward where the MP-5 lay. Dropping to her knees, she tried to pull it free, but the tree had landed directly on it. It was pinned.

Turning, she fell over. She wanted to cry. She wanted to scream. She despised feeling helpless. It made her angry. She slapped her hands on her belt and found the handgun. Good enough. It would have to do.

She staggered to her feet and picked her way over and around tree limbs and debris toward the front doors. The more she moved the better she felt, her head starting to clear, the world feeling less wobbly.

Once out of the building, the fresh air helped even more and she was able to break into a trot back toward the Mobile Command Unit. A snake of suspicion had wormed its way into her gut; something about the figure she had glimpsed fleeing the International Center had seemed familiar. She thought she knew who had taken over the security center. And she suspected she knew where he was headed. Now if only she could stop him from doing any more damage.

CHAPTER 60

Hand over bloody hand. Derek stopped, dangling thirty feet above the elevator car, to catch his breath. He may have miscalculated. He was in worse shape than he had thought and his muscles screamed at the strain. His vision kept blurring and the pain in his skull was a constant thumping tattoo. The climb was aggravating the wound to his ribs, which were starting to ooze blood again, soaking his shirt. He didn't know how much longer he could go.

Gulping a burning lungful of air, he gathered his energy for a last push and slithered his way up the cables, which were shredding his workpants and tearing into his thighs. The cloths around his hands were tattered rags, but the strips of leather belt were holding up reasonably well. Still, his fingers were scraped raw and bleeding.

Finally he was there. The top of the shaft was only about six feet above his head. Directly across from him was the elevator doorway to the workspace.

He studied the closed doors for a moment before continuing upward to the very top of the shaft. Above him were the gears and motors of the elevator mechanism. Toward the back of the shaft were steel plates — the elevator counterweight.

The doors to the workspace were at least four feet away from the cables he clung to. The ledge was only about six inches wide.

Sweat ran down his forehead and burned into his eyes. He blinked and shook his head, immediately wishing he hadn't as fresh pain blossomed behind his temples.

Tentatively, he reached out for the ledge with his left hand. Not even close.

Even more tentatively he reached out one leg, stretching. Close. Maybe twelve inches from the ledge.

With a forty foot-drop if he missed.

Craning his neck, he decided he really had no choice. The motor and gears overhead were housed in a steel box, which had a narrow lip he could grasp. Reaching upward, he gripped the underside of the equipment with his left hand, testing to see if the sharp metal edge would support his weight. It seemed to. He reached up with both hands and pulled himself over, hand over hand.

Thank God for pull-ups, he thought, as he dangled over the pit.

Swaying, he monkeyed across to the wall. He had to swing forward. He felt for the ledge with his toes, missing, swinging wildly back and forth. His battered, bloody hands pulsed with pain. He knew he was losing his grip — he only had seconds. He could feel his fingers slipping.

He tried again. The strength was leaving his hands. He couldn't stay here all day. He stretched. His toes came to rest on the ledge. He was able to take some of the weight off his fingers and hands. He almost wanted to laugh out loud, it felt so much better on his hands.

Taking a deep breath, he shifted his weight, and swung entirely onto the narrow ledge, hands pressed on either side of the elevator entryway. He felt like a spider climbing a wall.

He gripped the doorframe with one hand and wedged his left hand into the door opening, trying to muscle the door. It gave an inch. Then two. He swayed as a current of vertigo swept over him. He felt his body swing out, his center of gravity shifting, drawing him backward into the pit, where he would tumble, plunge, and die, body shattered on the elevator rooftop.

With a grunt, he shoved the door open and lunged inside, falling to the floor, gasping for breath.

After a moment, he crawled into the workspace. His muscles trembled; his body was soaked in sweat and blood. His heart hammered in his chest. Blood roared in his ears, air burning like molten lava in his throat and chest. Rest. He needed rest.

One minute. Three. Five. His heartbeat slowed, oxygen rushed to his aching lungs.

The workspace was long and narrow, about six feet high and six feet wide. It ran the length of the ballroom. There was only a narrow space to walk along the back wall. The entire floor was littered with cables and wires and cutouts for variously sized spotlights and lighting options.

He approached a cutaway for an overhead spotlight and peered down. Below him stretched the ballroom. He was almost directly above the stage. By shifting around he could see the leaders of the free world, strapped to chairs. And in front of them, performing for the television camera, was Richard Coffee, talking on a telephone. Derek watched in interest, getting the lay of the room. He heard Coffee say, "Delta, Delta, Bravo, Delta, Gamma, Alpha," and click off the phone.

A wiry, dark-skinned Latino crossed over to Coffee and they spoke in low tones. Derek got the sense they were disagreeing about something. Then the Latino stalked away, back to the TV camera.

Derek took the time to rest and consider his options. He had a hand-gun. He had a knife. He had an assault rifle. There appeared to be nine or ten bad guys in the room. He needed an accurate count. If he started sniping at them, they'd kill the hostages and the leaders.

He had to think. He needed a plan. A real plan. And at the moment, his mind was blank.

CHAPTER 61

Special Agent Lawrence Swenson stood in the middle of the Mobile Command Unit on the telephone talking to General Puskorius back in Washington, D.C. He was trying unsuccessfully to keep his voice under control. "Yes, General, I understand that. Yes, all of your Delta Force people have been recovered. Yes, all dead. Yes. Last report, all four enemy snipers were killed, as well as the infiltration unit masquerading as Colorado National Guard at Checkpoint Delta. Plan?"

Swenson swallowed. General Puskorius wanted to know if he had a plan for rescuing the world leaders. Events were so far out of control he hadn't had time to even start on a plan, especially since the Pentagon's plan turned into such a cluster fuck. "Sir, one is — no, sir. I'm working on regaining control of the International Center security center now —"

Swenson broke off as a muffled explosion echoed between the buildings. He looked at his second in command, Agent Laura Parrish. Parrish sat at a computer workstation, furiously tapping keys. She shook her head, tapped the screen for Swenson to check, and jumped up from her chair, and ran toward the door.

"Sir," said Swenson, "something's going on now. We're checking it out." He studied the computer screen. "And it looks like we've got some data on X Man. His name is Pablo Juarez, sir. A Colombian national. His entire family was killed by —" Another muffled explosion punctuated the air.

Parrish stepped back into the MCU. "Small explosions coming from the International Center."

Swenson nodded. "Excuse me, sir. I've got somebody working on the International Center right now. Um, back to Juarez. The intelligence I just received says, er, his entire family was killed by the Colombian government in a counter-terror strike aimed at one of the drug cartels about ten years ago. He joined the, uh, AUC as a result. I don't — I see, one of the paramilitaries, the United Self-Defense Forces of Colombia. But there is intelligence here, sir, that he left because they weren't — they booted him out, sir. I don't know. Just a moment."

He pulled out his walkie-talkie and pressed the talk button. "Special K. This is Superman. Do you read?"

Static.

He repeated the message. Nothing.

"Sir," he said into the phone, "do you have a plan? I — just a moment, sir."

The door to the Mobile Command Unit opened and FBI agent Vincent Silvedo stepped in. It took a moment for Swenson to recognize him. "Silvedo, where have you been? Hang on, I need a full —"

Silvedo tossed two hand grenades into the Mobile Command Unit and leapt out the door.

CHAPTER 62

In the White House PEOC, General Puskorius glowered at the telephone. Agent Swenson's call had been played over the speaker so everybody could hear it. Everybody heard the blast that resulted in the phone going dead.

Puskorius said, "Who the fuck is Silvedo?"

Director Johnston cocked an eye at Secret Service Director O'Malley, who consulted his laptop. "Silvedo, Vincent. Special Agent. One of ours."

Nobody said a word. Nobody knew anything. Had Silvedo just blown up the MCU? Or was that a coincidence? What had really happened to the MCU?

General Puskorius was punching numbers into his phone when the phone in front of Director Johnston buzzed. He picked it up and announced himself. "Yes —" His face grew pale. "Yes. I understand. Just a moment. I'm putting you on speaker." He hit a button on the console. He said, "This is Special Agent Brenda LeVoi. Go ahead, LeVoi."

The woman's voice was high-pitched and threaded with tension. "Sir, the Mobile Command Unit has been hit. It looks like somebody threw a grenade or something into it. There are no survivors. I repeat, there are no survivors. Agent Swenson is dead. Agent Parrish is dead." She rattled off the names of four more Secret Service agents who had been in the MCU.

Director O'Malley studied his computer. "Agent LeVoi, this is Director O'Malley. Do you see Agent Vincent Silvedo anywhere around there?"

Silence. "No, sir. I would have expected him to be trapped in the Cheyenne Center after the lockdown. He was originally stationed in the loading dock. That was the source of one of the explosions, sir. Nobody has heard from him since lockdown."

O'Malley glanced over at Johnston, who shook his head. O'Malley said, "We need an update, Agent. I believe you worked directly under Agent Swenson's group?"

"I led a — just a moment, sir. There's someone — it's Agent Silvedo. Just a moment."

Johnston was on his feet, shouting at the telephone. "Agent LeVoi! Agent LeVoi! Silvedo may be a mole. I repeat, Silvedo —"

But she was off the phone.

CHAPTER 63

Irina Khournikova raced toward the Mobile Command Unit. The explosion was distinctive and came from exactly where she was headed. She redoubled her efforts, skidding beneath the boughs of another blue spruce, watching as agents rushed toward the RV that was now smoking, windows shattered.

Her gaze shifted, searching for the muscular form of Vincent Silvedo. She was sure he was the figure that had slipped out of the International Center, another of Richard Coffee's Fallen Angels — an insider. And with his position at the loading dock he would have been key to getting Coffee and his people into the facility.

Agents fought their way into the MCU, reappearing a moment later dragging limp, bloody bodies. Irina counted five agents. Where was Silvedo? Had he disappeared? Did he decide this was a good time to exit the area?

A woman with short-cropped blonde hair and a narrow jaw seemed to be the agent in charge now. She looked vaguely familiar. Irina searched her memory. Over the last week of close preparation and over the months of setup, she had come in contact with most of the Secret Service and Bureau of Diplomatic Security agents working the summit. There weren't that many women. This would be — LeVoi, she thought. Brenda LeVoi.

LeVoi was on a phone now, her posture rigid. Irina thought LeVoi was talking to somebody higher up, apprising them of the situation.

Out of the corner of her eye she saw a muscular man appear. She focused her gaze, recognizing Vincent Silvedo. He was walking directly toward LeVoi and the knot of agents recovering the dead.

Irina brought her handgun around, focusing the sites directly on Silvedo's chest. She tracked his every step as he approached.

LeVoi turned to him, dropping the hand that held the telephone. She seemed to be speaking directly to Silvedo.

With lightning-like quickness Silvedo had a gun up and was pointing it at LeVoi.

Without hesitation Irina pulled the trigger.

CHAPTER 64

Irina Khournikova slipped out from beneath the blue spruce, arms wide, the handgun dangling from her index finger. She walked slowly toward the cluster of Secret Service and FBI agents who had hit the ground, guns drawn, as the bullets she had fired tore through Vincent Silvedo's chest.

Agent Brenda LeVoi was the first on her feet. She had her handgun out, aimed at Irina.

"I am Irina Khournikova, FSB, Russia," she said slowly and clearly. "I was tracking Agent Silvedo from the International Center. Swenson charged me with trying to retake it."

She now stood ten feet from the agents, who were all tense. Irina looked at Silvedo. His corpse looked like refuse. She wondered what had inspired him to turn traitor. She knew Richard Coffee was creative in his recruitment. Sometimes it was blackmail. Sometimes money. Sometimes it was just the right offer to the right person at the right time, part of Coffee's gift and charisma. Find a disaffected agent and stroke his ego, convince him he really was as brilliant as he thought and would be rewarded with The Fallen Angels.

Irina said, "He was going to kill you."

LeVoi nodded. "I know. Put the gun down, please."

Irina dropped her gun. "I have a knife, too. I'm reaching for it now."

LeVoi nodded. Moving deliberately, Irina retrieved the knife and dropped it to the ground next to the handgun.

LeVoi said, "Step away, please. Step back five paces."

Irina did so, hands still up in the air. LeVoi walked over and quickly patted her down. LeVoi's fair complexion was reddened by flames from the MCU, her jaw set in a stressed, determined way, yet her voice seemed calm and in control. "Identification?"

Irina handed over her credentials. She said, "Silvedo used hand grenades in the International Center. I was waiting for him to come out. I was up in a tree they had in the lobby, waiting, and he snuck out and tossed two grenades as a cover. I landed in the fountain when the tree fell over."

LeVoi said, "He used grenades in the MCU, too." Her voice cracked, but she shook it off. "You can take your hands down." She seemed to realize she had dropped her phone. She walked over to where she had let it slip from her grasp when she went for her gun, picked it up, and spoke into it.

"Director O'Malley? This is Agent LeVoi. Yes, the situation is under control." She briefly described what had happened. "Yes. Irina Khournikova. With the Russian FSB. Yes. Just a moment."

She handed the phone to Khournikova. "This is the president's Emergency Operations Center in the White House. You're on speaker with General Puskorius, the chairman of the Joint Chiefs of Staff, Director O'Malley, the Secret Service director, Director Johnston with the Department of Homeland Security, as well as the FBI and CIA directors and probably quite a few other people. Secretary Johnston wants to talk to you."

Khournikova knew the man by reputation only. What could he possibly want? She took the phone. "This is Irina Khournikova."

Secretary James Johnston's gruff, raspy voice came over the phone. "I guess we have to thank you, Ms. Khournikova."

"I was doing my job."

"Yes. Who is your direct supervisor?"

"That would have been Mikhail Alexandrov. But he is one of The Fallen Angels."

"Yes, we know. Ms. Khournikova, you're proving to be quite helpful to us. Do you have any ideas on how to end this siege?"

"Perhaps."

"Good. Let me talk to Agent LeVoi."

Khournikova turned the phone over to LeVoi, who listened for a moment, then nodded. "Yes sir. In five minutes? Yes. I'll be expecting it. I'll keep you apprised." She clicked off the telephone and looked at Khournikova. "You and I are now in charge of ending this mess. You told Secretary Johnston you had some ideas. I want to hear them. Right now."

Khournikova nodded and gestured to the ground. "Can I get my weapons back? I had an MP-5 in the International Center, but the tree fell on it. I'd like another. I also need some dry clothes."

"Absolutely. We'll get you a rifle ASAP and find you some fatigues unless you have clothes you brought." LeVoi turned to the agents and said, "I've just been made Agent-in-Charge. I want a full sit-rep in fifteen minutes." She looked at her watch and shook her head. "We've got to get to a TV. They're scheduled to come on and announce their new demands in about five minutes. Let's go."

A cloud of smoke rolled off the burning Mobile Command Unit. A team of firefighters was using extinguishers to try and douse the flames of the charred skeleton of metal and plastic. The fumes stung her eyes and bit at her nostrils. The smoke brought with it the stench of burned bodies, blood, and death. She shivered, clothes wet, the mountain air suddenly feeling cold despite the warmth of the sun. Khournikova said, "Do any of your snipers have thermal imaging capabilities?"

LeVoi, who had been turning toward the main complex, halted. "Probably. You have an idea?"

Khournikova nodded. "I have at least one."

CHAPTER 65

Sprawling on the floor in the workspace, eyes pressed to a crack around an overhead spotlight cutout, Derek studied the ballroom and The Fallen Angels' positions. Richard Coffee was staying close to the leaders on stage. Another one seemed to be sticking close to the TV cameras and their controls. There was a total of eight, all armed, spread out around the room. The hostages sat in chairs, some with their heads together, whispering, but most were silent, waiting.

He tried to puzzle out a plan. Leaning back, he inspected his MP-5. It was an assault rifle, not a sniper rifle, and he wasn't a sniper anyway. Although he had been trained in Special Forces, his expertise was biological and chemical warfare. He wasn't a sniper. He could probably take out one or two of The Angels from here, but that would result in a massive return of gunfire that he was pretty sure he would not survive. Unless —

He checked the rounds remaining in his sole magazine. Ten. Not good.

Not for the first time he considered the trapdoor in the stage. He was a long ways from there now.

He considered access to the roof. There wasn't any from here. There was a stairwell that led to the roof, but he was certain it had been wired.

For a moment he rested, monitoring his aches and pains. Resting probably wasn't a great idea. He'd been running on adrenaline for the last couple hours and he would only get stiff and slow if he rested too long. He closed his eyes, opened them, thinking that they had started out with a dozen men in the ballroom, and four on the perimeter. He had eliminated two of the perimeter men, then four of the Angels from the ballroom.

There were still two in the front lobby, but at the moment he didn't consider them a particular threat.

He wondered if it was possible to decrease the numbers in the ballroom from where he was.

He wondered if he could do it without getting himself or the world leaders or any of the other people in the ballroom killed.

Derek crept back over to the elevator doors and looked down the shaft, pondering the drop. Glancing back over his shoulder, he considered the coils of wiring and cable. His gaze lit on a roll of electrical cable, probably fifty or sixty feet of it. He crawled back over to it and checked its thickness. Rubber coated cable. He tested it. It was strong. Strong enough to support him?

What you're thinking is suicidal.

Derek crawled back and peered down at Richard Coffee. The angle was all wrong from where he was. He couldn't shoot straight down. If he was to try this, he would have to choose one or two of The Angels farther back, where he could have time to set an angle of fire.

You're crazy. Don't even consider this.

Derek put the coil of cable in his lap and started to unreel it, wondering if there was a way to minimize his risk. The thought made him want to laugh. He hadn't minimized his risk even once all day. Why start now?

From below he heard Richard Coffee's voice, talking to the TVs. "I want the world to know that the U.S. government —"

CHAPTER 66

El Tiburón clicked on the cameras. He did not have a good feeling about this. It was a feeling he had felt before — of a piece of cloth unraveling. It would start with a single loose thread, but soon everything would fall apart.

It was a feeling that reminded him of when he was a teenager, playing with his friends in the hills outside his village, hearing explosions and gunfire, smelling smoke. Running home, he discovered his family murdered, his house in flames.

It hadn't taken him long to join the AUC, to become a guerilla, to try and overthrow the corrupt Colombian government that had killed his momma, poppa, sister, and baby brother. He had channeled his rage into being the best, the most ruthless, and had gained a reputation as *El Tiburón*, the shark, the predator who didn't stop moving and killing or he would die.

But eventually the AUC became as corrupt, as weak, as institutionalized as the government they were fighting. So *El Tiburón* took his loyal men and fought their own war.

He could still smell the blood of his first kill, slitting the throat of a Colombian soldier on patrol. He could still feel how powerful it had felt, the hot blood gushing over his hand —

At the front of the ballroom, The Fallen stood before the world leaders. He said, "I want the world to know that the U.S. government has capitulated to one of our demands. They have released my fellow Fallen Angels from their prison at Guantanamo Bay, Cuba, given them helicopters and freedom to fly to Colombia."

The Fallen took a step forward. "The U.S. government has bought themselves time. I still require the release of Nadia Kosov. You have —"

El Tiburón stepped out from behind the camera and screamed, "No!

Enough! Don't you understand? Nadia Kosov is dead. There is no negotiating on that point. Move on!"

Coffee glowered across the room at him. Turning back to the cameras, he said, "You have one hour to release Nadia Kosov and have her
contact me or —"

El Tiburón snarled a wordless cry, raised his MP-5 and fired. The
rounds caught Richard Coffee in the chest. Coffee crumpled to the stage,
feebly reaching for his gun, which had fallen out of his hand. With a
groan, he toppled off the stage to the floor.

El Tiburón raised his hand and shouted, *"¡Ahora!"*

As one, six of the remaining Fallen Angels turned, raised their assault rifles and fired at Didier Christophe, the one remaining Fallen
Angel who was not one of *El Tiburón's* recruits from Colombia.
Christophe's rifle spat out a half dozen rounds as he died, falling to the
ballroom amidst screams and cries from the audience.

El Tiburón stalked to the front of the ballroom. He faced the cameras. "My name is Pablo Juarez, with the United Self-Defense Forces of
Colombia. We are now in control of the leaders of the G8. The Fallen
Angels no longer exist. You will answer to me now. Our demands are very
simple. Colombian President Pedro Gomez and his administration must
resign from office immediately, and turn over control of the Republic of
Colombia to Francisco Vasquez, current leader of the AUC. Under President Vasquez, all countries in the G20 present today will keep diplomatic
and economic ties open. If I am not informed of this transition in one
hour, I will kill United States President Jack Langston. To prove that I am
serious —"

El Tiburón leapt up on stage, aimed his handgun at European Union
President Waldenstrom and fired. He took another step, standing before
German Chancellor Heidi Braun, raised the gun, and fired. He turned
back to the camera.

"You have one hour."

PART IV
JUDGMENT DAY

CHAPTER 67

Derek, high above the action, rolled over on his back and closed his eyes. A lightning bolt of pain blasted through his head and quickly subsided. Momentarily he had a sensation of floating, of the vastness and antiquity of the universe, of the repetitive nature of violence. *If I quit now, so what? If crazies kill all the leaders of the world, so what? There are plenty of politicians itching to take their spots.*

He opened his eyes and thought, *Richard Coffee's dead again?*

He felt a little sad somehow. He and Coffee had been friends once. The kind of friends who watched each other's backs. The kind of friend you depended on to save your life in a sticky situation.

He had once thought Coffee was dead, exposed to biological and chemical weapons residue while in the first Gulf War. Then he had been miraculously reborn as The Fallen, a megalomaniacal cult leader and terrorist intent on destroying the world.

Crazy.

He rolled over and peered down at this new devil, Pablo Juarez. That was the problem with devils, he supposed. You killed one and there was always another one to come along.

What Juarez wanted was madness incarnate. Colombia wasn't represented in the G8. Not even the G20. Mexico, Argentina, and Brazil were their closest neighbors, and it was doubtful they would want that kind of unrest in their neighborhood. Not that Colombian President Pedro Gomez was too likely to step down and turn over the reins of power, no matter how much pressure was applied from the rest of the world.

Richard Coffee could make all the demands he wanted, but Derek knew they were all window dressing. Coffee had wanted chaos. Chaos on a huge scale, on an apocalyptic scale. Coffee, somewhere in his diseased brain, was venting his rage on the planet and all mankind, and, unfortunately, for the world, Coffee had been trained well by the United States government on how to do it.

Juarez, on the other hand, was a man with a different mission. No less crazy, perhaps, but he somehow thought his demands might be met. Or more likely, wanted the world's attention brought to bear on Colombia, the ongoing civil war, and the AUC's role in it. Just another suicidal terrorist who wanted to use other people's lives as a billboard.

Suddenly filled with energy, Derek picked up the cable he had been considering, but froze when he heard Pablo Juarez speaking again.

And he was calling Derek's name.

Derek crawled back to peer down at the man, who was talking into a radio, to the cameras. Juarez spoke in good clean English with a heavy Spanish accent, but Derek had no problems hearing him or understanding him. Juarez stood there in his dark pants and shirt, an MP-5 over one shoulder. Dark-skinned, dark hair, a confident, imposing figure on a stage before the world leaders, Peter Vakhach dead, Richard Coffee dead.

Another devil who wanted to dance on the grave of the world.

"Hello, Derek Stillwater. I know you are out there. Listening. I will not play games with you as The Fallen had. So here is an ultimatum. You must turn yourself into my men in the next five minutes, or I will shoot the Israeli Prime Minister and a dozen hostages here in the audience." Juarez looked at his watch. "Five minutes from now."

Derek swallowed hard. He felt paralyzed. What to do? The clock was ticking.

CHAPTER 68

Irina Khournikova and Brenda LeVoi and a dozen other agents watched Richard Coffee's death on a TV in the security office at the main resort building. News had spread of Vincent Silvedo's duplicity, and the deaths of Lee Padillo and Larry Swenson and the half dozen agents who had been killed along with them. The general sentiment was that these terrorists would be leaving Colorado in body bags.

The airwaves had been sizzling between Washington, D.C. and Colorado. It was obvious to the agents on the ground that the blame game was well underway and the D.C. pols were looking for the scapegoat du jour. Finally, it had been made clear that Brenda LeVoi and the Russian woman were now in charge. Khournikova thought it ironic that a foreign intelligence agent was being given a widely declared opportunity to share the blame if the day got any worse.

Khournikova watched the video unblinkingly. One of the Secret Service agents, a short, balding man with a Texas twang, muttered, "Jesus Christ."

Irina said, "We're down to six."

"Yeah," the agent said. "Maybe if we wait another hour they'll all kill each other, and we can all go home."

Brenda LeVoi shook her head, expression grim. "We're down to the core group, I think. They're all Juarez's people now. He's right. The Fallen Angels don't exist any more. This is a different threat now." She focused on Irina. "You have a plan?"

Irina nodded, surveying the group. She gripped the woman's arm and pulled her away from the crowd. "Do you trust them?"

Brenda studied her. "I have to."

Irina hesitated before saying, "Derek Stillwater has done a good job of thinning the numbers in there."

"You're sure it was him?"

Somebody said, "LeVoi. Incoming message from the secretary."

"I'll get right on it. Hang on." LeVoi turned back to Irina. "Are you sure?"

Irina nodded. "Yes. Who else?"

"Right." LeVoi seemed to think, then walked over to the agent who had tried to catch her attention and retrieved her notebook computer, bringing up the communication from Secretary Johnston. She studied the information for a moment. "All right, people. We've got intel. Somehow they've got somebody on the inside feeding them information. There appears there's some delay, but if we coordinate an op, we might be able to get almost real-time data on these guys' locations inside the ballroom. We have less than an hour. Khournikova, you have the floor."

Irina stepped forward. "I need at least two snipers with thermal imaging gear."

Two of the men stepped forward. They almost looked like twins. Tall, hawklike features, bold piercing stares, short dark hair. "We're all set."

Irina nodded. "Good. Get set up outside the front of the Cheyenne Center." She turned back to the crowd. "We have blueprints of the Cheyenne Center?"

A dark-skinned woman pointed to a computer file. "3D CAD/CAM. We've been going over it. You're considering a dynamic entry?"

Irina nodded. "We're going to have to blow our way in." She smiled. "But conveniently, The Fallen Angels already set the explosives in place. We just need to be ready for the timing."

"Aw shit," an agent monitoring the radio said. He was a blond built like a bodybuilder, with gray eyes and a sunburned face.

Everybody turned to him. He gestured to the radio. "This guy, Pablo Juarez, is communicating directly with Derek Stillwater. Says he's got five minutes to turn himself over or he's going to kill the Israeli PM and a dozen hostages."

Irina turned back to the two snipers. "Go! Do it now! You know what to do!"

With a nod they sprinted from the building.

LeVoi turned to Irina. "Not enough time. How well do you know this guy?"

Irina shook her head. "Not that well. But I know what he's — how do you say it in English? I know what he's made of."

"Will he turn himself in?"

Irina thought hard. "Maybe. But if he does, he will have something — I think the expression is, up his arm?"

"Up his sleeve," LeVoi said. "The expression is, 'He'll have something up his sleeve.'"

"Yes. I do not know if Derek Stillwater will comply with this man's demand. But if he does, he will have a plan to —"

Everybody paused, waiting for her to finish the sentence. Slowly, she said, "He will have a plan for disrupting Pablo Juarez's actions."

"Then let's get ready to help him out," said LeVoi. "People! We need at least two potential access points."

"The roof," the woman with the CAD/CAM programs said.

"The basement tunnels," said Irina.

"And," said LeVoi, "the loading dock."

CHAPTER 69

Secretary Johnston stood outside the PEOC, cell phone pressed to his ear. He was listening to his daughter Valerie whine. The connection was horrible, filled with static and dropouts, but Johnston wasn't sure he cared, because he wished his daughter would shut the fuck up.

"We really need you today, Dad. Mom's wackier than usual. Not violent, thank God, I don't know if I could handle that, but she's driving me nuts. The microwave was just the first thing. She's skinny-dipping now! She said she can't find her suit, so she just took her clothes off, went out in the backyard, waved to the neighbors, and jumped in."

"Bet Ed liked that." Ed Barron was their next-door neighbor, a retired accountant from the IRS.

"Dad, it's not funny! I was so embarrassed."

Johnston stifled his sigh. "Val, you do realize—"

"I need a break, Dad!"

"You do realize I'm in the middle of an international crisis, honey?"

"I don't care! It's always something. You've always put your job ahead of your family. Dragging us all over the world, and now this bullshit with Homeland Security. Mom needs you. I need you." Her voice was growing more shrill as she went along, gaining momentum. Johnston figured it was only a matter of time before she started bringing up every childhood grievance she'd ever had, every punishment, every missed concert, play, or parent-teachers conference. His thirty-eight-year-old daughter had her own problems including a bitter divorce and current unemployment in her chosen field of interior design, but most of her problems existed solely in her head.

"Valerie, this is a really bad—"

"Are you listening to me?"

"I am, Val, but I've got to go. I'll talk to you later." He clicked off the phone, powered it down, and rushed back into the PEOC just as Richard Coffee's next television appearance began.

Ten minutes later Johnston stared at the video monitor, now blank. He had spent his years in the military sending men and women on missions that would surely kill some of them. It was part of the calculus of warfare, and he had learned to live with it.

Still, he counted Derek Stillwater as more than one of his soldiers. He considered him a friend, and he wished now that he had never sent Derek undercover at the resort. Not that there had been any argument from Derek. Derek, who normally rejected any involvement with DHS, had a bond with Richard Coffee. And Johnston knew it was more than a desire for vengeance or justice. Derek wanted to believe that somewhere in the madness that was The Fallen Angel still lived Richard Coffee, U.S. soldier and friend.

He reached out with a shaky hand and downed half a glass of water. Pressing a hand to his stomach, he quelled a pang of stomach pain. Probably an ulcer, he thought. Or hoped. He hoped it wasn't something like stomach cancer that would leave his wife in the incapable hands of their neurotic only daughter.

He looked over at General Puskorius. Puskorius looked like he had swallowed a live cat.

"Go ahead," Johnston said. "Say what's on your mind."

"I hope your boy's got balls."

Johnston nodded. "He does, but that doesn't mean he'll turn himself in. Would you?"

Puskorius opened his mouth to respond when President Newman stood up. He did that whenever he wanted people to listen to him, Johnston noted.

"Don't you think turning over half this operation to a Russian is nuts?"

Johnston shook his head. "No sir, I don't. We're running through our chain of command so fast I'm glad to have anybody with experience in there. Besides, she's advising and consulting. She's not actually in charge. And I've read Khournikova's file, or at least as much of it as the FSB would release to me. She was so directly involved in the Pitchfork business that when it was all over I wanted as much information on her as I could get. She has been very insightful when it comes to The Fallen

Angels. She knows as much about them as anybody." He winced as another bolt of pain jabbed at his gut.

Secret Service Director O'Malley said, "I pulled up the file on Brenda LeVoi. She's a little green, but her track record is excellent. And frankly, she's just about as good as we're going to be able to do without flying people in. Think how many agents we lost inside the ballroom! Easily half our contingent."

President Newman snarled, "We need to find out how Coffee had so much inside knowledge. We need to clean house. Look how it's going to play to the world — Secret Service agents turned terrorists. O'Malley, you have to answer to this! And you, Johnston!"

Johnston, voice soft, said, "Let's solve the problem before we start pointing the finger, Mr. President. We're juggling flaming torches here and we can't afford to lose our concentration." He wondered if Newman wanted this problem solved. In his darkest heart of hearts, Newman probably wanted President Langston killed during this debacle so he could take over the reins of the presidency.

"Shit," Puskorius said. "The goddamned Fallen Angels don't exist anymore. Except in those helicopters over the Gulf." He turned to look at President Newman. "Mr. President, we have to make a decision about them and we have to make it now."

Director Ballard said, "The Colombian government was just on the line telling us they would shoot them down if they come near their air space."

"We'll shoot them down ourselves," the president said. He looked directly at General Puskorius. "Do it. That's an order."

"Yes sir." Puskorius reached for the phone.

CHAPTER 70

Derek checked his watch. Three minutes. He took a deep breath. Exhaled. Inhaled again. Moving over toward the lights, he raised the MP-5, prepared to smash the stock down on one of the fixtures so he could catch Juarez's attention, tell him he was coming to surrender.

He froze as a dim pounding reached his ears. What was it?

Crouching, he peered down below. Everybody in the ballroom had turned toward one of the doors near the stage that led out onto the hallway.

Juarez jerked his rifle, indicating to one of his men to check the door. He pulled out the PDA he had taken from Coffee, waiting. Three of Juarez's men gathered around the door, MP-5s raised and aimed at whoever was behind it.

"Now!" Juarez said, and clicked a button.

One of the terrorists shoved the door open. Maria fell into the ballroom, using a broom as a rude crutch. She shouted in Spanish, "Don't shoot! Don't shoot! It's me! Don't shoot *El Presidente* Langston."

Derek clenched his fists, cursing under his breath.

The terrorists picked her up by the arms. She cried out in pain as they dragged her toward the center of the room in front of Juarez. He glared down at her.

"Who are you?"

"My name is Maria Sanchez."

Juarez reached out and caught her throat in his hand, squeezing. "Who are you?" he snarled. "FBI? Secret Service?"

Derek swung his gun around. He slowly pushed it through the crack, widening it so he could see. He aimed the MP-5's sights directly on the back of Juarez's neck. It was an awkward firing position, and he was concerned that if he hit Juarez from this angle at this range with a 10-mm round it would go right through him and into Maria.

"Nobody," Maria croaked out. "I . . . I work for the resort."

He shook her, voice loud. "I don't believe you! How could you have killed so many? Are you a cop? A soldier? Who are you?"

Maria sobbed, voice weak. "Let . . . go. I'll . . . I'll tell you about Derek . . . Stillwater."

Juarez flung her away. She crumpled to the floor with an agonized scream, sobbing and gasping for air.

"Where is Derek Stillwater? Where? Tell me!"

"He's—" Maria sobbed. "He's dead."

Derek closed his eyes. *Maria*, he thought. *Be careful*.

Juarez's gaze was as flat and unblinking as a reptile's. Finally he brought his MP-5 around and pressed the barrel to Maria's forehead. She closed her eyes, but said nothing.

"How?" Juarez asked.

She opened her eyes to look at him.

"Some German."

Juarez seemed startled by this. "And the German? *Perro Loco*. What of him?"

"I shot him — while they were fighting."

Derek realized he was holding his breath and let it out slowly. *Good, Maria. Stick to the truth as much as possible. Please.*

"And Stillwater?"

She looked away, shaking her head. "Dead."

"How?"

"A . . . a knife fight. The German cut . . . cut his throat." She raised her hands to show the blood.

"What happened to your leg?"

"I fell. Down some stairs."

"Where is *Perro Loco*? Where is Stillwater?"

Derek tensed, waiting.

She didn't reply. Juarez bent over, caught up a fistful of her hair and pulled so she was looking at him. "Where are the bodies?"

"In the basement."

"Where?"

"In . . . in the furnace room."

He flung her away and started toward one of his men.

Maria turned from where she cowered on the floor and shouted at him. "What do you people think you're doing? Don't you realize this is suicidal? You can't possibly think you'll get away with this."

Juarez stopped, turned, and knelt in front of her. "My family was murdered by government soldiers. My mother and father and sister and baby brother were raped and murdered by those animals. They have to pay."

"Nobody's going to pay except you! Don't you realize you can't do this forever? It's only been a few hours. They'll figure out a way in. They'll blow up the doors and storm in here and shoot you down like dogs! All these lives will be wasted. The world already heard what you wanted. We've heard your message! But you can't—"

He reached out as if to stroke her cheek, but instead backhanded her across the face. His voice was low but clear. "Do you think we are fools? Do you think this is all we want? Did you not understand The Fallen Angel? We may be willing to martyr ourselves to a cause, but we will bring a plague onto mankind."

Derek pulled back the gun and pressed himself to the opening, straining to hear every word.

Maria, holding a hand to where he had hit her, sobbed out, "I don't . . . I don't understand. What plague?"

Juarez stood up. He laughed. "Let them come, Maria. Let them blow down the doors and take our lives. We will still succeed. Because The Fallen Angel and myself, The Angel of Death, have planted the seeds of the world's destruction in this building."

He laughed, hands on hips, and it was cold and crazy.

"They will never know," he said. "But The Fallen Angels and I planted a biological weapon in this building. The Fallen was mad, but he was a genius. Plans within plans within plans. He always had a backup. If they storm the doors, as you say, they will set it off. And every single person in this building will be infected with a plague that will spread around the world within weeks. So let them come! Let them come!"

He spun and pointed at one of his men. "Go! Verify that Stillwater is dead. Bring back his head." He turned and looked back at Maria. "You had better not be lying or I will cut your heart out as the world watches."

He punched a key on the PDA, and one of his men slipped out the door.

CHAPTER 71

Outside the Cheyenne Center, Secret Service snipers Bob Wingline and John Broadbent lay on a slight hillock beneath a birch tree about thirty yards from the entrance. Both carried HS Precision Pro 2000 HTR tactical sniper rifles mounted with DiOP TADS — thermal augmented day sights. Once they were set, they studied the front of the building through the video screen of the sights, which displayed black-and-white infrared images.

Wingline murmured, "Two bogeys."

On the screen the building was etched in shades of black, white, and gray as various heat levels came into play. They saw the metal bars of the security gates as one temperature, the windows as varying temperatures, the inside of the Cheyenne Center's lobby as yet another range of temperatures. And moving back and forth slowly at opposite ends of the lobby were two ghostly white human figures.

Wingline said, "I've got the one on the left."

Broadbent nodded. He tapped his microphone on and said, "This is Piper Two. We are in place. I repeat, we are in place. Two subjects. I repeat, two subjects."

Agent Brenda LeVoi's voice rang in their earpieces. "This is Eagle One. Confirm and hold."

Wingline tapped his microphone. "This is Piper One, Eagle One. Confirm and hold."

The two snipers watched the ghosts move slowly back and forth on the screens. Seconds ticked by. The afternoon sun beat down on the men, but they were two of the finest snipers on the planet, and had a mission they were very eager to perform.

Wingline moved the crosshairs of his rifle so they followed the figure on the left. He murmured, "Like pluckin' apples from a tree."

Broadbent muttered, "I bet I can get three into mine."

Wingline smiled. "You do and I'll buy the beer."

"You're on."

A slight breeze blew. It was eerily silent. There were no traffic sounds. There was a seventy-mile no-fly zone around the resort. The earlier clatter of small arms fire had died away as the snipers on the roofs and the National Guard had hunted down The Fallen Angels' snipers in the foothills.

LeVoi's voice sounded in their ears. "Proceed when ready."

Wingline said, "On three?"

"One."

Wingline said, "Two."

As Broadbent said, "Three," their fingers squeezed the rifle triggers. A burst of simultaneous gunfire broke the silence. Glass shattered and the ghostly figures on the infrared view screens disappeared, falling to the floor.

Bitter cordite filled the air around them. A slight blue cloud of smoke quickly blew away in the breeze.

Wingline said, "Got mine. Two in the heart. You?"

Broadbent smiled. "All three. You're buying the beer."

Wingline tapped his microphone. "Piper One. Mission accomplished. Over."

CHAPTER 72

Derek didn't have time to screw around. He leapt to his feet and stood on the edge of the open elevator doors, looking down the shaft. He would have to duplicate his route up, which should be easier on the way down. At least in theory.

Getting back to the elevator cables was no easy feat.

He stretched, reaching upward for the gearbox lip that had supported him before. His fingers barely scraped the edge. He stretched, groaning as a slash of pain ripped through his side.

He fell backward into the workspace, thinking. Back to his original idea.

Derek picked up the coil of electrical wire. He wasn't thrilled by it. He didn't know how much weight it could support. *No guts, no glory?* He hoped they wouldn't carve that on his tombstone.

Without thought his left hand rose and touched the St. Sebastian's medal and four-leaf clover he wore around his neck. *You're either lucky or you're dead*, he thought.

He unreeled the coil of electrical wire, dangling it over the edge. Hand over hand, quickly. When it hit the elevator shaft he hauled it back up, unreeled the same amount and swiftly braided the two strands together in a coil, knotting the end. Using his utility tool, he sliced the wire, found a metal I-beam in the exposed walls, and tied off the wire.

He still didn't like it, but time was running out. He slung the MP-5 over his back, gripped the braided wire, and slipped over the edge.

Almost immediately he felt the wire stretching taut under his weight. He picked up his pace, hands raw with pain in the effort to hold onto the thin line. He counted as he went. One. Two. Three.

Sweat drenched his body. His muscles burned.

Thirty. Thirty-one. Thirty-two.

The line snapped.

Flailing, he fell, dropping a dozen feet onto the top of the elevator with a loud crash that rattled every cell in his body.

Too much, he thought, gasping for air. *How much am I expected to do?*

Derek thought of Maria. Of what she had just done. Of how in order to make it from the power plant to the ballroom with a broken leg she must have already moved out of the furnace room into the hallway. Why? Probably to lose the company of the dead man and the heat. And he thought of the effort that must have taken. And how much courage it took for her to turn herself in like that. To risk sacrificing herself.

With a groan he rolled over onto his knees, quickly checked to make sure nothing was broken, and slipped into the elevator car through the top hatch. He took the MP-5 off his shoulder and checked his magazine. Half full.

Or half empty, he supposed. When life gives you limes, make Margaritas, and all that. He realized his brain was skidding around like a car hitting black ice, and forced himself to concentrate.

About thirty bullets. He clicked the weapon over to single fire. He couldn't afford semiautomatic, which would shoot three bullets per pull of the trigger, and he sure as hell couldn't afford full auto. He'd be ammoless in seconds.

Taking a deep breath, he opened the elevator door, crouching low in case this new hunter was close by.

Nothing.

Quietly, Derek slipped out of the elevator into the basement. Keeping to the walls, he began a slow recon down the hall. He stopped. Listened. Was that breathing he heard? Or the sound of his own heartbeat?

He approached the corner.

A figure exploded out of the darkness, rifle raised.

Derek dropped, kicking out, connecting with the man's knee. The terrorist fell with a cry, his gun firing. Bullets ripped into the fluorescent lights overhead, which exploded with pops, glass shards raining down, the immediate hallway plunged into gloom.

Derek tried to bring his own gun around, but the man was on him, hand around his throat, squeezing.

Derek tried to get at the man's own throat. Don't attack the hands. Fight back!

The pressure on his throat increased. He couldn't breath. Darkness.

Derek's hand caught on the handle of the Emerson knife where it hung from his pocket. He gripped it and swung it. The razor-sharp blade slammed into the man's thigh.

The terrorist arched back with an ugly snarl.

Oxygen rushed into Derek's lungs, flooding his brain. He twisted the knife.

An animal-like howl.

Derek rolled out from under the hunter, holding onto the knife, slashing upward through thigh muscle. Hot blood coursed over his hand.

The terrorist had short-cropped dark hair, a wispy mustache, and the face of an adolescent, all soft skin and round features, now deformed in pain and fury. His hand clamped down on Derek's wrist, squeezing. He kicked out, catching Derek in the ribs where he had been shot.

Derek lost his grip on the knife as the world burst into red-hot pain. It felt as if he had been stabbed in the ribs, not kicked. He dropped to his knees, holding his side, trying to suck in air.

The terrorist staggered to his feet, reached down and yanked the Emerson knife out of his leg, brandishing it in front of him, scarlet blood dripping from the blade as he advanced toward Derek. *"¡Está muerto!"*

He came at Derek like an experienced knife fighter, blade hidden in his hand, other hand forward. He slashed out not to stab, but to slice at a vital point — his throat, the inside of his arm —

Derek was instantly on his feet, shifting sideways, moving with the hand holding the knife.

Derek feinted with his right hand then lashed out with his left foot, hitting the hunter's wounded thigh. The hunter yelled and dropped to the ground, but not before he slashed at Derek's leg, connecting with his calf.

Burning pain seared across Derek's shin. He kicked out with the same leg, connecting with the hunter's jaw, slamming him backward to the ground. Hobbling forward, Derek kicked his thigh again.

The knife fell from the man's hand. With a grunt the man dropped to the ground clutching his leg and moaning.

Derek reached down and picked up the MP-5 and the Emerson knife. He brought the gun around, standing well out of range.

"Do you speak English?"

The man stared up at him. His eyes were half closed, his expression blank. Derek wasn't sure he was completely conscious. He repeated his question. *"Habla Ingles?"*

"Si," he muttered. *"Poco."*

The wound in the terrorist's leg was still bleeding, soaking his pant leg and pooling on the floor. Derek wondered if an artery had been severed.

Derek said, "What's your name?"

The man stared at him, uncomprehending.

"Do you want to die?" Derek demanded. "Do you want to die *now*?"

There was fear in his eyes and something else. Hope? "No." Barely a whisper.

"What's your name?"

"José."

"Okay, José. Put your hands on your head and keep them there."

With great effort José took his hands away from his leg and placed them on top of his head. Derek cautiously knelt next to him and rolled him back over on his stomach. He took the Emerson knife and slashed away the leg of José's pants, cut it into strips and used one to tie José's hands behind his back. Then he rolled him over and studied the leg. He wasn't entirely sure the man was still alive until he opened his eyes and looked at him.

"How old are you, José?"

Derek wasn't sure he was going to answer, but after a moment's silence the slurred response, *"Dieciséis."*

Derek thought for a moment, his own Spanish rudimentary and rusty. Sixteen. José was sixteen years old. A boy in a man's body.

He used the knife to cut off José's other pant leg, wadded it into a makeshift bandage and pressed it down on the wounded leg. Using the remaining strips, he tied it tight, not at all sure it would stop the bleeding.

Exhaustion ate away at Derek. It was now a physical entity, like carrying someone around on your back. He studied his own leg, which throbbed in time to his heartbeat. He gingerly rolled up his pant leg to look at the wound. It was bleeding and it was deep, but he didn't think it would kill him. He wanted to lie down. His ribs hurt. His head pounded. His hands were scraped and raw and bleeding. His back ached from where he had fallen on the elevator.

He reached over and cut the sleeve of José's shirt off. Derek fashioned it into a bandage on his fresh wound and carefully rolled his pant leg back down. *Death of a thousand cuts*, he thought morbidly. *I'll be like that knight in "*Monty Python and the Holy Grail*" that keeps coming even after you cut off his arms and legs.*

He looked at José. The kid wasn't doing so well. Derek could see that the bandage on the thigh was soaked with dark blood. He reached over and sliced José's shirt off him, folded it over and over and pressed it against the wound, then slowly rolled José over so he was lying on it, his back against the wall.

"You're going to bleed to death if that doesn't stop," he said. "But it's all I can do for you."

He looked into the boy-man's face, reached out and gently slapped him. José's eyes opened a little wider.

"I have a couple questions."

"Questions?"

"Uh-huh. I've helped you so far, José. But there are some things I need to know. You answer them, maybe I can end this and get you to a hospital."

José stared at Derek.

"Pablo said he and The Fallen Angel were going to bring a plague down. Did you know this?"

José hesitated. His head bobbed ever so slightly.

"What type of plague?"

"A germ bomb."

"Do you know where it is?"

"It . . . it is here."

"In the building?"

"*Si.*"

"Where?"

"Don't know. Pablo and Fallen. Placed it. I just did what I was told."

"Can Pablo set it off with the computer? With the PDA?"

Silence. Derek reached over and slapped his face again. His eyes opened wider, but the brown orbs were glazed and unseeing. "José! Wake up! Can Pablo set it off with the PDA? The little computer he got off The Fallen?"

Barely audible. "*Sí.*"

"Do you know where it is? Where they put it?"

Silence.

Derek slapped him again, but he didn't respond. The new pad of bandages was soaked with blood. Derek pressed his fingers into José's neck, feeling for a pulse. It was weak and thready and there wasn't a damned thing he could do about it. He slapped him again, harder. No response.

Then José's eyes opened and he muttered something. Derek leaned forward, close to the man's face, listening intently. "I can't hear you, José. Where is the germ bomb? Do you know where it is? Tell me where it is."

José muttered something and fell silent. Derek reached out and felt for a pulse. Nothing.

He wanted to feel angry. He wanted to shake him and bring him back to life and demand that he tell him where the bioweapon was.

But he was too tired. Too used up.

He moved around so his back was to the wall and leaned there, resting. He let his brain drift. He looked over at José and then bent down and checked through his pockets. Nothing. On his belt was a radio, which he took. He crawled over and checked José's MP-5. It had a nearly full magazine, which might prove useful.

With an effort Derek climbed to his feet, swaying there in the hallway. If José had known where the bioweapon was, he hadn't revealed it before his death. Derek would just have to find it himself. And with that thought, he pushed off from the wall and started walking toward the furnace room.

CHAPTER 73

Captain Jim "Beam" Lakemoore arced his F/A-18 Super Hornet into a turn, bringing it down to 2,000 feet. "This is Bravo-Delta-Oscar 1762. I have a sixty on target. Target is—I repeat—target is changing course. Evasive—target is—target is dropping to the deck."

The helicopters had slowed and were hovering. Lakemoore flashed overhead at 450 knots and was fifty knots out on turn-around. He checked his radar and called to Lieutenant Fred "Stooge" Collins behind him, "Can you get a visual?"

"Where the hell—? They're going due north. Shit. There's an off-shore oil platform—"

Beam dropped to a thousand feet. "This is Bravo-Delta-Oscar 1762. Target is moving due north. They are moving toward an off-shore oil platform. I repeat—"

Again they roared past the helicopter and brought the Super Hornet around.

In Beam's headphones the tower of the USS *Carl Vinson* said, "Bravo-Delta-Oscar 1762, can you give us coordinates?"

Stooge rattled off estimated latitude and longitude of the offshore oil platform.

The aircraft carrier tower said, "Can you acquire target without endangering platform?"

Beam brought the Super Hornet around again. "Window closing, sir."

"Lock on and hold. I repeat, lock on and hold. Confirm Bravo-Delta-Oscar 1762."

"CV, this is Bravo-Delta-Oscar 1762. Lock and hold. I repeat, lock and hold."

From behind him Stooge said, "We're going to lose them."

"Where's the second bogey?"

"Heading northeast. I'm keeping an eye on him."

"Shit. Where the fuck are they going? Disney World?"

Stooge laughed. "They aren't going far."

Beam: "CV, this is Bravo-Delta-Oscar 1762. We are losing target."

"Christ," Stooge said. "Are we going to fire on an oil platform?"

"I want a visual," Beam said, and dropped down to five hundred feet, bringing the Super Hornet in direct line with the offshore oil platform that jutted up out of the Gulf of Mexico like a skeletal monster.

"That's where they're heading. What do you say, thousand meters to go?"

"And closing," Beam said. Into his radio, "CV, this is Bravo-Delta-Oscar 1762. Target is one thousand meters and closing. I repeat, one thousand meters and closing."

Beam thought, nine hundred. Eight hundred.

They roared past and came back around. They were close enough that they could see dozens, maybe even a hundred small figures lining the walkways and work areas of the oil platform.

Five hundred.

Four hundred.

"CV, this is Bravo-Delta-Oscar 1762. Platform is in missile range. I repeat, platform is in missile range."

"Bravo-Delta-Oscar 1762, pull back. I repeat, pull back."

Beam pulled up, ascending back up to 2,000 feet and beginning a wide sweep above the oil platform. "We missed our chance."

"I don't know," Stooge said. He had binoculars pressed to his eyes. "Bring it back down for a visual."

"CV, this is Bravo-Delta-Oscar 1762. We're dropping down to five hundred for a visual."

A moment later Stooge said, "I see people jumping out of the chopper onto the landing pad—they're taking off again!"

"CV, this is Bravo-Delta-Oscar 1762. Target has dropped off passengers and is leaving the area. I repeat, target has dropped off passengers and is leaving the area."

"Hold."

They brought it past the oil platform again.

"Come on," Stooge said. "What's holding up the show?"

The radio crackled to life. "Bravo-Delta-Oscar 1762, this is CV. As soon as target is out of platform's range, you have orders to fire at will."

"Affirmative, CV."

The helicopter lifted off from the platform and headed northeast —toward the keys and the Florida coast. It was staying very low to the water, probably two hundred feet and it was flying fast. Stooge tracked it on radar, noting that it was catching up to the second chopper.

Stooge swore. "Radar target in sync with flight path. It's a cruise ship."

The helicopters were closing fast on the big white cruise ship that had sailed out of the Port of Miami several hours earlier.

"Weapons lock," Beam said.

"I don't know, Beam —"

The chopper veered, stopped its motion, and they overflew it again. Beam tore into a high-G turn, bringing it back around. "Lock."

"Ship is in target range," Stooge said. "Pull up. Pull up for god sakes!"

At the last moment they roared past the helicopter and the cruise ship.

"Bravo-Delta-Oscar 1762, this is CV. Abort. I repeat, abort."

"CV, this is Bravo-Delta-Oscar 1762. Missile lock canceled. Targets are hovering over cruise ship."

"*The Madeleine*," Stooge said. "Carnival Cruises."

The helicopter hovered and headed northwest again.

"Not this time," Beam said, and brought the Super Hornet around.

"Four hundred, five hundred." Stooge was reading the distance from the ship.

"Missiles locked."

"Six hundred, seven hundred . . ."

"Fire!"

They roared past the first helicopter as the two Phoenix AIM-54s dropped from their missile carriage and jetted toward the helicopters, which were coming in very low to the water. Suddenly the helicopters veered upward. Beam and Stooge saw bodies leaping from the choppers into the blue water below.

The missiles struck the helicopters, which exploded in a pair of red and gold fireballs.

"Targets have been destroyed, CV. I repeat, targets have been destroyed."

"Bravo-Delta-Oscar 1762, this is CV. Return to base. Good hunting. I repeat, return to base."

Beam brought the Super Hornet around and started flying back toward Cuba, and the USS *Carl Vinson*.

CHAPTER 74

Derek pushed his way into the power plant, slipping inside the door and standing against the wall. His gaze took in the stiffening corpse of the German, the litter of expelled shell cartridges, the drying blood.

When he was sure that he was alone, he limped over to the furnace and studied the system. From the main furnace ran two large metal ducts. One was the warm-air conduit. The other was the cold-air return. He knew there was a mechanical diverter for the air conditioning.

He tried to puzzle this out, wondering where Richard Coffee would have placed a bioweapon. The smartest thing would be to place it within the heating or cooling ducts, but to do so would require either access to the furnace room or to one of the ducts.

Derek's gaze followed the ductwork upward to where it split and split again. At the first split there was a trunkline that ran to the air-conditioning unit. There was a mechanical distribution switch there. The switch was a motor box that flipped a vent so hot air wouldn't get through if the air-conditioning was running, and flipped the vent the other way if the furnace was running. It had an access hatch.

Derek opened the hatch and peered in. Fishing through his pocket, he drew out a keychain. On it was a two-inch-long flashlight. He figured it would be a miracle if it hadn't been damaged during the day's adventures. To his surprise, a beam appeared at the touch of the button. He looked up and down the ducts. He saw nothing.

He shut the hatch and, with a sigh, climbed the stairs, stepping over the corpse of the German and letting himself out into an upper hallway. He scanned the walls in the hallway, counting two cold-air intake vents and three warm-air vents. He methodically checked each one, in two cases having to drag a bench over to get high enough to peer in. All were clean.

Coffee might have just placed it in the main ballroom somewhere all ready to go off when a rescue happened. It was possible. But it wasn't the impression he had gotten from Juarez's comments. Juarez indicated it was set to go off automatically if a rescue attempt was made. To Derek, that suggested it wasn't in the ballroom.

Coffee clearly knew the Cheyenne Center well. So did Derek.

Okay, Derek thought. *If I were to plant a booby-trapped bioweapon set to go off if a rescue attempt was made, where would I put it?*

He ruled out the front entrance and the lobby. The steel security gate would be a tough obstacle for any Special Forces or SWAT team making a dynamic entry.

The roof?

He liked the roof. The elevator shafts were obvious weak points. He knew at least one of them was mined. And he knew there had already been an explosion in the other. If the bioweapon had been there, Pablo wouldn't have been gloating about it still being available.

The loading dock? Same thing.

Derek considered the basement. There were two tunnels that connected to the Cheyenne Center. One led from the southwest corner of Cheyenne Hall to the International Center. The other led from the southeast corner of the Cheyenne Center to Colorado Springs Hall. The southeast corner would have been directly below the loading dock explosion.

Derek decided to investigate the southwest corner and started off in that direction. As he walked, something tickled at his memory.

He remembered passing two Secret Service agents by that doorway as he headed into the Cheyenne Center just before the summit began. One was on a ladder in the overhead crawlspace. The other—

Derek stopped, remembering. The other had been Pablo Juarez, dressed like a Secret Service agent. His partner—had it been Richard Coffee? Had he walked right past them as they were installing a biological bomb in the building?

He picked up his pace, his numerous aches and pains momentarily forgotten. Derek stopped at the closed steel doors that separated the Cheyenne Center from the tunnel to the International Center. The steel doors were wired with plastic explosives, a tangle of wires and infrared sensors.

Derek studied the wires. He was moderately knowledgeable about defusing bombs, having studied at the Redstone Arsenal in Alabama. That didn't mean he wanted to take on that door. He doubted if even the most expert bomb tech would want to. The thing to do would be to clear the area and set it off remotely, then rush through the breach. Which is undoubtedly why Coffee had set a bioweapon to go off during a rescue attempt.

Tricky bastard, Derek thought.

He backtracked, studying the ceiling. Slogging back to one of the meeting rooms, Derek grabbed a chair and returned. Standing on the chair, he removed one of the ceiling tiles and boosted himself up into the crawl space, a feat that got more and more difficult to accomplish as the day went on. He flashed the light around, got his bearings, and began once again to crawl along I-beams, support walls, and the drop-ceiling framework, the flashlight clenched between his teeth.

Sweat dripped down his forehead and into his eyes. Derek blinked. His ribs, thigh, and back screamed at the abuse. His vision blurred and his head pounded.

I am so tired of this shit, he thought. *If I get out of this alive I am going back home, getting on my boat, and taking a long goddamned vacation someplace warm.*

After about ten minutes—what seemed like hours—he saw red glowing lights, like the eyes of rats. He slowed to a crawl, studying every inch of space ahead of him, not moving until he felt comfortable with what might be there.

And then he saw it. A network of wires and photoelectric beams set up in a triangle around a cylindrical canister about one-foot long and seven or eight inches in diameter. He had found the bioweapon.

CHAPTER 75

Robert Mandalevo stood up and walked toward where Maria was sprawled on the floor. It occurred to him that leaving that chair might be the bravest thing he did in his entire life. He knew by rising to his feet he was painting a bull's-eye on his chest. He briefly thought of his daughters and kept walking.

Pablo Juarez glared at him, gun raised. "What are you doing?"

Mandalevo gestured to Maria. Everything about his body language and tone of voice was neutral and nonthreatening. At least he hoped so. "She's injured. I'm going to help her get comfortable. May I?"

Juarez continued to stare at him. After a moment he nodded. Robert knelt next to Maria and murmured, "I'm going to help you stand, all right?"

Maria nodded.

Mandalevo got his arm under Maria's shoulders and helped her to her feet. "Okay," he said. "You've done just great. Lean on me. We'll get you toward the middle of the room."

They began to limp toward where Mandalevo had been sitting. Without moving his lips, he murmured, "Is Stillwater really dead?"

Maria tried not to react. Mandalevo saw her flinch, nonetheless. "No," she said.

"Brave woman," Mandalevo said. "Good girl. Okay, here we are. Chair or floor?"

"Floor," she said.

Mandalevo gently set her down on the carpet. Tony Thoroughgood, an advisor with the British group, took off his jacket and rolled it up for her to use as a pillow. He shot Mandalevo a questioning look, but Mandalevo sat down, his hands in his coat pockets, working out a message on his BlackBerry.

Maria looked at him. "Thank you. Will . . . will this ever end?"

Thoroughgood caught Mandalevo's eye and nodded. Manadalevo realized the Brit knew what he was doing. He nodded in return. Thoroughgood was a short, square-shouldered man in his late forties with hair the color and texture of wet straw. He knelt next to Maria. "Hi there, I'm Tony. That was a pretty brave thing you did back there. How's your leg—"

He broke off as Pablo Juarez appeared next to them. Juarez aimed his gun directly at Mandalevo's face. "Hands out of your pockets."

Mandalevo froze. His heart skipped a beat and he felt a weight in his chest like a stone banging against his sternum. Slowly he took his hands out of his pockets, holding them up in the air.

"Stand up."

Thoroughgood jumped to his feet. "Hey, what's this—"

Juarez swung the butt of the MP-5 into Thoroughgood's face. The British advisor's nose went *crunch* and blood spurted through his fingers. Clutching his face, Thoroughgood stumbled backward, falling onto the floor with a groan.

Mandalevo climbed to his feet without a word.

Juarez waved over one of his remaining lieutenants. "Search his pockets."

The man patted Mandalevo down, retrieving the BlackBerry, which he handed to Juarez. Juarez read the screen.

"Who are you sending this to?"

Mandalevo said nothing. His gaze was flat, giving nothing away. He understood he was balanced on a tightrope and a strong wind had started blowing.

"Who?" Juarez screamed. "*Who are you in communication with?*"

"My office," he said.

Juarez gestured to his man. "Search him. Get his ID."

Mandalevo remained motionless as he was searched. The lieutenant came up with a wallet and handed it to Juarez, who glanced through it. He held up an identification card, studying it.

"You told me you were the assistant deputy political advisor. Here I see that you lied to me. That you are, in fact, the director of National Intelligence. And you have been e-mailing data to your government." He looked down at the screen of the BlackBerry. "What message did you send?"

Mandalevo remained silent.

Something passed between Juarez and his lieutenant. The lieutenant, a young-looking man with a barrel chest, bulging arms, and a round, dark-skinned face, punched Mandalevo in the left kidney. Electric shocks of pain spun through his back, pinwheeling in his guts. Mandalevo groaned and dropped to one knee.

"*What message did you send?!*" shouted Juarez.

A voice from the front of the ballroom said, "Tell him, Bob."

It was President Langston. Juarez spun. "Ah, you speak, *El Presidente*."

"Yes," President Langston said. "Although I think it is highly unlikely I still speak for the United States. By now Vice President Newman will have invoked the Twenty-fifth Amendment and been sworn in as the acting president. Robert was doing what he does best, Mr. Juarez. He was securing information. Go ahead, Bob. Tell him what the message was. No reason to take a beating for it at this point in time."

Mandalevo thought: *Oh, yes there is, Mr. President.* He said, "It wasn't complete. I sent an incomplete message that said there were five of you here."

The sound of muted breaking glass interrupted. There were shouts and screams, followed by silence. It came from the direction of the lobby. Juarez spun around, listening. He tapped his radio. "Manuel? Ricardo? This is Carlos. Check in. Do you read?"

Silence.

Juarez's face grew pale. Into the radio again: "Manuel? Ricardo? Check in. Check in. Over."

Mandalevo, voice quiet, said, "Your numbers keeping dropping, Mr. Juarez. Or is it *El Tiburón*? You are now five armed men trying to control nearly five hundred. As our conditions grow worse — as we get hungry or thirsty or require toilets — we will be more and more difficult to control. They can just wait you out, you know. We can sleep, take naps, but it will be difficult for you and your men to remain alert around the clock. Your message has been heard—"

Juarez rushed at Mandalevo, slamming the butt of the MP-5 down on his head. Fireworks exploded behind his eyes. Mandalevo groaned and collapsed to the floor next to Maria. Vaguely, far off, he felt the miraculous soft touch of Maria's hand on his forehead. He tasted blood.

Juarez screamed, *"I am in charge now! We will do things as I say! And I say that we are in control and our demands will be met!"* He stepped back, chest heaving, eyes dark with rage. *"Does anyone else want to challenge me? Anyone?"*

The crowd was silent, watchful.

From the front of the ballroom President Langston said, "President Pedro Gomez has done a great deal to bring your country's civil war to an equitable end. He has put democratic reforms in place, marginalized the drug cartels, negotiated truces, and is working to disarm the paramilitaries. Your efforts to overthrow his government will only hurt the people of Colombia. And your choice of a replacement is quite a puzzle to me. Francisco Vasquez can't even run his own organization, let alone an entire country. He's a very weak leader. Is that your goal? Try to get someone into office who will be somebody else's puppet? Or be overthrown in a very short period of time? The potential for starting up the civil war again is very high. You can't believe this will work. This is a no-win situation, Mr. Juarez."

From the floor, nausea churning his stomach, Mandalevo peered at the stage. Blood trickled into his left eyes. He blinked it away. "Shut up, Jack," he whispered. "For God sakes, shut up."

Juarez stalked to the front of the room, jumped up on stage, and crouched over President Langston. "The Gomez government has won their peace by supporting the drug cartels and turning the people into cocaine whores! They have slaughtered anyone who stands up to them rather than giving due process. The AUC has splintered into a hundred shards like a broken window, with most of the cowards' loyalties being bought with a few pesos and cans of food! You know nothing about my people! Nothing! And it doesn't matter, does it? You will be dead if they do not meet my demands!"

Juarez looked at the BlackBerry he still held in his hands, then dropped it to the floor and stomped it to pieces with his heel. He leaned closer to President Langston and said, "And if your foolish people attempt to rescue you, we'll take the world down with us."

CHAPTER 76

General Puskorius shouted into his phone, "What? Who...? *The Madeleine*? We need SEAL teams in there to retrieve them! Yes, scramble them now!" He was simultaneously pounding on the keys of his laptop, tracking down the right people to coordinate operations. "Yes—"

Secretary Johnston was also on his phone, talking to the Coast Guard commandant, Admiral Bill Dyce. "Yes." He eyed Puskorius. "They're pulling together SEAL teams now, Admiral, but you may have people in place. Yes, hang on." He punched another line and made sure the Naval officer was in on the call. "Admiral Dyce, I've got Captain Brockman with the USS *Carl Vinson* on line. He's going to provide the coordinates for you and we'll patch in General Puskorius to help coordinate—"

The PEOC was awash with mingled voices, the clack of keyboards, and the buzz of nervous energy. Johnston could practically smell the testosterone and adrenaline in the air. President Newman was pacing the PEOC, scowling. Puskorius and Johnston hung up at almost exactly the same time. President Newman said, "I want a report. General?"

Puskorius, jowls heavy, looked tired. He straightened his spine and threw back his shoulders as he described how The Fallen Angels had set some of their people off on an offshore oil platform and a cruise ship and how several of them had ditched into the Gulf of Mexico just before the chopper was blown to pieces by a Navy Super Hornet. "I've got three SEAL teams going after them, sir."

"With orders to shoot on sight, I assume."

Puskorius hesitated. "Sir—"

"Shoot them on sight."

"Yes sir, but it's possible that they will try to take hostages. I'm still waiting on intel about the oil platform. There could be a couple hundred people working on it. And the cruise ship could have anywhere from a thousand to two or three thousand people. And we're spread a little thin."

"Thin?"

"The closest SEAL teams are at the Naval Surface Warfare Center in Panama City, Florida, sir. They're heading out as we speak, ETA twenty-five minutes."

"That's too long."

Johnston said, "The Coast Guard's on their way. We'll be coordinating with the SEAL teams."

Newman continued to pace. Johnston thought Newman was struggling to look presidential. Not necessarily act presidential, but to be perceived as presidential. For a moment he felt sympathy for the man. Learning the job in the middle of the crisis wasn't easy, and few could live up to it. Still, he thought Newman was thinking about political repercussions more than thinking about the actual crisis at hand.

Newman said, "I don't like it. This has gone to hell. Puskorius, why in hell didn't your people shoot down that helicopter before they offloaded?"

General Puskorius said, "Civilians were in the area, sir." He wrenched his gaze off President Newman and studied the conference table, littered with coffee cups, notepads, and the remnants of a hastily eaten lunch. He glanced over and caught Johnston's gaze, who shot him a brief head nod to indicate he was backing him.

Puskorius said, "It was a bad idea to allow these prisoners free, sir. The United States has a policy of not negotiating with terrorists." The words hung there like a noxious cloud of gas.

Johnston thought that President Newman was trying to point the blame somewhere else, and Puskorius threw it right back at him. He wondered how long Puskorius would last as chairman of the Joint Chiefs if Newman turned out to be the long-term president. He knew that if this day didn't end with a living, breathing Jack Langston that left Newman president, his own political career would be over as well.

President Newman's eyes fixed into slits. "As I'm sure you're aware, General, the United States has a *public* policy of not negotiating with terrorists, but we have often had back-channel negotiations ongoing when there have been hostages involved. And that doesn't change the fact that the military screwed up!"

Puskorius was about to respond when Lt. General Akron raised a hand to get everyone's attention. "We've got another message from Secretary Mandalevo—" He trailed off as he brought the incoming e-mail up on the main plasma screen.

5 BG NOW. DS OK. NEG ENTRY. BI

They studied the message. FBI Director O'Malley said, "5 BG NOW? Does that mean they're down to five?"

Secretary Johnston's phone rang and he picked it up. "Johnston here." He listened for a moment and said, "We believe there are only five of them left in the ballroom now. We don't know why the numbers have dropped. And yes—"

Johnston said to the room, "Snipers took out two of the terrorists who were patrolling the lobby of the Cheyenne Center."

"Thank God!" President Newman said.

Johnston didn't respond to that. Back on the phone he said, "We have reason to believe there are five of the terrorists remaining, and that Derek Stillwater is still alive. We're not sure—" His gaze flicked to the message on the screen. "Hold off on your entry until we give the signal. Yes. Hold." He hung up and looked around the PEOC. "What the hell does "NEG ENTRY and BI mean?"

Akron swallowed. "The message appears to have been cut off. At least, I think so."

CIA Director Ballard was on the phone. "Admiral? Yes. I want to know if that BlackBerry signal is—" Ballard's round face grew pale. "Yes sir. Thank you." He slowly hung up. "The NSA says Robert's BlackBerry is either turned off or dead. The signal's gone."

All cell phones, including BlackBerry's and other wireless devices, kept in constant communication with local cellular towers unless they were shut off. The National Security Agency had tapped into all cellular and satellite communications in a fifty-mile radius of the Cheyenne Resort and had their entire staff monitoring all communications.

"What does that mean?" President Newman said. "Is he dead? Did his battery die? What?"

Ballard said, "We don't know, Mr. President. It's possible he was caught."

President Newman eyed the messages: NEG ENTRY. BI. "What does NEG ENTRY mean?"

Akron said, "It might mean we shouldn't try to enter the building."

"Why?" President Newman demanded. "Why would Mandalevo say that? Is it possible that these people — *El Tiburón* or Pablo Juarez or whoever the hell he is — caught Bob sending messages and is sending one of his own to confuse us?"

Silence fell as everybody considered that. It was Akron who said, "I suppose it's possible, sir, but why tell us that the numbers were down to five? And would Juarez tell us that Stillwater was still alive?"

Johnston tried to think of what BI might mean. Or what it might start, but came up completely blank. "Sir," he said to President Newman. "Agent LeVoi and Ms. Khournikova are getting set up to enter the building. We need to let them know our decision. Should they go in or not?"

President Newman clenched his jaw. He turned and studied the cryptic message on the computer screen, then turned back to Johnston. "Tell them it's a go."

"Mr. President," interrupted FBI Director O'Malley, "with all due respect, perhaps we should —"

"Director O'Malley, it's already been pointed out to me that we shouldn't negotiate. Juarez said we comply or Jack Langston dies. We and the Colombian government can't comply and I do not want Jack Langston to die. Director O'Malley, order your people to proceed."

With an uncomfortable feeling in the pit of his stomach, Secretary Johnston watched the Secret Service director phone Agent Brenda LeVoi. "Agent LeVoi, proceed with your operation when ready. The timetable is yours."

Johnston thought: *Did Newman just sentence everybody in that building to death?*

CHAPTER 77

For a moment Derek stared at the bomb. With a hiss, he quickly scuttled backward until he reached the opening to the crawl space and dropped to the floor. He felt ill. His stomach churned, his head throbbed, and his hands shook. He knew it wasn't just all of the day's battles catching up to him. It was him.

He fell to the floor, back against the wall, and propped his head in his hands. The world swirled around him and his stomach roiled. Sprawling on his hands and knees, he vomited, sucking bitter air in and out of his lungs. Spangles and fireworks danced on the screen of his closed eyelids. The unmistakable sweet smell of rotting bodies filled his nostrils. Derek shook his head, instantly regretting the action as his headache intensified.

He crawled away from his mess and lay down on the hard floor, forearm over his eyes.

Coffee, you bastard!

It was just like Coffee, a master strategist, to create backup plans within backup plans. They had been trained in the same place in the same way by the U.S. Army. While Derek had specialized in biological and chemical warfare, Coffee had focused on Psyops — psychological warfare. A linguist, he had often been charged with interacting with locals, both as a trainer and as a propagandist. Derek doubted if Coffee had much more than basic field training from the CIA before slipping into Chechnya undercover and infiltrating the culture. Of course, while there he had led Chechen rebels in guerilla warfare and terrorism against the Russian government, as practical a training ground as any for becoming a full-fledged worldwide terrorist.

He drifted for a moment, lost in his own thoughts, a million emotions and memories flickering through his brain. He thought of his ex-wife, Simona. Reaching into his back pocket, he retrieved his wallet. The ID in the battered trifold identified him as Michael Gabriel, as did all the other supporting evidence. But there was a photograph of Simona.

He wondered if he would ever see her again, then gave himself a quick mental kick. He hadn't seen her in years. She was a doctor in Texas. She'd never remarried. Neither had he. Sometimes, when he let himself, he wondered what that meant. Did she still love him? Did he still love her? It was his career that had trashed their marriage — years in the military, followed by years working with U.N. weapons inspection teams. He had been thinking about her a lot over the last couple years.

Biological and chemical warfare and terrorism were the tiger tail he had caught early in his military career. It was like the fascination of watching two scorpions try to sting each other to death. Fear of it drove him to try to prevent it. Yet he couldn't let go of it, couldn't look away. He had seen its devastation firsthand in Iraq. Included in his files were details of secret missions into North Korea and Iran, Pakistan, and Africa, where he worked as a contract analyst for the CIA. What he had seen struck fear deep in his gut. A shrink once told him, "You've spent most of your career looking through the gates of hell. You'd be nuts not to be a little bit nuts."

Why couldn't he let it go?

Images: rotting bodies of Kurds in northern Iraq, sprayed with sarin gas from helicopters; nighttime grave digging in Pakistan, performing field autopsies on corpses believed infected by biowarfare agents, victims of surreptitious government-led testing on human beings; staring at huge corroded bioreactors in Russia that showed all evidence of manufacturing genetically engineered smallpox to be used in long-range missiles.

Get it together, Derek!

Derek sat up, looked down the hallway and spied a restroom. He walked down to it, pushed his way in, and turned on the cold water, splashing it on his face, washing his hands, rinsing out his mouth. He looked at himself in the mirror. His face was covered with small scratches and scrapes. His hair was littered with dust and debris, and his eyes looked sunken and dark.

"You look like shit," he said.

The image in the mirror nodded and grinned. He thought the grin made him little a little bit demented.

"What do you think?" he asked himself. *"Can you disarm it?"*

On the sink in front of him he laid out his tools. The Emerson knife. A small flashlight. A screwdriver he'd been dragging around with him all day. A set of keys and his utility tool. The utility tool was like a Swiss Army knife with a number of gadgets including scissors, knife blades, a corkscrew, and a pair of pliers.

Around his neck was a St. Sebastian's medal, a steel four-leaf clover, and ju-ju beads, the latter given to him by a friend who survived Somalia. *They saved my ass, dude. And you need luck more than I do.*

St. Sebastian had been an officer in the Imperial Roman army, a captain of the guard in the third or fourth century. He was reported to have healed the wife of a fellow soldier, and then began to convert soldiers to Christianity. He was arrested and tried as a Christian, tied to a tree, and shot with arrows. Sebastian miraculously survived and continued to preach, though his ministry was short lived. The emperor had him rearrested and beaten to death.

Derek thought there was probably a lesson there. You could view Sebastian surviving the arrows as a miracle and a sign of God's favor, but what were you to make of the second and final execution? That God decided to bring him home, he had proven his faith the first time? Or that God was sending you a message the first time and you were too stupid to pay attention to it?

During the fourteenth century plague victims prayed to Sebastian, which is how he became associated with plague. Which is why Derek wore his medal around his neck, figuring he could use all the benevolent oversight he could get.

Derek wasn't quite up to praying to saints, but he rubbed his thumb over the medal, thinking very dark thoughts. Taking a deep breath, he put all his tools away, turned, and walked back toward the crawl space. He was as ready as he was ever going to be.

CHAPTER 78

A Bell UH-S Huey military helicopter roared in over the main building of the Cheyenne Resort and landed in the circular drive in front of the central entrance. It had barely touched down when the hatch door slammed open and a dozen armed soldiers jumped out and sprinted for the front doors, where Secret Service agents waited.

The Special Forces team quickly assembled in a conference room that had been turned into an operations center. Special Agent LeVoi stood at the front of the room with Irina Khournikova. As the twelve men gathered around, LeVoi felt a sharp twinge of doubt.

She was not military. Brenda had a law degree from the University of Michigan. She had always wanted to be part of the FBI. It was, she often thought, her first love — which probably explained her three failed marriages. She was finally accepting that it was okay; she was doing good things in the world.

And she had ambitions in the bureau. She'd like to be the first female director of the FBI. Now it was time to live up to her ambitions. She felt in over her head, but she had asked for this and it was the time to rise to the occasion. LeVoi did the talking, not wanting to cause problems with the soldiers' chain of command by having them take orders from a Russian.

LeVoi pointed to the 3-D CAD/CAM images of the Cheyenne Center and the troika of the Cheyenne Center, International Center, and Colorado Springs Center projected on the walls. She drew their attention to the sketches of the Cheyenne Center. "Group Alpha?"

A soldier raised his hand. He was tall, broad-shouldered, with short blond hair and a square jaw. "Captain Ray Stanchfield. I'll lead Group Alpha. Lieutenant Jorge Ruiz —"

A wiry soldier with dark penetrating eyes raised a hand.

"—will handle Group Bravo."

LeVoi nodded. "We've got our people as well. We have very little time to coordinate. You will be running the entry op; I'm coordinating from here." She introduced Irina Khournikova. "She'll be going in with Group Bravo. She is very familiar with the tunnel."

Ruiz eyed her. "You got combat training?"

"Yes," Irina said. "Russian Army and FSB. You are familiar with *Spetsnaz*?"

"Yeah," Ruiz said. "Bunch a pussies."

The team laughed. Stanchfield started to say something, but Irina smiled and said, "Then I'll make sure you go in first, Lieutenant. I'll cover your ass. You wouldn't want a pussy to show up your Special Forces, would you?"

LeVoi said, "Enough. Group Alpha takes the roof. There are three Service snipers up there already. We will download all these maps to your PDAs and we have printouts as well. Who are your demolition experts?"

Two of the soldiers raised their hands. "Good," LeVoi said. "The tunnel doors are apparently wired from the inside with Semtex. Our evaluation is it's booby-trapped. It can also be set off by a signal from a PDA that the lead terrorist, known as Pablo Juarez, has with him. The world leaders are also wired with explosives."

One of the demolition experts, a slight man with sensitive features and a whispy red mustache, stepped forward to study the CAD/CAM configurations. He said, "We can get those jammed, right?"

"Yes, but it causes problems with our own equipment."

He scratched his jaw and looked at Stanchfield. "If the timing's right, though—"

Stanchfield nodded. "I'll see to it."

LeVoi ran them through the logistics of the two-pronged entry plan. She didn't like the short preparation time. It was that lack of intel and planning that had killed the previous assault team. She hoped there were no more surprises, but didn't think that was likely. Operations of this complexity always went to hell minutes after they started. She didn't express her doubts, but said, "People, time is very tight here. We have to move in the next five minutes."

She hesitated, then brought up a photograph of Derek Stillwater on one of the walls. "This is a friendly. He's been picking these guys off all day, one at a time. We have evidence to suggest that he's still alive. If you see him, do not shoot him. He may be a very valuable asset. He's a troubleshooter with DHS and a former Green Beret."

Ruiz said, "A *brotha*."

"Keep an eye out for him."

"Will do," Ruiz said. "We're ready to kick some terrorist butt."

Stanchfield gave LeVoi a thumbs-up. "We're ready."

LeVoi turned to Irina Khournikova. "You?"

Khournikova nodded. She reached down and picked up an assault rifle that had been propped in one corner. She looked at Lieutenant Ruiz. "Ready to rock and roll, Lieutenant?"

Ruiz grinned. "Ladies first."

Khournikova led Group Bravo out of the resort at a brisk trot.

Stanchfield was on his radio to the U.S. Space Command stationed at Peterson Air Force Base. "When I give the signal, shut all satellite and radio communications down around here for five minutes. Five off, then on until my next signal. And, Captain, that next signal will mean we want the leaders safe and they have to be shut down. Understand?" He waited. "Affirmative. Out."

He turned back to LeVoi. "Let's go." His group ran after him and loaded into the Huey, which promptly lifted off and flew toward the Cheyenne Center.

LeVoi was on the phone with Secretary Johnston and everybody at PEOC. She checked her watch. They had twelve minutes before Pablo Juarez planned to kill President Langston. The clock was ticking. "Sir, Project Judgment Day is underway."

CHAPTER 79

Derek crouched in the crawl space and studied the bomb. He thought, *I am way in over my head with this thing.* He was trained to defuse bombs, though it wasn't his primary expertise. It wasn't the bomb itself that worried him — well, okay, it worried him. What worried him the most were the tripwires.

He settled back to think. The bomb appeared to have two kinds of triggers. One was physical — Coffee had set up a crisscross of what looked like fishing line around the device. The second was the lasers, not unlike those used in garage door openers. The actual beams weren't visible, but Derek had no problem seeing the lasers themselves with their glowing red eyes.

He wasn't convinced they were the only two triggers, either. He thought it might be possible there was a radio link, so Coffee could have set it off using the PDA. That wasn't his biggest concern.

His biggest concern was whether or not Coffee had put some sort of vibration sensor or mercury switch in the device.

Derek focused his flashlight, peering closer. It appeared to be made of molded plastic, perhaps some sort of PVC piping, a sort of modified pipe bomb. Pipe bombs were typically jammed with ball bearings or scrap metal to give the weapon destructive power. In the case of a bioweapon, that was not typically the case. Usually there was some sort of explosive whose main purpose was to disperse the biological agent without incinerating it.

The weapon was situated next to an air duct, very close to the foundation wall of the Cheyenne Center, right opposite the tunnel leading to the International Center. As a result, the crawl space stopped at the wall, except above the tunnel itself. And that had been wired with Semtex, as had the steel doors.

Derek froze. He thought he heard something. He strained his ears to hear, wondering if Juarez had sent somebody else in his direction. Then he heard it again. It seemed to be coming from the tunnel. A faint sound, perhaps subliminal. A change in the atmosphere, a sense of movement.

He shifted his focus back to the bomb. What if there was a vibration sensor?

He heard — or sensed — movement. The presence of at least one other person nearby. Holding his breath, he tried to extend his hearing, his eyesight, to throw his brainwaves out and try to sense what and where and who was approaching.

C'mon, baby. It's time for the arrival of the cavalry. A little fuckin' backup from the rest of the world.

It was soft. And light. And it came from the tunnel.

"Hello!" he called out, his voice hoarse. "Hello? Is somebody over there?"

The sounds stilled. He waited. Listening.

"Hello? Hello? This is . . . this is Derek Stillwater," he called out. "Who's there?"

A faint voice said, "Derek? You're alive?"

"Irina?"

"Yes."

"The door's wired."

"We know. Are you alone?"

"Yes."

"We have a demolition expert with us. We plan to blow the doors."

"No! You don't want to do that!"

"Hold on."

Faint whispers drifted to him like dandelion puffs dancing on the air. A dozen feet away a glow of light appeared and temblor-like vibrations ran through the catwalk. "Easy," he called out. "Don't make too much movement."

Sweat broke out on his forehead and dripped onto his hands. He gulped in air. A voice said, "I'm Sergeant Terry McCormack. You're Stillwater?"

"Yeah." Dimly through the catwalk area above the doors Derek saw a long, angular head. He could barely see him because the crawl space was not only wired with explosives, but crammed with electrical wires, conduits, and heating ducts. A wave of relief washed over him. Finally, somebody who didn't want to kill him.

"We want to put a controlled explosive on the door that will set off the Semtex so we can enter. You'll need to move down the hallway as far as you can."

Derek hung his head. Well, maybe they didn't *want* to kill him, but they sure were *going* to kill him if they weren't careful. "There's a problem," Derek called out, and described the bioweapon.

A moment of tense silence followed. Finally McCormack said, "Hang on. Don't go anywhere." The head disappeared.

Derek tried to make himself comfortable. It wasn't easy. His hands, slick with sweat, wouldn't stop shaking. His vision doubled, tripled, then returned to normal as his head pounded in sync with his heart. A moment later Irina's head popped up. "We've put a hold on our entry. How did you find out about this?"

He quickly sketched out what he had heard Pablo Juarez say.

"Do you think there is more than one?"

"I don't know. Probably not."

"Can you defuse this?"

"I don't know. I don't know much about it."

"Hang on."

Irina disappeared and McCormack reappeared. "Describe it."

Derek did. McCormack was quiet a moment. "What's it on?"

"On?"

"Yes. It's next to the air duct."

"Is it strapped to the duct, to an I-beam, or what?"

Derek flashed his light on the bomb. "It's resting on one of the ceiling tiles."

"Good. That's really good. Is it screwed down or anything?"

"No."

"Bastards might have screwed up after all," McCormack said. "What kind of tools do you have with you?"

Derek told him.

"Sharp knife?"

"Yes. I've got the Emerson knife. It's very sharp. Sharper than the knife on my utility tool."

"Okay. You have steady hands?"

Fuck no, Derek thought. He said, "So-so."

"Ought to work. Okay, Stillwater—"

"Call me Derek."

"Sure. Call me Terry. Okay, Derek. I'm going to walk you through dismantling the sensors. The lasers first, then the wires. That ought to be pretty straightforward. Then comes the tricky part."

"If we get that far."

"We'll get that far. But we have to start now. Time's running out."

Derek took a deep breath. "Hang on." He leaned over and wretched violently, dry heaving until his ribs screamed at him to stop. Panting, he fought the panic, trying to calm down. *Plan B*, he thought. What's *Plan B*?

McCormack called out, "You going to be okay, Derek?"

"Peachy. Give me a few seconds, okay? I've had a bad day."

"When you're ready."

Derek rubbed his forehead. *When you're ready?* He sucked in a bitter, dusty chest full of air. He thought, *the weather forecast for hell is cold with a chance of snow and likelihood of ice.*

"Okay," he said. "What do I do first?"

CHAPTER 80

On the roof of the Cheyenne Center, Group Alpha, led by Captain Stanchfield, approached the northwest elevator housing. He was accompanied by one of the Secret Service snipers, who was briefing them on his evaluation of the tripwires.

"We breached the maintenance door without any problems, but we think they've got the door wired so if we try to go through it'll blow. When we went into lockdown we were told to hold station, so we did. But I checked things out, and we discussed our options should an op come into play."

Stanchfield frowned and looked around. The sky was clear and blue, Pikes Peak visible in the distance. The roof was flat, covered with black tar that absorbed the sun and felt mushy beneath their feet. A satellite dish and radio antennas bristled skyward from the low, flat elevator housing. "How'd you get up here?"

"Up the elevator. There's a work area that overlooks the ballroom. Once the elevator hits the top, you can enter the work area. If we could get in there, we can see down over the ballroom. It'll be a great sniper nest. From the work area you can access the roof through here, but it's locked and we have reason to believe —"

Stanchfield interrupted. "You can't tell if it's wired from this side?"

"Come look."

Stanchfield followed the Secret Service agent — Cauldwell — over to the square cinderblock elevator structure. Cauldwell wore black sniper gear and moved with a bowlegged stride. Stanchfield wasn't sure he trusted him, and flashed his team to watch his back. These snipers had been up here all this time and never tried to enter the building. He understood they had been directed to stay put, and dynamic entry wasn't their job, but still — He didn't get it. It made him suspicious.

Cauldwell pulled open the steel door to reveal the motor housing for the elevator. There was another steel door across from him, but it wasn't what attracted Stanchfield's attention. It was the six monofilament wires that crisscrossed the room around the motor housing.

"Not too subtle," Stanchfield said. Now he understood why they hadn't tried entry.

"No. And if you carefully lean over this way —" Cauldwell showed him, "— and shine a light, you can see at least one of the detonators and Semtex."

Stanchfield followed his directions and could, indeed, peer through a square opening in the housing and see where one of the wires was attached to a device linked to a packet of plastic explosives. He stepped back and waved over Furilla, his demolitions expert.

"Check it out," he said, but was distracted when his radio chattered. It was Agent LeVoi.

"Alpha, this is base. Hold. I repeat. Hold operation. Bravo has encountered Stillwater and what appears to be a biological bomb. Bravo is attempting to defuse weapon. I repeat. Hold operation."

Stanchfield clicked on the radio. "Alpha One here, Base. Confirm."

Cauldwell said, "One damned thing after another."

Stanchfield nodded. He pointed a finger at Furilla. "Get set up."

With a nod, Furilla waved over one of his teammates, Johanssen, and took off his backpack and withdrew a fiber-optic scope. He attached the pack to his belt and studied the wires. "I'm going to lie down," he said. "I need some help keeping it steady because of the wiring."

Johanssen nodded. He was the youngest member of the team and looked it. He was twenty-three-years-old, blond-haired, blue-eyed, originally from Minnesota. There was a guileless, naïve quality to his appearance that was a total crock, but he used it to his advantage with women, who liked to baby him. Furilla said, "You know the drill."

The fiber-optic scope was about eight feet long and Furilla could control its direction. It had a telescoping wand so it could be extended into different sites like locked rooms, air vents, gas tanks, or automobile interiors. It was one millimeter in diameter and he could slip it under most doors, if necessary. Furilla didn't have that in mind. He was going to push it through the hole in the housing they had used to see the detonator. He just wanted help holding it steady so they didn't accidentally bump the tripwire.

Sprawling on the floor, Furilla settled down, holding the scope's small, handheld monitor in front of his face. With Johanssen's assistance they inched the snakelike scope toward the opening. Once there, he peered at the image.

"Another inch or so straight in."

The scope moved forward into the opening. He could manipulate the lens at the end of the scope to peer around 360 degrees. He studied the obvious detonator, then started a slow counterclockwise rotation.

"There's number two. And three. I can see the wires, but not four. I think there are five." He scanned further. "Okay, pull it out."

They pulled back. Stanchfield, standing nearby, cocked his head, asking for an update. Furilla tapped his pointed chin and pursed his thin lips. He had pale blue eyes beneath a heavy brow, which was wrinkled in worry. He licked his lips and looked at Johanssen and shrugged. "Can't disarm it. Probably have to blow it. I think that'll make the elevator go crashing to the basement."

"They have brakes," Johanssen said. "Elevators don't crash."

"Yeah, but I'm looking at probably half a pound of Semtex that I can see. I think it'll tear that elevator car loose from its moorings with probably about two or three thousand pounds of counterweights, not to mention most of this structure." He gestured at the cinderblock room.

Johanssen nodded. "So we follow it down. Put the snipers into the work area, the rest of us drop straight down the shaft."

Stanchfield said, "Which might be so filled with debris we can't get through."

"Hmmm."

Furilla said, "I want to see if I can scope the door."

Stanchfield frowned. "Could you see it before?"

Furilla shook his head. "No."

They moved their gear over and Furilla crouched down by the door. He moved the scope along the bottom edge, which had a tiny space between the bottom and the concrete floor. He scanned along the door without seeing anything.

"Okay. In we go."

He nudged the scope through the crevice, quickly meeting some resistance.

"Does it fit?" asked Johanssen.

"I'm not sure. It should. I'm going to move it over —"

The explosion was immediate and devastating.

CHAPTER 81

Derek crouched uncomfortably over the bioweapon with the screwdriver in his hand, very gently unscrewing a plate off the back of one of the lasers. He had to hold things as still as possible so as not to jerk the laser off its receiver, which would trigger the bomb.

An explosion shook the entire building. Startled, Derek fumbled the screwdriver, dropping it. It clanked off a wire support and dropped harmlessly to the tile.

He overbalanced, falling backward. He pushed off so he would fall away from the bomb and not onto it. With a thud he landed on a tile. It held for about one second before collapsing beneath his weight. He crashed eight feet onto the hard floor and lay there for a moment, waiting for the bioweapon to explode directly over him.

It didn't.

A screech of metal reverberated from somewhere in the building, shrieking like demons. It was followed by a grinding roar that gained volume as it went, suddenly ending in what sounded like an enormous collision of metal on metal. The entire building shook again. A wall of dust rolled down the hallway.

He struggled to his knees, his back protesting. Derek's heart pounded, chest swelling. He shut his eyes and turned his face into his sleeve as the dust covered him. For a moment he was totally blind. The dust started to settle, but the air was still filled with a gray fog that smelled of dust and mold and smoke. He coughed and spat, his mouth tasting dry and chalky.

"Everybody okay?" he shouted.

"Derek? You're alive?" It was Irina's voice.

"Yeah. Sort of."

A babble of voices drifted over from the other side of the wall.

Finally, McCormack's voice rose over them. "Where the fuck are you, Stillwater?"

"I fell through the ceiling."

"What's going on with the bomb?"

"What the hell happened?"

"We're on it, Stillwater. Focus! Check the bomb!"

"Yeah, yeah, yeah," he muttered. "I'm not dead, am I?" Limping to a chair, he climbed on it and boosted himself back into the crawl space. It was harder than it had been. His energy was ebbing fast. He spidered his way back to the weapon, every muscle, bone, and nerve ending in his body protesting.

"It didn't blow up," he said.

"No vibration sensor then. What about the lasers? Are they still aligned?"

Derek studied the bomb. On one end was a small plastic square. Before the explosion a tiny light had glowed red. Now it was blinking.

"It's armed!" he shouted. "Take cover. It's armed!"

McCormack shouted, "Is there any—"

Derek didn't listen to him. He reached out, grabbed the bomb, hefted it with both hands, eyes closed, expecting it to detonate immediately. When it didn't he tucked it under one arm like a football and jumped through the hole in the ceiling, landing hard on his feet. He took off at a sprint, ducking into the door for the power plant. He ripped open the door to the janitor's closet and dropped the weapon in a bucket. He snagged two bottles of Clorox bleach, ripped open the caps, and poured them both on top of the weapon.

The red light continued to blink, mocking him.

He spun on his heel and leapt through the door, sprinting for the far end of the corridor. The explosion behind him blasted a hole in the wall and knocked him off his feet. He was stumbling upright when a second explosion at the tunnel end of the hallway erupted. The percussion wave caught him and flung him to the floor. Everything went red, then black.

CHAPTER 82

In the ballroom, the first explosion blew a small hole in the corner of the roof, letting in shafts of sunlight that pierced the dust. Fist-sized chunks of debris dropped to the floor. The lights flickered off, on, then returned before a third of the lights went dim, casting the room in shadow. The crowd screamed, many cowering, hands over their heads. Some of the more savvy bureaucrats, suspecting that a rescue attempt was being initiated, threw themselves to the floor or ducked beneath tables.

Pablo Juarez also suspected it was the beginning of a rescue attempt. He leapt onto the stage and stood next to President Langston. "So, your Secret Service has decided it is time to risk your life rather than negotiate or capitulate."

President Langston raised his chin. "You had no intention of negotiating, and if you expected the United States or any other government to give in to your demands, you were a fool."

Pablo jammed the barrel of his gun into President Langston's throat. "Who's the fool, *El Presidente*? The one tied to the chair or the one with a gun in his hand?"

A high-pitched, heavily accented voice said, "I am willing to negotiate directly with you."

Pablo turned to stare down the row of world leaders to Crown Prince Talal, the current head of Saudi Arabia. He wore the traditional white cotton thobe, with tagiyah, ghutra — head scarf — and agal, the thick cord that held it in place. A short, heavyset man, he was sixty-four years old and considered to be a moderate reformer in many ways. Pablo strode over to him.

"What did you say?"

"I will negotiate with you," said Crown Prince Talal.

"What could you possibly have to negotiate with?"

"We are a very rich country. Although Colombia has significant oil supplies, we can open markets for you. We could apply pressure to the current regime to get them to promise — how do you say? — certain concessions to your organization."

"Concessions."

"Yes." Crown Prince Talal licked his lips, his head shaking slightly with nervousness. "And — or perhaps instead — we could arrange for funds to be delivered into a bank account of your choosing."

Juarez grinned. "You're bribing me."

Crown Prince Talal stood straighter. "I am negotiating, sir."

President Langston said, "You can't negotiate with a terrorist. He's not —"

"*Shut up! Shut up! Shut up!*"

President Langston cocked his head. "Mr. Juarez, you can't believe you'll survive this. Your people are stretched too thin. This can't continue. Now would be a good time to surrender."

"Surrender?" Pablo stalked back toward President Langston. "*Surrender?* You think we have done all this only to surrender? I will *never* surrender! *Never!* Do you understand me?"

President Langston said nothing. Pablo screamed, "*Do you understand me?*"

"All too well."

Crown Prince Talal interrupted. "And my offer? Will you consider it?"

Pablo grinned. It was the toothy, carnivorous grin that had earned him the nickname *El Tiburón*, the shark. There was no humor in it, only predatory hunger. He moved back toward the crown prince. He cocked his head and rubbed his chin in a parody of consideration. "Hmmm, will I consider your offer? Let me think. Ah. No."

And he raised his gun and shot the Saudi prince twice in the head.

Juarez stepped back and glanced up and down the line of world leaders. "Does anyone else wish to negotiate with me?"

Silence.

"Then we understand each other. The die has been cast. Events are in play that can't be stopped." He locked eyes with President Langston. "They cannot be —"

Another explosion, this one almost directly beneath them, rocked the building. The lights flickered again before shutting off completely. The ballroom was lit only by emergency lights along the walls and the sole shaft of sunlight through the hole in the roof.

Juarez staggered, face growing pale. Puzzlement danced across his features. Turning, he looked up at the hole in the ceiling, then around at his men. He withdrew the PDA from his belt, tapped it on, and brought up an image. He walked back and forth, studying the screen.

He pointed to his men. "Be prepared to deal with —"

Another explosion rocked the building and this time he was ready. He studied the PDA screen and said, "I think your people are *dying* to rescue you, Mr. President."

CHAPTER 83

Pain. It was the first sensation Derek felt. It was followed by pressure, as if a cow had fallen on him. Slowly, he started sorting through the various sensations, trying to figure out what had happened. But the sensory information was overpowering his more rational thinking. He didn't think he had blacked out for very long. But the first thing he felt was weight on his body and pain that shot out from the back of his head. His ears ached, too.

Blinking, he looked around. The hallway was almost completely black. Here and there were emergency lights, but they only seemed to glow in the darkness and the dust, providing little in the way of illumination. *The explosion knocked out the electricity*, he thought, *but somehow the backup generator's still running. At least for a while.*

He tried to roll over, but couldn't. Reaching out with his hands, he felt what appeared to be the steel frame of a wall and chunks of drywall. The explosion must have knocked over at least a section of one interior wall. He tried to move and more pain shot through his head. He touched his scalp. It felt wet. He peered at his fingers, but visibility was so poor he couldn't really see them.

Derek held still, trying to think. "Hello?" he called out. "Hello?" His own words were barely audible. He yawned hard. His ears popped with a painful snap. He tried again. "Hello?" Better. A little better. The overpressure from the explosions had affected his ears, hopefully not permanently.

"Derek?"

"I'm over here."

More light, but he couldn't see where it was coming from. Beams, cutting through the haze and dust that hung in the air. They shined here and there, eerily arcing through the debris-filled hallway.

Irina Khournikova appeared out of the gloom and knelt down next to him. "Are you okay?"

"I've been better."

So had she, apparently. Blood oozed from a cut across her forehead that had been hastily taped shut. One eye was swollen, a large bruise growing purple on her cheekbone. A swarthy, wiry soldier appeared next to her. "Let's get this shit off you, man."

"This is Lieutenant Jorge Ruiz," Irina said.

"McCormack?" Derek asked.

Ruiz shook his head. "He was practically next to the doors when they went off."

"How many?"

"Everybody but me and Irina here." His voice was sober.

Irina said, "Are we . . . the bomb that went off — ?"

"I had it in bleach. It didn't stop it from exploding, but maybe it killed whatever bug they had in it." He didn't add that he didn't know if the container had been airtight or if the brief exposure to the bleach during the actual detonation would be enough to kill the germs they'd had in there.

Ruiz said, "I'm gonna lift this off you, man. Let us know if it hurts."

"It hurts."

Ruiz gave a soft laugh. "I haven't moved anything yet."

"Yeah, well, that's the kind of day I've had."

"Me, too, brother. On three. One. Two. Three."

Ruiz hefted the wall off Derek with a grunt and he slithered out with Irina's assistance. Ruiz dropped the wall back down with a dull thud. It kicked up another cloud of dust and grit. Derek pushed his way across the debris and leaned against the wall, sliding to the floor. Irina took out a first-aid kit and studied his scalp. "You get all this from this explosion?"

"No. There've been a few other problems. Couple knife fights, got caught in two other explosions, fell through the ceiling a couple times, and I've been shot at least once."

Ruiz said, "Okay, you win, man. Your day has been worse than mine."

"What about the first explosion? That crashing sound?" Derek asked.

Irina frowned. Ruiz answered for her. "Team Alpha was going in through the roof. They set off a booby-trap. It took out four of them and there's no access any more. The entire elevator shaft collapsed and is filled with debris. There's a hole about six inches wide that they can use to look into the ballroom, but that's about it. It's just us."

Derek rubbed his forehead. "Got any Tylenol?"

Irina went through the first-aid kit and found some pain medication, offering it with her canteen. "We can call for backup."

"Time?"

"Going right on by." Ruiz peered down the hallway. "Can we get into the ballroom from down here?"

Derek nodded, wincing. "Give me a second. I have an idea."

Irina waited patiently. Ruiz got on his radio and called Agent LeVoi, explaining their status. He got off a moment later. "She's sending another team through the tunnels."

Derek snapped his fingers. "I do have a plan." He looked at Ruiz. "Can they jam signals?"

"You bet. That was the plan, before everything went to hell."

"Good. Make sure we still can. When we go busting in there, I don't want them blowing everything up around us."

Ruiz got back on the radio. Irina knelt beside him. "Coffee is dead. So is President Vakhach."

He thought about that a moment. "You're saying you don't have a lot of motive to be here."

"As good a motive as any now. This has to end. Thanks to you, we're down to five terrorist targets. But five terrorists with automatic weapons and plastic explosives in a room with five hundred people can do a lot of damage and cause a lot of death in a very short period of time. Is this a good plan?"

"No. Sorry. It's not a good plan. I don't have any good plans today. My good plan went to shit before noon. I'm way past plans A, B, C, and D and well on my way to plan Z. I just hope to survive plan Z."

Ruiz turned back to them. "*El Tiberón* killed Prince Talal of Saudi Arabia. We've got orders to go in now before they kill anybody else. The backup team's five minutes away. What do I tell them?"

Derek held out his hand and Ruiz helped him to his feet. "Tell them to plan on blowing out the doors to the ballroom and going in hard, aiming for the bad guys. Just before they do, we want all communications jammed."

"You're right," Irina said. "It's not a good plan. It'll get everybody killed. Including us."

"What about us?" Ruiz asked. "We gonna just sit here and direct traffic? Have us a little picnic? Because I forgot the beer, man, if that's what you had in mind." His words were light, but Derek heard the pain and fury behind the bravado. Ruiz was a joker, the guy who laughed in the face of death, making light of a situation gone to hell on the express train. But he knew Ruiz was pissed — he'd lost most of his team. It was there in his coiled body language, in the slithering creature behind his dark eyes.

Derek's smile was hard and tight. "We're going to be stars of the stage, my friend. Our job is to get to the leaders before all hell breaks loose and take out this head guy, *El Tiburón*, before he kills somebody else."

"Three on one," Ruiz said. "I like those odds. How about you?"

Irina raised an eyebrow. "It sounds better than it did before, but I'd like a few more details."

Ruiz grinned. "Hey, this guy's Special Forces. He's got cojones the size of cannon balls. He's done okay without our help so far."

Irina said, "He's also lucky. His luck won't last forever. I'd like to get out of this alive."

"Babe, we get out of this alive, I'm taking you out to dinner."

Irina grinned back. "Jorge, we get out of this alive, I'm taking you up on it."

"It's a date."

Derek rubbed his neck and shook his head. "Jesus, you guys. You want to be alone for a little while?"

"Maybe later, man. I got a reason to live now. Got a hot date planned for this evening. Dinner and dancing —"

"Tick," Irina said, "tock. Time's a wasting."

Derek flashed her a salute. "You heard the lady, Ruiz. Anybody have a spare set of night vision goggles?"

Ruiz handed him a set.

Derek pulled them on and clicked the switch. The hallways lit up in shades of green and black. "First, anybody seen my screwdriver? You never know when you're —"

Ruiz handed him one.

"Good. Now I'm fully armed. All right. Plan Z. Follow me."

Ruiz hefted his SCAR L assault rifle. "To hell and back, *vato*. To hell and back."

CHAPTER 84

Derek led Irina and Ruiz down the corridor, staying as quiet as possible. He was limping like an old man, he thought. His whole body screamed at him to stop, quit, lay down somewhere, rest. His hearing was muffled, his head ached, his ribs and arms and hands burned from cuts and abrasions and wounds. He knew the clock was ticking on his endurance. The fuel gauge was just about on empty.

As they moved away from the tunnel area, the hallway cleared. Farther down the hallway he could see the destruction caused by the collapse of the elevator shaft. Rubble filled the hallway nearly to the ceiling.

He led them into the storage area beneath the stage. Part of this room had suffered damage as well, one wall partly collapsed, cinder blocks and chunks of concrete scattered on the floor.

Ruiz tapped him on the shoulder. He turned and Ruiz tapped his ear, indicating the radio. Moving close to Derek, he whispered, "Backup's in the tunnel, coming into this building."

Derek nodded. He turned and pointed to the trapdoor that opened onto the center of the stage. Ruiz stepped close, flashing a light on it at an oblique angle. He pointed at the padlock. Derek smiled and showed his screwdriver.

Together they moved a table over beneath the trapdoor. Derek climbed up on it and began to loosen the screws that held the hasp on the door to the stage. Irina prowled the area while Ruiz held a light for Derek to see. It took about two minutes because he wanted to minimize noise and vibration, but finally the hasp and padlock dropped into his hand. He set it aside, and waved Irina and Ruiz to the other side of the room to talk.

In the dust on the floor, he drew a sketch of the stage, the location of the world leaders and how the backstage area was laid out in comparison to the ballroom and the trapdoor. "Only one person can go through at a time," he murmured. "Luckily, the door opens toward the back of the stage, so you can go straight up and out. But if you're not quick it can be a bottleneck. You've got to go up and get out of the way for the next person. I'll go first—"

Irina shook her head. "You're too slow. I've seen you limping around. You're cut to pieces. You've been shot. It's amazing you're still moving. You open the door, I'll go through first."

"No way, babe," Ruiz said. "I'm first up. But I agree with her, *vato*. You're an old man compared to me and you're hurt. You push up the door and I'll go through first."

Irina scowled at him. "I'm first through because you're going to boost me through as soon as Derek pops the lid. I can't do that for you nearly as well as you can for me."

Ruiz scowled right back at her then grinned. "Babe, I can tell you like it on top. Okay. You ready?"

They moved back to the trapdoor. All three of them perched on the table. It wobbled precariously under their weight. Irina had her MP-5 ready. She dropped into a crouch. Ruiz called Peterson Air Force Base and gave the go-ahead for all radio signals to be jammed beginning in one minute to last for ten minutes. He studied his watch, immediately tapped the radio, and subvocalized into the throat mic. "This is Bravo One to Gamma One. One minute and counting from now!"

Derek stood beneath the trapdoor, hands pressed to it. Ruiz crouched next to Irina, hands around her waist, eyes on his wristwatch. She kissed him on the cheek. "This better be a great restaurant."

His eyes sparkled. "You bet. The best — seven — six — five —"

Derek tensed, sucking in a chestful of air.

"Four — three — two — one!"

CHAPTER 85

Pablo Juarez was prepared for an assault, but not from behind. He was standing on the lip of the stage, facing the crowd, his assault rifle at the ready. The PDA was in his hand, the signal to blow the explosives on the world leaders only a button click away. His men had moved toward the center of the ballroom, herding the crowd closer together, away from the doors.

Behind him a section of the wooden stage slammed upward with a bang. Juarez spun. A tall woman with auburn hair burst out of the stage opening as if she had bounced off a trampoline.

Before the woman had even landed on her feet, multiple explosions ripped the ballroom as the doors slammed inward.

Juarez was already moving, finger punching the key to set off the suicide belts.

His eyes widened when nothing happened.

Gripping the PDA, he jabbed at the button. Rage rushed through him. The screen read: No Signal.

He screamed, an inchoate, wordless venting of frustration and anger.

The woman hit the floor in a crouch and immediately sprinted for the world leaders. Another man appeared in the hatch, this one keeping low and rolling. Unlike the woman, this one wore camo fatigues.

The woman's gun swung toward him.

Pablo dived forward and swung an arm around President Langston's neck, jerking him out of the chair and to his feet, using him as a human shield.

"Go ahead and shoot!" he screamed, backing away from Irina and Ruiz. "Go ahead!"

In the main ballroom Secret Service and FBI agents swarmed

through the doors. The crowd, screaming, was mostly huddling to the floor. Some of those closer to the doors rushed the openings. Pablo's men opened fire. FBI shooters, crouched by the entryways, took out the terrorists in a calm, methodical fashion, one by one.

The ballroom was filled with blue smoke. Gunfire chattered amid screams and the thud of falling bodies.

President Langston shouted, *"End this now! Shoot him!"*

Pablo Juarez cursed. Dragging President Langston with him, he leapt across the stage, firing as he went, and tumbled through the trapdoor into the room below.

CHAPTER 86

Derek was coiled to leap through the hatch when two men fell through on top of him. All three slammed to the tabletop, which collapsed beneath them. A suffocating cloud of dust rose up. Derek rolled and rose to his knees, searching for his gun, which had fallen from his hands on impact.

Pablo Juarez struggled to his feet, clutching President Langston close to his chest. His MP-5 was somewhere on the floor. He pulled out a handgun and held it to President Langston's head.

"Don't move or I'll kill him! I will!"

Derek stayed in a crouch, poised. He fought back a choking cough from the dust, blinking it out of his eyes. Voice calm, he said, "Mr. President. How are you doing?"

"Is that you, Derek?"

"Yes, sir."

"Shoot us. Don't worry about me."

If Derek had a gun, he would have. He didn't know where the damned thing was. Somewhere in the debris. Out of reach. He said, "Pablo, put the gun down. It's over. It's all over now." He slowly got to his feet, bringing his hands down along his sides.

"I said don't move!"

"Easy! We can talk. We're reasonable men, aren't we?" Blood sang in his veins. Pressure built behind his ears. Above him he heard screams and the rattle of gunfire.

"Don't move!" Pablo's voice went up in pitch, his tone reedy with anger. "I said, do not move!"

"Is this your idea of being a hero for your people?" Derek asked. "To hide behind an old man? Use him as a human shield? That's a coward's way, don't you think? Let him go and face me. Man to man. Come on, Pablo. Come on, *vato loco*. Show me who's got the balls! You're a dead man anyway. You know that. It's only a matter of time before this room is flooded with agents. Some sharpshooter will put a bullet in your head from twenty feet away."

Pablo took the gun away from President Langston's head and aimed it at Derek. "Shut up! Shut your mouth!"

Derek stepped to the side. Just one step. His chest swelled. One misstep and Juarez would pull the trigger and this shitty day would be over for good.

"Impulse control problems, Pablo? Feeling a little stressed out? That's because you're cornered. You're like a rat in a trap, *vato*. There's no place for you to go. Even if you set President Langston free and run out that door, this building is surrounded. They'll gun you down like a dog in the road. Won't that be a brave, heroic end for you, eh *vato*? I don't think you're an *El Tiburón*. You're not a shark. You're more like a little fishy. A goldfish. How do you say guppy in Spanish, Pablo? Eh *vato*? *El guppo*?"

Pablo, face twisted in rage, flung President Langston to the side and rushed toward Derek, gun thrust forward.

Derek dropped to his knees. As he did, he swung the Emerson knife up out of his pocket. Pablo loomed over him, a guttural blood cry echoing around the room. Derek swung the knife up and into Pablo's stomach.

The battle cry turned to a breathless whistle. Pablo dropped the gun and gripped Derek's wrists with both hands. Pablo's eyes grew wide, expression twisted in pain and surprise. And something else. Regret? Sadness?

Putting all his muscle into it, Derek lunged upward, driving the blade up through Pablo's diaphragm. Hot blood gushed over his hand.

Pablo grunted. His mouth opened to speak, to scream, to moan. No sound came out. He choked, trying to bring in air, unable to because of the ravaged diaphragm. He opened his mouth again. Blood sprayed from his lips.

Derek twisted the blade, the feeling of gristle and bone and flesh parting beneath his hand filling him with horror. And primal satisfaction.

Pablo's face went blank. His hands still clutched at Derek's wrists.

Derek lunged again, twisting, ripping upward and back.

Blood spewed from the wound. Pablo sank to his knees, clutching his stomach then slowly fell over sideways. His lips moved as if in silent prayer.

Derek knelt next to him, trying to hear.

Pablo tried to speak again. Then he was still.

Derek knelt there next to him for a long moment. Exhaustion weighed on every cell in his body.

President Langston awkwardly climbed to his feet. Thoughtfully, respectfully, Derek wiped the blood off the knife using Pablo's shirt. He looked into the empty eyes of the dead man for a moment, repulsed by Pablo's actions and by his wasted end. With a shake of his head, he climbed to his feet, groaning. He limped over to the president and cut off the plasti-cuffs, then took off the "suicide" vest.

President Langston, rubbing his wrists, looked down at Pablo Juarez. "What did he say there at the end?"

"*Madre. Perdone.*"

President Langston shot him a quizzical look. "Mother?"

Derek nodded. "Mother. Forgive. Maybe he was trying to say, Mother, forgive me."

CHAPTER 87

Coast Guard Captain Paul Billings was met at the offshore oil platform by Bob Ravenshield, the drill foreman. Ravenshield was a burly, broad-shouldered man in his fifties with whispy gray hair and a perpetual squint. He looked at Billings and said, "They stole our fucking boat."

Billings nodded. "What kind?"

"Sixty-four foot cabin cruiser. Owned by the company. We use it to ferry personnel back and forth. Named *Lady Okie.*"

Billings was lean and tall, sandy hair blowing in the mild breeze. "How many people?" He sighed and thought better of it. Get the story first before asking questions. Billings recognized a first-class cluster fuck when he saw one, and he knew there would be investigations for years into who screwed up. "Just tell me what happened."

"That fuckin' helicopter dropped off five people. They came blasting in here, ran right past us, and down to the boat. We tried to stop 'em, but we don't have guns or anything."

"Did they? You said they came blasting in here. Were they armed?" *Hell, they shouldn't have been armed. As far as he was concerned they should never have been given a helicopter.*

"No. That's just an expression. No guns or weapons. But they seemed to know right what they were doing. They got on the boat and when one of my guys, Ben, tried to stop them, well, I mean, Ben's a big guy, but this guy just sort of reached out and broke his arm like it was a matchstick, you know? Told him to back off. And then they were gone. I mean, it happened so fast—"

Billings took notes and directed Ravenshield to help his people search the platform.

"What, you don't believe me?"

Billings nodded. "I do believe you. But these are international terrorists. We want to make sure."

Ravenshield scowled, turned, and spat over the railing. "Yeah, yeah. Go ahead."

Billings went back to his boat and made a call. He was patched directly through to Secretary James Johnston, which gave him pause. That was just about as high up the food chain as he'd ever been and the air was a little thin up there. He thought again about who was going to get blamed for this mess, and was determined not to have the shit fall on his shoulders. He gave the secretary a carefully worded sit-rep — situation report — and awaited directions.

Johnston's groan came over the line. "Same story with the cruise ship. Go looking for the boats, Captain. Keep us informed. We'll have the whole damned Navy and Coast Guard out looking for them now."

"Yes, sir."

"And Captain?"

"Sir?"

"Shoot on sight."

"Sir?"

"You heard me."

"Yes, sir."

Billings clicked off and swallowed. He looked out over the horizon and shook his head. He headed for the radar room. Maybe they could get a bead on these guys. But he had his doubts. It was a big ocean.

CHAPTER 88

Derek followed President Langston up onto the stage. The remaining Angels were either dead or kneeling on the floor, hands cuffed behind them. The room was crazy, people talking, people weeping, people milling around. The world leaders were discussing whether to hold a press conference immediately. Medics were trying to triage patients. There were dozens of corpses scattered around the room, mostly security people from the various countries.

Derek scanned around and spotted Maria in the center of the room. He ran past the president and Irina, jumped off the stage and pushed his way through the crowd. He knelt down next to her and hugged her close. She hugged him back.

"You're alive!" she said.

He couldn't stop smiling. "Of course I'm alive! But you! Are you crazy? Why didn't you just stay where you were?"

"It was better for you to do your thing. See how good it worked out?"

"Maria! You're crazy!"

"You bet. And don't forget, you promised me a trip on your boat."

"As soon as your leg's okay."

"Now go. You have work to do, right?"

Derek nodded. He needed to make sure nobody rushed out before they could get the area tested for biological contamination.

Secretary Mandalevo stood a few feet away. He said, "You must be Dr. Stillwater."

Derek looked at him. "Secretary Mandalevo, right?"

"Yes."

Derek nodded to him. "See she's taken care of, okay?" He then told Mandalevo what needed to be done. Mandalevo nodded. "It'll be taken care of. Take it easy. Get your wounds taken care of. You're done for now, Doctor."

Derek nodded and looked at Maria, who winked at him. He turned and started to walk away when Mandalevo said, "Dr. Stillwater."

He turned to look at the man. Something passed between them, an understanding, and maybe some type of informal agreement. Derek knew that he would meet the man again in the near future.

Mandalevo, face tired, but eyes sharp and alert, said, "Well done."

Derek nodded and walked toward the front of the room. He looked for Irina, but didn't see her at first. Then he spotted her kneeling near the base of the stage. When he got to her, he saw she was kneeling next to the body of Richard Coffee. A medic was kneeling next to her.

She looked up at him. "He's still alive."

He stared at her in disbelief.

The medic glanced up. "Barely."

Words caught in his throat. He didn't know what to say. Or even what to feel or think.

He saw the gun on Irina's belt. His first reaction was to grab her gun and empty it into Coffee's head. He could see similar emotions in Irina Khournikova's eyes.

President Langston appeared at his side. "He's alive?"

Irina nodded. "Yes, Mr. President."

President Langston's face flushed. "He murdered my wife and children."

Derek nodded. The world leaders were watching them now. Dozens of people were watching them. President Langston couldn't seem to take his eyes off Coffee's body. He held out his hand to Irina. "Give me your gun."

Silently she handed it to him.

President Langston aimed the gun at Richard Coffee. A long moment went by as a million emotions flitted across his face. Then he seemed to sag, and he dropped the gun to his side. "Take him to the hospital. Put security around him."

The medic nodded. "Yes sir."

Derek knelt next to Coffee. He felt a heavy weight on his chest. His emotions spun out of control. Richard Coffee — his friend. Richard Coffee — his enemy.

Coffee stirred. His eyes opened a sliver. Recognition seeped onto his face. He croaked, "Derek?"

"Yes."

"Over? Did . . . you . . . win?"

"Yes."

A sigh escaped Coffee's lips. His eyes closed. Derek thought he was dead.

The medics placed Coffee on a stretcher and hooked up an IV. Coffee's hand fluttered. "Derek?"

Derek stood next to him. Took his hand. "I'm here."

"Nadia?"

"She's dead, Richard. It was an accident, but she's dead. I'm sorry."

Coffee's chest heaved. He coughed once and groaned.

His chest stopped moving. Derek felt Coffee's hand go limp. The medic double-checked his vitals and shook his head. "He's gone."

President Langston rested his hand on Derek's shoulder. "The man called himself The Fallen Angel. He's evil. I should have shot him."

Derek didn't disagree. He didn't know if he could have pulled the trigger under those circumstances either, though. Richard Coffee the friend had been gone for a long time. Richard Coffee who called himself The Fallen Angel wasn't somebody Derek wanted around. The world was better off without him.

He saw Irina watching him. Her face was tight and pale. She had hunted Richard Coffee for a long time. He had killed her lover. What was she thinking right now? What was she feeling?

She stepped close to Derek and kissed him on the cheek. Without another word she turned and walked away.

President Langston removed his hand from Derek's shoulder. "Good work, Dr. Stillwater. Very good work today. We stopped the devil today."

Derek shrugged. "There's always another one to take his place, sir." He turned to follow Irina out of the ballroom.

EPILOGUE

The Salacious Sally, Derek's cabin cruiser, sailed through the calm waters of the Gulf of Mexico in a southwesterly direction. Atop the flying bridge, Derek studied the GPS. He glanced off his port bow toward the distant island of Cuba. The sun beat down on his bare shoulders. His hair had grown out and was bleached from the sun. Even some of the scars were healing, although some of them refused to tan, no matter how much time he spent on deck with his shirt off.

There were other scars, though, unseen, but felt. He still didn't sleep well, the nights torn by nightmares of everything going wrong. Of being caught in explosions, being a step too slow. Nightmares of missing the biological bomb Coffee had hidden away, of the deadly plague he had installed in it infecting the G20 leaders and staff, all the survivors taking the diseases home with them.

A forensic analysis of recovered bomb fragments found DNA and antigenic evidence of a strain of virus that caused Venezuelan equine encephalitis, which could be transmitted to horses, humans, and birds. There was no evidence it had escaped the bleach or the explosion. There was some discussion as to whether or not Coffee had gotten the weaponized viral material from a lab in Venezuela, but it was entirely possible they had cultured it themselves from infected animals in Colombia or Mexico.

A voice behind him said, "Ever been there?"

He glanced over his shoulder and smiled. Irina Khournikova appeared behind him in a black string bikini carrying a pitcher of Margaritas and two glasses.

"Cuba?"

She nodded, set the glasses down and poured two margaritas, invitingly green. She'd even added salt to the rims.

He smiled, remembering. "Oh, I spent a little time at Gitmo. In and out."

She cocked her head, then leaned close and kissed him. Derek snaked an arm around her waist and brought her close. He kissed her back. She tasted of salt and tequila and lime. Once the events in Colorado had wrapped up, Maria had been made offers by TV producers for the story of her life. She'd gotten offers to act in a Spanish-language TV series and do some modeling. Derek Stillwater — or perhaps Michael Gabriel — had been quickly forgotten, which was probably just as well.

Sergeant Jorge Ruiz had received commendations and immediately been promoted and transferred to Afghanistan. Derek had asked Irina out instead. And now they'd been on *The Sally* for two weeks, currently heading for Cancun, Cozumel, and probably down to Aruba. Maybe even Costa Rica. He heard it was nice. He'd never been there.

"How about you?" he asked. "Ever go to Cuba? Last bastion of Soviet-style Communism?"

She smiled. "Yes. I spent a year there working with the *Dirección General de Inteligencia*." She took a sip of her margarita and then leaned forward to kiss him again. "And interestingly enough, I read a file on a Canadian businessman by the name of Richard Blankman who looked surprisingly like you."

Derek blinked. "That's, um, interesting."

"They were doing research into biological weapons at the Center for Genetic Engineering and Biotechnology laboratory, you know."

Derek took a drink. "Yes, I know."

She cocked her head. "I know you know. You disappeared from the country shortly after you broke in."

"Um —"

Irina placed her fingertips over her mouth and laughed, then pointed toward Cuba. "I liked Cuba. Very warm. Great beaches. Not like Moscow at all."

Somewhat relieved to get off the subject of his classified adventures in Cuba, he grinned. "I believe it. Moscow isn't known for its white sand beaches." He took a sip of margarita. "What *is* Moscow known for?"

She laughed. "Vodka, opera, ballet, and corrupt bureaucracy."

"Here's to Cuba then." He raised his glass and she clinked it with her own. Her gaze wandered the blue horizon. "I wonder what they'll do."

He knew who she was talking about. The remaining Fallen Angels, Coffee's people who Vice President Newman ordered released. The Coast Guard and the Navy had recaptured six of The Fallen Angels. Three were believed dead when they ditched into the Gulf of Mexico when their helicopter was shot down. That left twelve who were still missing. "I have no idea," Derek said. "Hopefully they'll die of boredom somewhere. I hope I never hear from them again."

It was a hope; not an expectation. He didn't believe the world had heard the end of The Fallen Angels, although now that their leader was dead, perhaps they would go about their business being arms merchants or mercenaries.

Irina brought him back to the present by leaning against him. It was a very effective way of getting his attention. All that firm tanned skin. "Let's not talk about such things," she said. "Let's live today. Now."

He smiled and took a sip of his drink. He set his glass down and wrapped his arms around her. He kissed her and let, for the moment, his worries about the future slip away. It was a beautiful day. The sun was in the sky, the water was calm, and he was in the company of a gorgeous woman.

The devil may very well have his day. But not today.

ACKNOWLEDGMENTS

I would like to acknowledge the continued support and assistance of Leanne Terry, Ian Terry, and Sean Terry; my agent Irene Kraas; my team at Oceanview Publishing, Pat Gussin, Bob Gussin, Susan Greger, and all those seen and unseen, Mary Adele Bogdon, John Cheesman, George Foster, Sandy Greger, Joe Hall, Susan Hayes, Maryglenn McCombs, Cheryl Melnick, and Gayle Treadwell; Scott Schafer for background on helicopters, and Eric Glick for introducing me; Allison Scott at The Broadmoor in Colorado Springs, Colorado; and finally, Naida Harrington, Carolyn Ann Killea, and Joan Miller for pointing me toward better Spanish.